A Better Man

A Better Man

by

Enid Harlow

VAN NESTE BOOKS
Midlothian, VA 23113

Library of Congress Cataloging-in-Publication Data

Harlow, Enid.
    A Better Man / Enid Harlow -- 1st ed.
    p.   cm.
    ISBN   0-9657639-7-8 (cloth)
    I. Title.
    PS3558.A62426B4   2000
    813'.54--dc21   99-29126
                                   CIP

Manufactured in the United States

VAN NESTE BOOKS
12836 Ashtree Road
Midlothian, VA 23113

For Michaelis

ONE

HERB WAS IN a phone booth on the northeast corner of Lexington Avenue and 59th Street. Six-foot advertisements hemmed him in. A half-empty bottle of orange soda perched on the ledge beneath the phone. Seven or eight small white stickers, haphazardly pasted over one another, covered the phone's black handle. The stickers on top had jagged edges, suggesting they'd been clawed at by people desperate to get to the ones beneath. Shiny metallic numbers stared Herb in the face. He tightened his grip on the newspaper beneath his arm and wondered what the hell he was doing in here. The phone booth had no door. Wind whipped up under his overcoat. His back felt exposed. He might as well be standing on the street wearing nothing but a hospital gown.

Automatically, Herb did what he often did in moments of unease: He tugged on the brim of his hat. Turning, he saw New York City's rush-hour crowds, augmented by streams of Christmas shoppers, packing the block behind him. Frenzied by the season, hunched against the cold, lurching north and south through the evening darkness, indifferent to civility and carelessly churning yesterday's snow into slush beneath their feet—those were the culprits who must have pushed him into this booth.

Every fifth or sixth person held a portable phone to his ear. The *Wall Street Journal* predicted that this proportion would rise to one out of four within two years' time as cellular phones got cheaper and lighter. To Herb's mind, few things looked sillier than a bunch of adults walking down a city street talking into little toy-like black boxes. But deals depended on their calls, reservations had to be made or canceled, appointments confirmed or rescheduled, and movie and theater tickets purchased, regardless of the surcharge. Damn the expense, it was the time they couldn't spare. The *New York Times* had reported that scientists were pointing to the radiation emitted by those phones as a likely cause of brain cancer. But you couldn't tell that to the people packing this block. They were true New Yorkers: willing to risk death, disease, and mutilation to save themselves a minute's wait.

Herb turned back to confront the bottle of orange soda. Had a bicycle messenger left it there after calling in to answer his page? Herb admired the nerve of those kids in bucking city traffic. But what was he to make of the stickers? Most were torn and illegible, picked apart, perhaps, by the nervous fingers of people making the most difficult calls of their lives. Two stickers remained sufficiently intact for him to see that they were mini-business cards. One advertised a fortune teller, evocatively named Madame Rosa, the other a car service. Both, conjectured Herb, were services one might well find oneself in need of when stranded in a phone booth. Madame Rosa. Herb said the name to himself. Rosa. Rose. Rosy. The future could be rosy. And Madame. Madame. A weighty word. A woman of solidity and strength. A woman whose advice could be trusted. Herb considered placing a call to Madame Rosa. He'd ask her how he happened to be in this booth, for certainly he hadn't walked in under his own volition, and now that he was here, what did she think he ought to do. He stared at the phone, keeping his elbow tight to his body. The newspaper jammed up under there felt like a friend. Madame Rosa, if she were worth her weight in smoke, would tell him to get the hell out of here and go home. He could nearly hear her voice now, low and husky in his ear, a heavy Russian accent: Get out. Go home. Herb fully intended to do just that. He had, in fact, never intended to make the call. Not actually intended, in the sense of intentional will. Not willed at all. Not fully.

All he had intended to do was go into a store and buy Maggie a present. "What, you? Shopping?" his secretary, Ethel, had cackled. "I could give it a try," Herb replied. "Well, I never," Ethel said, and turned on her heel, conspicuously insulted, and stormed out of his office.

Herb didn't see why he couldn't do it. How hard could it be to go into a store and buy his wife a Christmas present? That he had never done such a thing in twenty-two years of married life—and not just a Christmas present but one of any kind—he recognized as a strike against him. Not that he hadn't bought Maggie presents. He had. Hundreds of them. Thousands, he'd venture, over the years. And if you regarded as presents all the things she had bought for herself and their daughter, Phoebe, and charged to him, the count was astronomical. But he had never physically gone into a store and picked one out. Ethel attended to that. She had been attending to it since he and Maggie were married. It was part of her job. And she did it spectacularly well—keeping track of holidays, anniversaries, and birthdays, diligently marking them off on her office calendar, and going out as those occasions approached to make whatever purchases would help Maggie celebrate them in the style to which Herb had made her accustomed. Ethel brought to the shopping the same efficiency she brought to everything else she did about the office—classifying homeowners' policies and updates, tracking periods of enforcement and pending renewals, writing up forms and endorsements, answering letters, and entering a bewildering amount of policyholders' personal information on her data base.

And never once had Maggie complained about the system. "Why, Herb, how did you know?" she'd cry when presented with a gift purportedly from him, but knowing perfectly well Ethel had selected it. "It's just what I wanted." She'd throw her arms about his neck and cover his face with fluttery little kisses. "What wonderful taste you have." Acting had been Maggie's girlhood dream, a dream she had traveled from the Midwest to Manhattan to pursue, and had seemed to awaken from the very morning after they were married. "Glad you like it, sweetheart," Herb would say, feeling the little kisses like small birds running across his face and locking his wrists behind her back to make the moment last. "I'm not a prisoner," she'd often snap then, with surprising intensity, breaking his hold and pulling away. "You have to let me breathe!"

To brave the stores himself was the honorable thing to do. But could he do it? It would give Maggie the surprise of her life. But was he capable? She'd have no choice then but to forgive him for his part in the terrible argument they'd had last night. That settled it. He'd go into a store and buy a Christmas present for his wife. Millions of men around the country—billions, if you took in the world, subtracting for Buddhists and atheists and Muslims and Orthodox Jews— were doing it this very minute. And he was a man like other men, as he'd told Ethel, or meant to, before she let out that cackle and stormed from his office, sweeping up as she went in a practiced if bony hand the pile of mail from his outgoing box.

Today that pile, as it happened, had included a substantial supply of checks for settled claims in addition to the usual business correspondence and notices of quarterly premiums due. As Herb looked at the checks, sweeping with Ethel out the door, he just had time to think what welcome presents they would make at this time of year, then the outer door had slammed and Ethel was gone, and he thought he saw his father standing in a darkened corner of the room, surveying an office that had once been his.

"A nice bonus, eh, Pops, those checks?" Herb had said aloud to the shadowy image in the corner. Having grown up idolizing the principles of insurance the way other boys of his day idolized the Lone Ranger, Herb couldn't wait to go to work for his father, something he had started doing the day after his high school graduation. Insurance protected persons and property. Insurance saved families from bankruptcy when their houses flooded and their homes burned to the ground. Insurance rode to the rescue when the breadwinner unexpectedly keeled over at his desk. Herb was proud to be in its employ. "Covering your ass is nothing but basic business sense," his father had often told him, and when his father died, Herb was surprised to learn he had inherited not only the business sense but the business as well. He also had inherited his father's small stature, large nose, brown eyes, dark, then silver, hair, his unquestioned loyalty to facts, friends, and figures, and the promise of longevity in his genes. The small hands were his mother's. "How is it possible?" Maggie would sometimes ask, a look of utter bewilderment on her face, turning his hand over in hers as if expecting to find something different on the other side. "A hand this small on a business tycoon?"

Herb sat in his father's chair and worked at his father's desk—an antique mahogany roll-top with an upper row of small drawers pulled by almond-shaped brass knobs—which his father had kept in this very office on the thirty-first floor of this very building for forty-five years in the exact center of the room, just where Herb kept it now, and he would die at it, too, he expected, just as his father had done, doubling over in the middle of a phone call to his broker twenty-six years ago this month.

"Sort of a gift on the company?" he added as an afterthought about the checks, although he suspected his father would not be pleased to think of them as gifts, for he had never much liked seeing a claim resolved in a client's favor. They differed there. Herb had made a go of the business in the years he'd had it under his control and didn't mind paying out a claim now and then. "It keeps us honest, Pops," he said to the image in the corner. "And you always stressed honesty when in doubt. Do what's right was how you put it."

The image shifted its footing and Herb thought he could almost make his father out: fingers curled on his chin, lips slightly pursed, big, bushy eyebrows, grown gray over time, raised high on his forehead. A look of expectation in his eyes. It was that look that got to Herb. Every day of every year that he had worked for his father, he would walk into his office, see his father look up, his eyebrows head for his forehead, and that look of expectation appear in his eyes. The great brows would hang over the look a moment like nails holding it in place. Then they'd come down, and gradually the look would fade. Herb had imagined it would fade entirely in time, but time had proved him wrong. He worked for his father for sixteen years, and on each working day, no

11

matter how quietly he turned the handle on his father's big oak door or how lightly he tread across the beige plush carpet on his father's floor, he would see his father glance up, raise his eyebrows, flash him that expectant look, hold it a moment, and let it fade. Herb had never figured out what the old man was expecting. Something from him, he'd always assumed, some great achievement or profound mark implanted on the conscience of the world, but now he supposed it might only have been a phone call his father was expecting, bringing word about some claim.

Honesty when in doubt.

Herb was in doubt now. Serious doubt. He put his hand on the receiver. He took it off.

Get out. Go home.

Do what's right.

He and Maggie had had arguments before, but nothing like the one last night. That wasn't an argument. It was a cataclysmic misunderstanding, a breach in the lines of human communication, a chasm of gigantic proportion, a drop through space. As far as Herb could figure out, it had started because he was scratching his hand.

"Don't do that, Herb."

His skin got so dry in the winter.

"It itches, Maggie."

"You'll break the skin."

Her eyes on his hand made the spot itch all the more. He scratched the back of his hand. He scratched his knuckles.

"Stop it, Herb. You'll scratch straight through to the bone."

He scratched at his arm beneath his sleeve which he'd unbuttoned and rolled back to keep the newsprint off his cuffs.

"Stop it," she said again, and when he didn't stop, she sighed her sigh of exasperation and left the room. Moments later, she returned with a bottle of lotion.

"That's all right," Herb said.

"Sit still," she replied.

"Really, Maggie, it's all right."

"Give me your hand."

"It doesn't itch any more."

"Give it to me."

She rubbed the lotion into his hand and up his arm. She turned his arm over and rubbed more lotion into the underside. She rubbed gently but clearly with purpose, leaving a fine, greasy film from the tips of his fingers to the bend of his elbow.

"Now the other one."

"I'm holding the paper."

"Put it down."

"I'm reading it."

"Hold it in your other hand."

"I'll get grease all over it."

"Damn it, Herb! I'm offering. I'm offering and offering. What more can I do?"

Stymied by the exact nature of her offering, but knowing that to pose the question would only enrage her further, Herb held his peace.

Maggie hurled the bottle of lotion across the room. Spurts of thick white liquid ejected from it as it flew.

"I try so hard," she said. "I'm always trying."

"I know it, Maggie. I know you do. I know."

"You know?" she yelled into his face. "What do you know? Stocks?" She spit out the word and looked around for something else to fling. "Bonds? Is that what you know? Stocks and bonds? Insurance? Highs and lows?" A crystal glass, the color of Scotch, caught her eye. "Bonded in blood, you'd think, for all you know. Bonded in gold." She grabbed the glass off the shelf and hurled it at him. It sailed past his ear and smashed against the wall behind. "You know the trouble with bonds, Herb?" she demanded. "They come unbonded, that's what! They split apart like atoms. They lose their grip."

The power of hysteria held him. He sat, mesmerized, in its grip. Generally, the merest hint that Maggie might resort to shouts or dissolve into tears was enough to get him to accede to her least demand. But lately, she had done away with hints entirely and gone directly for the real thing. Last night, she came at him, fingers splayed, long red nails sharpened to points. She seemed intent, not on wounding merely, but on actually eviscerating him. Rending flesh, ripping out organs. He smelled sherry on her breath, the diet of the week. Her eyes seemed loose in her head. He tried to rise from his chair and failed. Her nails raked his throat.

"There's blood on your shirt," she said afterward. "Your precious white shirt."

"It doesn't matter," he replied.

"What does, Herb?" She was shouting again. "What matters to you? What really, truly matters?"

He gazed at her, towering above him. Even when he was on his feet he had to tilt his head at an awkward angle to meet Maggie's eyes, but seated here, beneath her, gazing up into her superior height and burgeoning rage, he had to twist his neck and slide down in his chair to get her fully in view.

"Sorry, Maggie," he said.

"I know." Her voice went suddenly, alarmingly quiet. "I know you are, I know. You're a good man, Herb. A man with a heart of gold."

Then she had leaned over and pounded her fist into his chest.

"A gold heart, a tin ear, and a three-piece suit of armor."

She plucked at his vest, tugged at the knot of his tie.

"A veritable metallic man."

"What is it, Maggie? What's wrong?"

"A newspaper under your arm like a sword in its sheath."

"You want a glass of water or something?"

"Water? What good would water do? You think water can help? You think water can solve anything? My bones are turning to chalk."

"No, sweetheart. They're not."

"Yes, Herb. They are."

"Turning to chalk? How could they be?"

"I hear them crumbling at night."

Sweat broke out on her brow and upper lip. It ran down her throat and into the V of her sweater. It pooled between her breasts where, magnified in the lens of his glasses, it stood out like fat beads of oil. Herb took her arm and tried to urge her onto his lap. Her skin was clammy and cold. Sweat dripped off the ends of her hair and dropped onto his face, jumping like terror from her to him. He offered her his handkerchief—one of the extra large white cotton handkerchiefs she bought for him by the dozen at Saks Fifth Avenue.

"Tell me what to do," he said.

"Go change your shirt," she replied. "You're going out."

"I don't have to go tonight."

"No? Won't you turn into a pumpkin if you don't?"

"How about coming with me then?"

"To Manny's?" She tossed her golden-red hair and laughed. "I hardly think so."

"I'll take you anywhere you say."

"Thanks, but I'm not hungry."

That didn't surprise him. Maggie was rarely hungry these days. She had been existing primarily on sherry for a week. The week before that it had been bananas. Next week it might be cabbage leaves, for all he knew, or she might abruptly turn ravenous. She did that sometimes, out of the blue demanding he take her to Le Perigord or La Grenouille or some other fancy place with a menu he couldn't read and food too rich for his blood. But it had been a month now, he calculated, since their last dinner out. Le Veaux D'Or it was then. Maggie had called him her Iron Henry, the way she sometimes did, for whatever reason he never understood. She'd nibbled at his ear, ignoring the stony eyes of the snooty French waiter standing close at hand. She'd erupted into startling, high-pitched peals of laughter, which he couldn't tie to any humorous remarks either of them had made. She'd ordered soup and paté and duck in orange sauce and shoveled each course down with an uncharacteristic disregard for etiquette. She'd even had dessert, unheard of for her. But since that night she'd declined all his invitations to dinner and spent most of her time in bed.

"Go on, Herb," she had said to him last night. "Go change your shirt and go to Manny's. I know you want to. I know how happy that place makes you and I want you to be happy."

"You're sure you won't come? I'd love to take you."

"Another time."

"You'll be all right?"

"I'll be fine."

And so he had gone. He wasn't proud of it, but it was a routine, a habit he couldn't break. He'd been going to Manny's long before he met Maggie. It was his place. He liked the food and the company and the ambiance. The waiters spoke his language and knew his name and what he liked to eat and on any given night, three or four of his friends were liable to wander in. Last night there'd been two besides Manny, who, as owner, was a given—Eddie Taylor and Bill Schummacher. They'd had a few and played a couple of rounds of poker and by the time he got home, Maggie was asleep. And this morning at the office, he had yelled at Ethel. He remembered that now with shame. First he'd shouted at her for misplacing the Miller file, then he'd insulted her with his resolve to go shopping.

"You're not yourself today," she had said.

"Then who the hell am I?" he had shouted back.

She stared at him, stunned and palpably hurt. But he'd be damned if he'd apologize. He didn't often raise his voice to Ethel, but when he did he found himself hoping for an excuse to do so again. Ethel rarely rose to the challenge and that morning had been no exception. For most of the day, she had simply left him alone, and when they were obliged to confer over some business matter, she was distant and thorny and when, just before five, he announced he was going shopping, she'd taken that for the last straw and turned on her heel and stormed out of his office.

Herb had waited a few minutes after the outer door slammed to give her time to get down in the elevator and out through the lobby. Then he got up and put on his hat and coat and headed for the door himself. But could he really do this?

He had walked back to his desk and sat down again to think it over. Maggie was the one who did the shopping in the family. Department stores were her natural habitat. And not just department stores. Jewelry stores, antiques stores, specialty shops, shops where shoes, hats, bags, china, crystal, furniture—anything, actually—was sold revved her up like a drug. She could spend all day in stores, and frequently did, going from one to the next from morning till night, and coming home flushed and breathless, eyes bright, throat parched, blood up, yet not a hair out of place.

Shopping transformed her. It not only lifted but could actually reverse her spirits, altering her complete outlook on life. Herb had seen her leave the house in a mood tinged with despair, head for a store to buy a hat or a dress or a teapot, maybe some handkerchiefs or shirts for him, a skirt or scarf for Phoebe, and return with a smile on her face and her belief in the system of free enterprise fully restored. For as long as he had known her, Maggie had gone to stores the way other people went to houses of worship. But since September, when Phoebe left for college, Maggie had seemed to find in shops not only spiritual renewal but her true reason for being as well. Until a week or so ago, when she had all but stopped going out entirely.

Do what's right.

The right thing was to get up from his desk, walk the few blocks to the department store, and buy something nice for his wife. So Herb had stood up, crossed his office again, gone down the thirty-one floors in the elevator, picked up the evening *News* at the lobby stand, which Max had saved for him as he did every night of the working week, proceeded north on Lexington Avenue through the cold and the crowds, and without a thought for his own personal safety, plunged in through the store's revolving door.

He might have landed on Mars or on the ocean's murky bottom. For a moment he couldn't breathe. He had trouble clearing his vision. Unidentifiable shapes swirled before him, no order or pattern discernible in their movements. Then slowly, the shapes turned to people, or parts of people, heads, arms, shoulders, finally faces. What he saw in their eyes looked desperate, as if there'd been a fire and all the people on the upper floors had converged on this one and now, dazed and frantic, were searching for the exits. The crowds heading north up the aisles didn't stay to the right nor those heading south to the left, as every stairway monitor in every public school Herb had attended insisted, for the sake of order and decorum, people ought to do. Where the long, glass counters met at intersections, the traffic on the right refused to yield, which was the law in every state in the union, so far as Herb knew, and, likely, every country in the world with left-wheel drive. But here, in this store, people took to the floor as they pleased, jettisoning concern for human decency and the rules of the road. They cut one another off without signal or apology, made quick, rude, inexplicable turns, stopped short, backed up, circled recklessly, and sprinted with expressions of open desperation on their faces to examine items that had only just caught their attention. What was needed, Herb saw at once, was a traffic cop. He thought of raising his hand and shouting, Halt! But he'd been swept out into the middle of the floor and turned about. He felt dizzy and lightheaded. He'd lost sight of the door that led onto the street. He considered calling for help and decided against it. He could do this, he told himself. It was simply a matter of staying on his feet. He took a step, then took another. He kept his head, maintained his balance. He negotiated the crowds, actually approached a counter. Look at me, Ethel. I'm shopping!

"Sorry," he said, taking a sharp jab to his left eye. "Pardon me," he muttered, feeling a briefcase apparently loaded with bricks smash into his groin. "My fault entirely," he murmured, stepping aside just in time to avoid being trampled by an oncoming stroller. His left shoulder was hit, then his right; he spun about like a top. He grabbed his hat, righted his glasses, and found himself facing an assortment of handbags. Good, he thought. Maggie loves handbags.

But they came in so many different shapes and sizes and colors. The choice undid him. Some appeared to be silk, others leather, others made entirely of beads. Some had long straps, a few had none at all. Each was conceived, even he could tell, for a specific purpose. What if he misjudged Maggie's purpose, brought home something for which she had no use whatsoever, or, worse, something of which she already had dozens? He could hear her laughter ringing in his ear. "Why, Herb, you silly man. What on earth were you thinking?"

A woman's shoulder collided with his chin, sending him into a perfect one-eighty and bringing him face to face with the jewelry counter. Perfect, he thought. A place of outlandish glitter and unabashed extravagance, it seemed designed with Maggie in mind. But again, the choices confounded him. He drummed on the glass. He was lost and then, miraculously, found.

"May I help you, sir?"

He looked up into the face of a lovely young saleswoman.

"I'm looking for something for my wife," he replied, and tipped his hat. "Her eyes are violet."

The young woman smiled.

"Something to go with her eyes."

She nodded and focused her attention on the case below and Herb, on his side of the counter, did the same.

For several minutes, he and she stood, heads bowed, gazes lowered, earnestly peering through the glass. The brim of Herb's hat hovered just above the young woman's head. He saw it as a shelter under which she might stand for as long as she liked, protected from life's impending storms. She spoke to him softly while pointing to the glittering objects below. Tirelessly, she pulled out narrow drawers lined with felt, removed rings and bracelets from the drawers, proffered brooches and pins in the flat of her hands and dangled necklaces from her long graceful fingers for his inspection. In slow, careful detail, she explained the relative merits of rubies and diamonds and sapphires and pearls. She made pertinent remarks about lockets and chokers and earrings and anklets. She offered patient and informed advice about the merchandise in her domain and, guided by her counsel, Herb eventually made his decision.

"I'll take the bird," he said.

Maybe it wasn't a bird. He took a second look as the lovely young saleswoman plucked it from its felt perch and held it out to him in the palm of her hand. Certainly it wasn't like any bird he had ever seen. It had diamond wings and a gorgeous ruby eye and was more in the nature of a fanciful creature, a phoenix, or something out of a dream or a storybook, than any real-life, actual bird. But that ruby eye was a stunner. Maggie would like it, he knew she would. Or he hoped she would. It was hard to tell what Maggie liked or didn't like these days. Just last week she had stood at the door when he came home from work, white roses in his hands, and screamed, "Get them out of my sight! This isn't a mortuary." With a brutality that had left him speechless, she'd ripped the flowers he'd sent Ethel out to buy from his grasp and flung them into the foyer. "I detest white roses," she'd told him. "They're hideous. They're evil!" He had to take her at her word although he would have sworn she'd once said they were her favorite flower. Still, there was something about that bird—the ruby eye, especially, and the way the wings were flared as if for flight—that he thought Maggie would like, and so he said he would take it.

"Could you gift wrap it, please?" he ventured, and when the sweet young woman had so cheerfully taken the brooch away and so cheerfully brought it back again, all done up in shiny white paper decorated with gold stars and curly red ribbons, Herb thought the least he could do to show his gratitude was to give her a sizable tip. He had his hand in his pocket, about to do just that, when something told him it wasn't right, not in here, and so he extended his hand over the counter instead, letting it hover there a moment above the diamonds and emeralds and sapphires and pearls until, after the briefest hesitation, the young woman shyly met it with her own.

Herb felt the warmth of that hand even now as he stood in the phone booth, clutching his paper under his arm and contemplating the bottle of orange soda on the ledge. He recalled the hand's lightness and shape, the slenderness and length of its fingers, the softness of its skin, and the memory brought with it the memory of one other hand in his. Her face and figure, too, as it was in days gone by and as it was again, taking him utterly by surprise, there on the street, not far from his office, unbidden, unaccountable, when he'd bumped into her the other day. The sheer possibility of another life passed through him like a breeze, and he lifted the receiver off its hook.

Get out, go home. The four words, heavily weighted by Madame Rosa's Russian accent, flew around the inside of the phone booth.

Herb had pulled the flap of his overcoat aside to drop the handsomely wrapped diamond bird with ruby eye into his jacket pocket. He remembered giving the box a tap for safekeeping as he turned away from the jewelry counter. The next thing he knew, he was catapulted through the revolving door, unceremoniously shoved in one side and out the other, and now here he was, in this backless booth.

Since he was inside anyway, it seemed only sensible to make use of the thing.

Do what's right.

He slid a quarter in the slot, dialed information, and asked for the hotel's number. He was surprised that he even remembered the name of the hotel, for he hadn't thought he was paying particular attention when she'd mentioned it. Certainly he hadn't made a point of remembering where she was staying, hadn't written down the name or filed it away in the back of his mind for ready reference or anything like that. But the name came back to him along with the memory of her hand in his, her gentle touch, her easy laugh.

The coin dropped a second time and, like a bystander who out of idle curiosity had stopped to watch, Herb witnessed his fingers punching the numbers the operator had given him into the metallic pad. He decided to suggest a quick dinner. For old time's sake, he'd say. She'd know where.

Maggie was nineteen years Herb's junior. A kid, he'd thought the first time he saw her. The most beautiful kid on the planet.

Eddie Taylor had dragged him down to Zack's one night in December of 1976 when Herb had already had enough of an evening and would have been content to return to his hotel and crawl into bed. He was living in a single room on the second floor of a Sixth Avenue hotel back then, and the thought that evening, when it was already well past two and his head was swimming from a few too many at Manny's, of his comfortable bed in that unprepossessing little room was a decidedly appealing thought.

"Count me out," he'd said.

"Come on, old fart," Eddie had countered. "The night's still young."

Yielding to the elegant persuasion, Herb had gone along. At the last minute, Manny Green, Chuck Zimmer, and Bill Schummacher had decided to join the party, so the five of them had taken the subway to 18th Street and walked across to the tiny club on 20th between Ninth and Tenth.

"Trust me," Eddie had whispered in Herb's ear as he held the door to the club open for him. "There's a little filly here will knock your eye out."

And when Herb had taken his seat and watched Maggie dance once across the stage, his life as he'd known it turned out to be over.

"Christ," he muttered. "Christ."

"Didn't I tell you?" Eddie said, poking him hard in the ribs. "Didn't I?"

Maggie stood center stage, tall as a Grecian column, slim as a penny, her hair alive as fire in the lights. What there was of her costume . . . sequins, threads . . . shimmered on her body like a second skin. Her breasts might have been made of snow or porcelain, her legs of light.

"Christ," said Herb. "Oh, Christ."

She took a spin across the stage and turned his head and in all the years since it had never turned quite straight again. Almost before she had finished her first number, Herb was on his feet, clapping like crazy. He made the guys at his table stand up and keep the clamor going, applauding and banging their hands together, hooting and hollering and whistling like cowboys, until she got the nod to do another. And when she had finished that one, Herb stood up again and started clapping, and Maggie looked him straight in the eye and without a nod from anyone, began to dance again.

She danced as if dance were her first and only language. To a guy who could barely keep his balance in a fox-trot, she seemed a creature from another world. And in that costume that almost wasn't, even looking at her from a distance seemed more than he deserved. When she had finished the dance, she came over to his table and stood before him, her washboard-flat, shimmering abdomen going in and out only inches from his hand, and he found himself staring at her belly button, his eyes sucked down past concentric circles of naked flesh into vortices of mystery so deep he thought he ought to turn away.

"Thanks for the endorsement," she said. "You bought me another week's work."

Christ, Herb thought. Oh, Christ. "Glad to be of service," he replied.

After that, he rarely missed a night at Zack's. The guys gradually fell off, tired of going or having other things to do, but Herb hardly noticed their absence as he sat at his place night after night. It took him three weeks to get up the nerve to send a note backstage. Swept off his feet was putting it mildly. Shot from a cannon was more like it. Rocketed to the moon.

It took him another year and a half to pop the question (although he knew the minute he laid eyes on her that if he didn't marry Maggie Ellsworth he'd never marry anyone). During that year and a half he took Maggie to supper every night after her performance, usually taking two or three of the other dancers along as well, for those girls always looked to Herb like they could stand a meal and he didn't think dancing in clubs was any kind of life for a woman. Especially a woman like Maggie. She was nineteen when they met and had only been in the city for three years, having boarded a bus in Ohio, she eventually told him, and leaving the farm and the only life she'd ever known behind forever.

"New York was my destiny," she said with a solemnity that made him think it was true.

"But sixteen?" Herb asked. "On a bus across country? What about your parents?"

"My mother found some movie magazines under my mattress. She said they were trash. She said I was trash."

"And your father?"

"My father was a prince." Maggie tossed her head and laughed. The sound of her laughter washed through Herb like liquid gold. "When I was six, he rode off on a white horse."

Herb could have said it then: "I'll take care of you. I won't ride off." For at that minute he saw himself bolted to Maggie's side, her support and protection for life. But he'd only known her a couple of months and couldn't risk scaring her off with a statement like that, and so he offered to take her to dinner instead.

"Thanks," she said. "That'd be swell."

"Gee," she said when he gave her money for a decent pair of shoes.

"You're too good to me," she said when he threw in for a semester's worth of acting classes after she told him she couldn't afford them any more.

"Honest, Herb. You're one in a million," she told him when he let her charge a winter coat to his account.

"You're the man of my dreams," she announced when he found her an apartment in a safer neighborhood and paid six months' rent in advance on the lease.

Herb didn't think much about the young men he occa- sionally saw leaving that apartment as he arrived to pick

Maggie up. They were all "in the business," as she put it—actors or models or dancers, or wanting to be. She took classes with them, she explained, or ran into them at auditions, and afterward they went out for coffee or came back here to her place to discuss their dreams and what it would be like when they finally made it big. Sometimes, when Maggie talked about the life she'd have on the stage or screen, her violet eyes lost their focus and a distant, dreamy look came into them, and Herb would feel as if she had stood up and walked out of the room and left him behind.

Could he actually ask her? Did he have the courage? And if he was going to do it, shouldn't he do it soon? But what if it was too soon? What if she tossed her hair, laughed her golden laugh, and refused him? He'd die, that's what. So wasn't it was better to spare himself the pain and keep his mouth shut?

"Why, sure I'll marry you, Herb," Maggie replied almost before the words had passed his lips. "It will be the happiest, proudest day of my life."

He remembered exactly where they'd been standing when he finally got the question out—waiting for the light to change at 59th and Fifth. Maggie was standing on his left with her arm hooked through his. They were going to the Plaza for lunch. He was planning to ask her then, bolstered by the solid wood surroundings of the Oak Room Bar, and by a stiff Dewar's, of course, but suddenly a breeze took him and he couldn't wait. The sun was shining. It was the 15th of June. If he didn't get the words out that very minute, they would stick in his throat for life. The exact location of the sun, almost directly overhead, was forever pinpointed in his mind, for when Maggie said yes, Herb had raised his eyes to the sky, half in jubilation, half expecting to see a lightning bolt hurled from above, and there, instead, was the shining sun.

"I've been waiting and waiting for you to ask," Maggie cried and hugged him hard. Then she dropped his arm abruptly and ran around to his other side, putting his body squarely between hers and the horse hitched to its hansom cab on the corner. "I hate horses," she said, grabbing tight to his arm. "We had two on the farm when I was a kid. I've always hated them. My father used to take my hand and press it against their huge, sweaty flanks and laugh when their quivering and snorting made me jump."

"Horses won't hurt you," Herb told her. "Especially that one," he added, pointing at the ancient mare hitched to her cab and wearing a beat-up straw hat with holes cut out for her ears.

"You don't know that," Maggie said, and shook her head emphatically. "You can never tell what a horse will do. They're like Chinese people. They can read your thoughts with their awful slanted eyes."

The light changed then and they crossed the street and walked over to watch the water cascading softly down the statue of the naked woman in the double-tiered fountain across from the Plaza. Suddenly Maggie raised her hand like a kid requesting permission to leave the classroom. "See, Herb?" she said, and passed her palm back and forth through the air as if she were wiping a cloth across the face of the sun. "Just like that, I marry you and wipe the slate clean. Every bad thing that ever happened to me is gone as of this moment. From this day forward, I will have a perfect life."

She looked to Herb like something out of a painting, standing there with her hand lifted to the sky, the sun glinting off her golden skin. And as he gazed at her, that unfocused, distant dreamy look came into her eye and just for an instant, he wondered if he hadn't made a mistake. But he was a gentleman and had given his word.

"You're a man with a heart of gold," Maggie declared, and hooked her arm through his again. "Everyone says so. It's an honor to have a thing like that said about you. Now I'll have an honor too, the honor of being your wife."

On the day of the ceremony, she took the breath from his body, and he had to fight to get it back, seeing her come down the aisle so graceful and tall on her dancer's legs, wearing white satin shoes and with a crown of tiny pearls in the center of her flowing golden-red hair. She hadn't invited her mother, and Herb was sorry there wasn't a man at her side to give her away, but her father was long gone and she could claim no other male relative. The manager at Zack's had offered to fill in, as had the whole gang at Manny's, but Maggie wouldn't hear of it. "This is my life," she said sternly to Herb. "Of my own free will I'm uniting it with yours. I don't need anyone to help me give my life away."

Startled by the sound of the telephone ringing in his ear, Herb held the receiver away from him, stared at it in confusion a moment, then replaced it on its hook. He retrieved his quarter from the slot and closed his fist around it. He hadn't quite thought this through. Invite Pat to dinner, yes, and tell Maggie what? That she was welcome to come along? "You go," she'd say, as she normally did when it was a question of Manny's. "Go to that place with your so-called friends."

That sort of remark wounded Herb for she was talking about men he had known long before he knew her—not so-called friends, but real ones. Men like Manny himself and Chuck and Eddie and Bill, guys from the old days, before wives and children became permanent fixtures in their lives. Thirty-five years ago, when Manny opened his place on 46th, west of Broadway, the guys had begun the routine of meeting there every night for dinner and beers. Christ, was it possible? Maggie only eight at the time? They ate and drank and talked women and business and sports. They were a club, a group, a clan. It became a tradition Herb found himself unwilling to break, and if, over the years, he held to it more stringently than the others, it was because they expected it of him. "You at your table proves order in the universe," Eddie had assured him once. That did it. If the guys needed him there, that's where he'd be. Same table, same time, night after night—center of the room, toward the back, beneath the overhanging black-and-white TV, open kitchen beyond. The guys would come in when they could, see him there, wander over, clap him on the back, order their beers, light up their cigars, lay down their bets on whatever sport was in season, and the night would begin. Manny's was a given, a constant, a haven, a home. The place never changed. Marbled floors, mirrored walls, standing mirrored columns, good food, great waiters, a place where men could be themselves, and even after he was married, and the rest of the gang too, some for the second or third time, Herb didn't see any reason why it shouldn't go on being just that. Maggie could come along whenever she liked, he meant it when he told her so. And on those rare occasions when she took him up on the invitation, having suddenly, inexplicably changed her mind and called out for him to wait, rushing in to her bathroom, fixing up her face, putting on her heels, and come back down the hall, saying of course she'd go, of course she would, she'd love to, nothing made him prouder than walking her in on his arm and showing her off to his friends.

"They don't like me, Herb. I know they don't."

"Sure they do."

"I know what they think of me. Gold digger, slut."

"No, Maggie. They don't."

"Just because I like to wear pretty clothes and fix myself up like somebody cares."

"They don't think that, they don't."

"Go on. Get out! You're happier with them than with me."

The phone was before him, the quarter in his hand. It seemed wasteful not to put the two together. He dialed Pat's number again and counted the rings. Five just to get reception on the line. Hotels weren't what they used to be. Another two before he was connected to her room. He heard her voice, said what he had called to say, and hung up fast. Then he snatched the bottle of orange soda off the ledge, poured the remaining contents into the gutter, threw the bottle in the trash, and headed for the uptown local.

TWO

THE SLUSH UNDERFOOT didn't slow Herb down. He was a born New Yorker and walked like one: briskly and with a tension in his step, winding through a maze of pedestrians on a packed street without breaking stride and beating a flashing "don't walk" sign without half trying.

The subway entrance was less than a block from the phone booth he had just left. Not the entrance he normally used, but then he didn't normally go shopping after work. Or make phone calls to women he hadn't seen in a decade. Nothing he had done since five o'clock that afternoon was normal for him, and he found the break in his routine unsettling. It left him feeling the way he often told Eddie he felt after one too many at Manny's—a little mixed up.

Digging in his overcoat pocket for his MetroCard (an innovation his father would have approved, being in favor of anything that legally kept you from spending more money than you had to), Herb felt the small bulge of the gift-wrapped box in his jacket beneath. I did that, he thought. Braved a store, made a purchase. He was momentarily so taken with himself he considered giving the present to Maggie that very night instead of making her wait until Christmas. "This one's from me for real," he'd say, "not Ethel."

Better not, he reconsidered, taking the steps down into the station at his usual clip. It would only arouse her suspicions, and why create a problem where one didn't exist?

Subways were Herb's kind of transportation. Like himself, they followed a routine and adhered (more or less) to a fixed schedule. Like himself, they ran along pre-determined routes: north and south throughout Manhattan, east and west at 42nd Street. Some, like the B, D, N, and R, meandered east from Times Square, south to Wall, out to Brooklyn and back again, and the E and F would get you to

Queens, but he never had occasion to take those trains. Manhattan was his beat. The Number 6 from home to office and office to home; the 6 again to Grand Central for Manny's; the Shuttle to Times Square, a short walk up Broadway, and the whole thing in reverse to get back.

Herb slid his MetroCard along the slot, waited for the green "Go" prompt, hoping not to encounter the "Swipe Again" command, the one serious drawback to these cards, capable as it was of holding up a whole line of travelers, enflaming tempers, causing words, ugly looks and missed trains. When the signal to proceed appeared, Herb did as he was told and walked resolutely to the middle of the platform. Once there, he turned, walked halfway back, strode to the edge, secured his paper beneath his arm, held his hat, and leaned out. No train in sight. Opening the *News* to the sports page, he folded it down the middle for subway travel as his father had taught him when he was a boy, and prepared to wait.

What a paucity of papers existed today. In his father's day, there had been the *New York Sun*, the *Herald* (famous for its foreign news coverage), the *Tribune,* then the *Herald-Tribune*, the *World,* and the *Journal-American* as well as the *Times,* the *Post* and the *News.* These days he had to supplement with the *Financial Times*, *Forbes*, *Fortune*, *Newsweek*, and *U.S. News and World Report.* When Phoebe was small, Herb had made a point of buying the *Post* on Sundays just so she could read the funnies. 1893, Pops! he recalled answering quickly to one of his father's impromptu quizzes on the evolution of funny papers in the United States. Which paper, kid? The *New York World.* Who owned it? came the next question. Joseph Pulitzer, the instant reply. What'd the critics call that colored supplement? Yellow journalism, Herb would snap back. He had all the answers, then. His father was three at the time the first newspaper funnies came out and he told him when he saw those brightly colored pages lying on the floor where his own father had tossed them, he had crawled over, attracted by the colors, picked up a corner of one page and put it in his mouth by way of introduction. Thus began his lifelong infatuation with the printed page. Herb always liked that tale. It was the closest thing to a bedtime story he'd ever had from his father. His mother may have told him some, but Herb didn't remember that; he barely remembered his mother for she had died of influenza in 1947 when he was ten.

Heralded by a rumble on the rails, the train came chortling down the track, the big red number 6 hanging like a welcome mat in the window of the front car. Long as he had been riding the trains, Herb still thrilled to their approach. Their head-on rush into a station infused a track, lying fallow and desolate only a moment before, with sudden power and noise, with reinforced steel energy and the irresistible promise of near-instant access to a string of New York neighborhoods just down the line. Screeching to a halt, the 6 threw open its doors and disgorged its passengers—tired business people and weary Christmas shoppers—the bulk of whom were likely headed for the very department store Herb had just left, which was staying open until nine every night from now until Christmas to accommodate them (not to mention serve its own interests). Herb stood back to let the people off, then elbowed his way onto the car, packed solid with riders. A seat was out of the question, but he had only two stops to go, so, claiming his territory, he planted his feet near the door and grabbed the overhead rod.

When the doors slid closed, he bent his knees just enough to brace himself for that moment to come, which gave him as much of a kick today as it had when he was a kid first riding the trains on his own, when the car would lurch forward and he would lurch back and the ground would be pulled from under him as by a giant iron fist and the train would hurl itself forward into the long dark tunnel ahead. And when, inevitably, the moment came, Herb gave into it with a little bounce, allowing his ankles and knees to absorb the impact, and let himself be carried off. Trains relaxed him. They took the pressure off. Whatever happened between one station and the next—shootings, muggings, delays due to fires on the track, police investigations, sick passengers, yanked emergency cords—was out of his control. He held his newspaper in front of his face, content to leave his life for the moment in the capable hands of the Metropolitan Transit Authority.

The train was deep in its tunnel, the overheads flickering, when, from the bottom right corner of his paper, Herb saw a portion of a bushy gray eyebrow emerge. He pulled the paper aside half an inch. The lights came back and a man in his eighties gazed up at him from the seat below. Two gray eyebrows, arched high on his forehead. A critical look. Understood. The phone call had been a mistake. But he hadn't meant anything by it. Dinner, that's all. Things with Pat had always been easy. She made him laugh. Her laugh had come back to him in that one startling moment of bumping into her on the street and had opened a place within him that he hadn't realized he wanted so badly to be filled.

Before he'd reached the age of twenty-five, Herb had reconciled himself to never marrying. The women he knew in high school and, later, those he met in the business classes he took at night, treated him more like a friend than a suitor, and that was all right with him. It kept him focused and on-track. But Pat was different. Pat had showed him true consideration, and Herb would always love her for that. They'd had some fine times, though he'd have to say he sensed an inclination toward the end on her part to take it to some other level, but it was over the minute he'd laid eyes on Maggie. This came as no surprise to Pat, who seemed to know what he was going to say even before he broke the news. "Maggie's got the dazzle," she replied. "I can't compete." "We'll always be friends, Pat," Herb told her, wishing there were another way to put that. "More than friends," she answered softly. And when Maggie, for reasons not fully known to him to this day, accepted his proposal of marriage, Pat was the first to wish him happiness. "If you ever need me," she said. "Call."

And so he had called, Herb explained to the man with the bushy eyebrows on the train. Dinner, that's all. And a few laughs. Pat got his jokes. She liked his friends. In those days she'd go to Manny's with him in a heartbeat. And, what's more, he told the eyebrows, still raised high on the man's forehead although his gaze had drifted off, she understood how much running his father's business meant to him. Improvement plans, expansion strategies, benefit packages, policy riders and amendments filled his days. Property covered and perils insured against infiltrated his dreams at night. Medical, dental, religious, personal and sick days, parental and vacation leave, company travel time and just compensation for overtime loomed large in his thoughts. Maintaining contact with his father's old clients was a particular priority. Herb made a point of paying them regular personal visits to renew and update their policies, to inform them of whatever new coverage he believed it in their best interests to carry, and to meet and properly insure their descendants as they came along. In the years since his father's death he had acquired a respectable client list of his own, both individual and corporate, which included, but was not limited to, Manny's restaurant, Manny's customers, Manny's home, the homes and businesses of Manny's friends, and those of his own personal friends and business associates as well. The day he had convinced Chuck Zimmer to tack on flood insurance to his homeowner's policy ranked as one of the proudest in his life. "Floods, Herb?" Chuck had balked. "In Manhattan? You gotta be kidding." But the very next month, a water main had broken outside Chuck's garden apartment and that little piece of paper saved his neck. Early on, Herb had tried impressing Maggie with his ability to recite entire policies by heart, including supplementary coverage, exclusions, and deductibles, but he gave up the effort fast.

"Insurance!" she'd cried. "What a bore! You need to find some other line of work. Something more suitable for a man of your caliber. Now let me think." She tapped a forefinger against her upper lip. "What might that be? A financial wizard, a business tycoon, a king of the office. That's it!" She threw up a hand. "'The king was in his counting-house . . . ,'" she chanted. "Banking! That's the job for you, ' . . . counting out his money.' And I'll be the queen eating bread and honey. It's perfect, don't you see?" And in the sparkle that lit up her eyes he almost did. "The bank will be your castle," she told him. "You'll have pigeons on the ledge, blackbirds I'll bake in your pie. And the maid . . ." She took up the chant again. "'The maid was in the garden, hanging out the clothes.'" She paused a moment, then clapped her hands in glee. "Of course! Ethel's the maid! 'Along came a blackbird and nipped off her nose.' That's just what I'll do. I'll nip off her nose."

But the insurance business was not a bore to Herb. It was an enterprise embodying courage and compassion, dealing as it did with high risk and immense vulnerability. He saw the policies he sold as far-sighted and generous. He viewed them as encompassing the dangers of fire and flood, theft, irreparable loss, personal accident and mortal peril, as well as exploded boilers and burst pipes. All parts of a house, including its foyers, dens, guest rooms, basements and attics, additions and garages fell within his company's purview. Interiors from top to bottom, exteriors to the north, south, east, and west were insured against disaster. And should all else fail, death, too, was covered. What could possibly be boring about that? In all the years they'd been married, Herb had never been able to say this to Maggie, but he saw each policy he sold as an instrument of love.

Married life took Herb by surprise. He hadn't expected it to be so complicated or to involve such radical change. The changes began even before the wedding day. His single room on the second floor of the Sixth Avenue hotel turned into a penthouse. "It isn't right for a man like you to be cooped up in a tiny room like that," Maggie explained, after having come to the hotel one day while he was at work and directing the staff to move him to the penthouse. "What's the matter with you, Carmine?" Herb had demanded, having retrieved his key from the front desk and gone up to his room to find that it didn't fit, and having to go back downstairs again. "I've been living here seven years and you don't know which key is mine?" "Oh, didn't she tell you?" Carmine replied. "Miss Ellsworth dropped by and had us move you to the penthouse."

Herb rattled around in that six-room penthouse for two months until they were married and then the six rooms on 54th and Sixth turned into fifteen on 77th and Madison. The co-op Maggie made him buy had a long, white-tiled hall that ran like a river of milk connecting all the rooms. A woman came in every day to scrub that hall. Other women came to dust the furniture, vacuum the carpets, polish the wood, wash the clothes, iron and fold the linens, prepare the meals and put away the dishes. Never had Herb's life been so full of women. Busy, industrial women. Specialized, competent women. Seeing them at their various tasks, he was impressed by their expertise and attempted to remember their names, but no sooner did he get one set of names straight than the women to whom they belonged disappeared and he had to learn a whole new set. If he noticed an absence, he might inquire of Maggie what had become of Mary or Abigail, hoping he had the names right, but whenever he asked, a look of such infinite sadness would flood her eyes that he always wished he hadn't. "I try to keep them, Herb. Honest, I do. I try as hard as I can to make them stay, but something always goes wrong."

The women who left his employ were quickly replaced by others and those were frequently joined by an array of strangers who came not necessarily to clean things, but to repair or replace or deliver or remove them. Herb viewed this endless stream of people like a company of actors, strutting across the floors of his apartment as they might across a stage: decorators, painters, plumbers and repairmen, dressmakers, florists, butchers, cooks, and wine merchants, laundresses, housekeepers, and eventually, to his profound astonishment and joy—nursemaids and governesses. None of it ever seemed quite real to him as he watched, more or less dumbfounded, from the wings. Now and then he'd find himself accepting a bit part in the production, coming in at the last minute to save the day, carrying not a spear but a checkbook. It was a part he could play with his eyes closed and often did, Maggie complained, accusing him of being blind to every single effort she made about the house.

"Do you think I do it for myself?" she regularly demanded. "Is that what you think? Well, I don't. I do it for you. For you and Phoebe. I do it to make things nice."

Floors came up, curtains and fixtures came down, walls were painted and papered over, entire rooms were demolished and new ones constructed in their place. Minor adjustments wouldn't do for Maggie. She worked with antiques and on a grand scale. Venetian chandeliers, Baccarat vases, Louis this and Louis that, French Provincial, Italian Renaissance. The terms she bandied about meant nothing to Herb, but once a period had been established and a room or group of rooms designed to reflect it, he adjusted. Somehow, he settled in. Early American, Art Nouveau, whatever it was, he learned to live with it. Then only a few months later, he'd come home from work and find everything changed. Whole countries had been abandoned, entire centuries obliterated.

"Like it, Herb?" Maggie would say and point to a new sofa with matching chairs, a new dining room suite, a new dining room. Herb tugged on his hat and said, "Sure." Then he taught himself a little trick. He learned not to notice. By the time their third wedding anniversary rolled around, he could walk into a room and hardly see a thing. And when Maggie asked, "Like it, Herb?" he could answer in all candor, "Like what, sweetheart?" His trick became a habit. The habit became entrenched. It drove Maggie to distraction. "Damn it, Herb! Are you blind?" She'd take him by his ear, drag him across a room, stand him in front of something she proclaimed a work of art, and force him to look. "Look at it, can't you? Just look. Can't you see how beautiful it is? Can't you see that?" Glass would shatter. "I only do it for you!" Objects would fly. "To make things nice. To bring a little beauty into your life."

How someone like him who didn't need more than a bed, a table, a good reading light, someone who had lived happily in a single room in a hotel for seven years, had acquired so many rooms and so many possessions long remained a mystery to Herb. Eventually, however, he came up with the only possible solution: The rooms must belong to somebody else. The possessions were those of some other man. The life he was living was another man's life. That had to be it. And then on the day the child appeared, the baby girl they named Phoebe, the mystery deepened. How was it possible to love with such a bewildering force? And to love something so small, something that had not even existed the day before?

Herb was forty-four when Phoebe was born and had about given up hope of ever having a child of his own. But there she was: pink, slippery, formidable, helpless, and his. His? "Of course she's yours, Herb. What do you think?" He didn't know what to think. He didn't know anything about babies, baby girls especially. "But she's so little," he protested. Maggie laughed. "They come that way." Phoebe. His little girl. His.

Maggie gives the baby a toss. "Isn't she wonderful, Herb? Isn't she the most perfect thing you've ever seen? Go on, take her."

The child comes flying toward him.

"No, Maggie. Not me."

Like a satchel, she's snatched away.

"Not till she's bigger."

The infant flies into the air again.

"Careful, Maggie."

She heads for the ceiling, drops back into her mother's arms.

"'Bye, baby bunting . . . '"

Once more, the baby sails toward the ceiling.

"You think you ought to be doing that?"

"'Daddy's gone a-hunting . . . '"

"Couldn't she throw up or something?"

"'Up to the ceiling, down to the ground . . . '"

"Couldn't she—— ?"

"Oh for God's sake, Herb! Can't I ever have any fun?"

But these days, Herb reflected, feeling the gentle rumble of the subway rails coming up through the soles of his shoes, Maggie wasn't much interested in fun. For the past few weeks, she had rarely left the house. And for days before that, the apartment had looked like a warehouse. Boxes were stacked in the kitchen. Cartons and crates, evidence of her last major shopping spree, lined the front hall. "We coming or going?" Herb asked one evening, tripping over a box as he walked in the door. "Aren't you going to open these?" Maggie didn't answer, and the boxes and crates remained where they were. Soon Herb stopped asking anything at all about them, and then one day, they disappeared. It turned out Maggie had called all the stores and told them to come and take everything back. She slept most days now, but only fitfully at night. Sometimes, waking before dawn, Herb was likely to hear her in the distance somewhere, prowling about the apartment. Several mornings in a row he got out of bed and walked through the house and found her leaning against a wall, surveying a room and whispering, while tapping a finger against her upper lip, "It's not right. It's not quite right."

Then briefly last week she'd rallied, and Herb thought the crisis had passed. "Phoebe's coming home for Christmas!" Maggie announced, the old excitement in her voice. "I almost forgot. I have to finish the tree." But the project soon seemed more than she could handle. A few days ago Herb came home to find half the tree decorated. The day after that he found all the ornaments removed from the half she had finished and placed on the other half. The following day, the tree had been stripped bare, and Maggie was in bed. Last night, a single bulb adorned its branches. Moods, he figured, or a vitamin deficiency. He suggested she see a doctor. "Doctors," she replied, and turned onto her side. "I've been to so many I've lost count. They never see what's wrong."

Standing here now on the train, Herb thought of the days when Maggie would leave a gift for herself next to her breakfast plate, or in the large cut-glass bowl on the hall table where she placed the mail, or under her pillow at night. The gifts were usually small and each was wrapped in bright paper and bows and came with a card, declaring the item was from him. "How sweet of you, Herb!" Maggie would exclaim, making a great play of having come upon the package unawares. "Oh, what a sweet thing to do," she'd say, reading the card with cleverly feigned surprise. "Thank you, Herb. Thank you so much." "You're welcome," Herb would reply, automatically taking up his part. Then Maggie would tear open the box, examine its contents with such enthusiasm while expressing such unrestrained delight that Herb would almost forget she had spent hours picking the gift out herself. "I love it! I do! It's just what I wanted. What wonderful taste you have!" she'd declare, and cover his face with kisses.

Sometimes she'd toss the package aside and saunter over to the green leather chair by the living-room window, where he sat at night to read his papers, and take the one he was reading out of his hand and drape her lovely arms about his neck and lower her body onto his lap and nibble at his ear. And when she did that he would think she was right, he had damned good taste.

"I'm glad you like it," he'd say.

And if it were a dress or a hat or anything else that might be worn, she'd rush in to put it on and come back out and model it for him, twisting her hips and flinging her glorious golden-red hair from shoulder to shoulder until it looked as if bright sparks from a setting sun were flying about the room.

So convincing were her performances, by the time they were over Herb had begun to wonder if it weren't possible that somehow, some part of him, like a shadow part, had, without any other part knowing, gone into a store and actually selected whatever it was that had brought his beautiful wife such unalloyed delight. This feeling of having a shadow part within him that operated without the knowledge or consent of any other part of him crept over Herb increasingly with married life. The first time he fully became aware of it was one evening, long ago, after he'd acceded to Maggie's passionate requests that he take her to a movie.

"It's *Cover Girl*, Herb," she'd said. "Come with me. Oh, please, you've got to. It's my favorite movie in the whole world."

"I don't go to movies much," he told her, and suggested she go with someone else.

"I don't want to go with anyone else. I want to go with you. It's *Cover Girl*," she told him again. "You've seen it, haven't you?"

He told her he hadn't.

"Not even once?"

He shook his head.

"With Rita Hayworth and Gene Kelly?" she prompted, as if that would make him remember.

"Sorry," he said.

"Oh, Herb, no. I can't believe that. I really can't."

She looked as if she might cry.

"I must have seen it twenty times." She brightened at the memory. "It's at the Beacon. Tonight only. You've got to come. Please, Herb. Please."

The minute the film began, Herb knew he was in trouble. He had thought the title meant the girl was a cover for something, like a Red agent, and kept waiting for the story to prove him right. When it didn't, he grew restless and confused and leaned over to Maggie to ask her to explain things. "Is she a spy or isn't she?" "Later, Herb," Maggie whispered, her eyes straight ahead. "Watch how she dances. Watch how her long hair flies." Herb looked back at the screen and struggled mightily with the plot, but when before long it escaped him completely, he turned to Maggie again. "What's going on——?" he started, and looked at her face and his heart nearly stopped. Her beautiful eyes were filled with tears.

"That could have been me," she said, "up there on the screen, singing and dancing."

All through the rest of the picture Herb had looked at Rita Hayworth from a wholly different point of view. With her long legs kicking and her red hair flying, she really did look an awful lot like Maggie. Soon it wasn't any stretch at all for him to see how it could have been his own gorgeous girl up there on the screen, dancing her heart out. After that, he started seeing himself in the Gene Kelly role. Not in his youth or piano playing, and for sure not in the way he went through most of the movie whining like a sick cat, but in what he did in one of his dances. In that particular number, Kelly split off from himself and became two men. Or not two men exactly, but one man and one shadow, dancing round and round each other. Something about it struck a chord in Herb, for it seemed to him that sometimes, just like Kelly up there before him, going round and round himself on the screen, he split off from a part of himself and went round and round himself in life.

It was as if one part submerged and another part washed up and became all there was to him. At times the visible part was the one Maggie found so boring, the part she claimed cared only for money, for business. At other times the part that surfaced and swept the first away was the part she, for reasons known only to herself, called her Iron Henry. The two parts followed one another like Gene Kelly and his shadow, one surging while the other receded, then the two changing places, the one behind coming forward, the one in front falling back, the two splitting off and dancing round and round each other across a room or down a street.

"Are you sorry you married me, Maggie?" Herb asked when they came home from the movie that night. "Are you sorry you gave up your career?"

"Dance with me, Herb," she said. He had only just opened the front door.

"You know I can't dance," he protested.

"Oh, but you can," she replied, and took his hand and placed it on the small of her back.

Clouds of Chanel No. 5 and Charles of The Ritz engulfed him.

"You're light as a feather on your feet," she said, and took his other hand in hers. She pressed her cheek to his. She hummed softly in his ear. The smell and feel of her lifted him right up off the spot where he stood and soon he became light as that feather she said he was and was dancing with her down the long, white hall.

Later that night as he lay in bed, the hallway's gleaming white tiles spinning in his head, Maggie rose up on an elbow and brought her face close to his. She kissed his lips, her hair grazed his nose, and at her touch the years dropped away. He was a young man again, bold and strong as that Iron Henry she liked to compare him to. Maggie brought it to him like a prize, a trophy of his former self. She whispered something in his ear but he couldn't quite make out her words. He wanted to say something back but didn't know what to say, so he put his arms around her and held her close and neither of them said anything after that. She clung to him and he clung to her, two speechless, shadow parts going round and round each other in a spinning room. The thought flashed through his mind that maybe Maggie didn't have the words either, that maybe there was a part to her as there was to him that she went round and round with, a part of her that matched that part of him and was the reason they were together, and that maybe their two shadow parts were meeting then and dancing mutely in the dark.

Oh, Maggie. Oh, Christ. What wouldn't he do to have her back the way she was. He'd phone Pat, call off dinner, do what's right.

He'd confess all, tell Maggie everything, honor his father's policy and come clean. Confess what? Tell her what? That he had accidentally run into Pat in front of a store? That out of all the streets in New York and all the millions of people milling about on them during the course of any one day, he'd been on the one street on the one day that Pat had happened to walk out of a store? Tell that to Maggie and expect to be believed? Or perhaps he should tell her that Pat looked great? That she hadn't gained an ounce? That the old days had burst into life at the sight of her? Was he out of his mind? Maggie's anger was like a third person in the room. Even when she sat quietly in a chair, it hovered close, waiting to pounce. And when it leapt into action, his very survival was at stake. She came at him geared for battle, fingers curled, eyes narrowed to slits and scanning the shelves for weapons. Anything at all would do—a dish, a tea cup, a flower pot. Clearly, she wanted more than to make a point. Annihilation was her goal, eradication of his very core.

The train pulled into the 68th Street station. Hunter College. A fine school. Only one station stop away from his. No reason Phoebe couldn't have gone there. Or Columbia. Or NYU. But no, they were too close to home. She had to pick some goddamned place halfway across the country. Michigan or Illinois or wherever the hell it was. Phoebe, in college. It didn't seem possible. Just yesterday she was in diapers, or in those frilly white panties Maggie put on her to cover the diapers. His little girl, a college kid. He could hardly believe it. He remembered the day she had come to his office to meet him for lunch and Ethel had asked her what she wanted to do when she finished college. "Christ, Ethel!" he'd shouted. "What the hell's the matter with you! College? She hasn't even finished high school yet." And Phoebe had thrown him a look of surprise, with maybe, he'd thought but couldn't be sure, a flash of admiration in it too, for she had never heard him yell at his secretary before. Then she'd cut in with that smart-alecky tone she sometimes used and Maggie claimed she got from him: "Yes, Ethel, I know what I'm going to do. I'm going to be a truck driver." Truck driver! Who was she kidding? Herb didn't hold with talk of women in the fire departments and flying for the Air Force. Driving a plane or a truck was a man's job. Even getting into a cab these days and seeing it

43

driven by a woman gave him a jolt. He knew this town, its streets and crazy drivers, its pot holes and motorcycles, its brave but reckless bike messengers zigzagging through traffic, risking their necks to make an extra buck by racing the wrong way down one-way streets. Truck driver! In college now?

Two kids, maybe from Hunter, boarded the train. Arm in arm, lost to the world. Baggy jackets, baggier jeans, sneakers even in the snow. With the luck of young lovers they found seats as soon as they stepped aboard. The older man with the bushy eyebrows and a woman Herb hadn't noticed sitting next to him got off just as the kids got on, and the two slid into their seats as if they had their names written on them. The boy hooked his arm around the girl's neck. He pulled her to him and opened his mouth wide enough for Herb to see his tongue dart out and slither into the girl's mouth. Hers came out to meet his and, like small reptilian creatures, the two tongues touched, pulled back, glided forward, gyrated, curled and flattened, rubbed sides, and rolled over and under one another. These kids were seventeen. Eighteen, tops. Phoebe's age. His baby, the truck driver. He thought of her in a boy's arms, stopped the thought before it could form of her with her mouth opened like that. And the doors slid shut and the train shot forward, fast as time. Only a minute ago Phoebe was in her crib and he, hands clasped firmly behind his back, was bending over her, fearful of getting too close, of breathing whisky or cigar fumes into her face. She was a baby, and then she was a kid, too young to read, having stories read to her at night, and now she was in college, off on her own in some faraway school in some goddamn distant state.

"'Rapunzel, Rapunzel . . . ,'" Maggie's voice came back to him over the soothing hum of the rails.

He'd been in his bathroom, shaving, as he did every night before going out to Manny's. His bathroom connected to Phoebe's room on one side and to his and Maggie's on the other. The door leading to Phoebe's room was open a crack.

"'Let down your hair to me . . .'"

He stood in the doorway, his face covered with shaving cream, the razor forgotten in his hand.

"'Rapunzel, Rapunzel, let down your hair . . .'"

He opened the door wider to watch Maggie's face as she read. She lay next to Phoebe on the child's bed, her hair spread loose on the pillow. He listened to her read about Rapunzel's hair being as fine as spun gold. Her own hair was as fine as that. He listened to her read about Rapunzel unfastening her braids and throwing her hair out the window for her prince to climb up. The red in Maggie's hair grew bright in the lamplight coming from the side of the bed, and Herb thought of the sun setting low over the Hudson, and from that night forward, Maggie's hair for him was the color of sunset, no matter what color it was.

"I'll wait," he'd said when she had finished reading the story. "Get a sitter. Come to Manny's with me."

"You go," she replied. "Go to that place with your so-called friends."

THREE

HERB GOT OFF the train at the Lenox Hill Hospital stop, crossed to the west side of Lexington, dropped the evening *News* in the trash can, and picked up the *Post* at the corner stand.

Rami, huddled in his little window behind the rows of candy bars and packets of gum, had the paper held out for Herb as he approached.

"I have saved you one," Rami said in his precise Indian diction and lilting tones. He had already rolled the paper into a tube to save Herb the trouble of doing so. "You are late tonight, Mr. Larrimore."

"Thanks, Rami." Herb took the paper from him with one hand and handed him the exact change with the other. "Shopping held me up."

"It is that time of year."

"You can say that again." Herb noticed that Rami was not wearing a hat. "Wind's picking up," he said, "gonna be cold tonight."

"It is not usual for you to be late," Rami replied.

"You warm enough in there?"

"Each night of the week you are here for your paper by twenty past five or twenty-five past at the very latest."

"Oughta wear a hat in this weather."

"It is now six-eighteen. Many times I have checked my watch."

"Present for the missus."

"I have been worried."

"Don't worry, Rami. It's bad for the digestion."

"When I do not see you by twenty-five past the hour, I worry."

"You keep warm now. A hat's good in the cold." Herb gave him a wave and, lowering his head against the wind, walked quickly on down the block.

At the corner, forced to stop for the light, he surveyed the avenue. Park Avenue: most pretentious street in town. North of 96th, things got real, but here it was all fancy apartment houses, gray or green awnings, snooty doormen and snootier dogs. The Christmas trees running down the Avenue's center island were stunning, he'd give it that, especially at night with the trees' bright white lights sparkling against a dark sky. Still, they didn't hold a candle to Maggie's tree. Park Avenue trees were as uniform as pyramids, solid white, and pretentious as the street itself. Maggie's tree had life to it. Color and shape and life.

Year after year, he'd come home from the office in the week before Christmas to find her in a sweater and jeans, a bandanna on her head, laboring away on the tree and looking like a kid working her tail off on some school project. Cartons of ornaments opened around her, half the glass balls still wrapped in the cotton she'd painstakingly packed them away in the year before. Face flushed, skin heated, breasts straining against her sweater, Maggie came alive as she worked. Everything about that tree had to be just so. Wide bands of actual cotton on the dining room floor—a sheet wouldn't do, she said, it was far too flimsy—radiating from the foot of the tree in wider and wider concentric circles to form a field of simulataed snow. Wood and glass and ceramic figures lined up and waiting on the floor beside her to fill their designated places in the snow and take up their parts in the Christmas scenes, biblical, secular, or whimsical, in which they were featured.

Maggie allocated a corner of the dining room near the window as the Christmas tree's place of honor. She assigned each ornament a specific location on a branch and had the finished product complete in her mind, down to the tinsel and angel hair, before she placed the first glass ball. And she would brook no interference. "No, dear. That doesn't go there," she would say to Phoebe when she was small and wanted to help, or to Herb himself when he occasionally tried to give her a hand. Very gently, she'd remove the ornament from the branch where he or Phoebe had hung it and place it on one above or below, or even leave it on the same branch, but move it farther back or forward. Herb didn't pretend to understand her system, but he cherished the excitement he saw in her face as she worked. Stepping close to the tree to dress its limbs, stepping back at intervals to assess her progress, she came to life as the tree took shape.

"Just wait, Herb. You'll see," she'd call into him every now and then as he sat in the living room, reading his paper. "It's going to be magnificent."

Two days before Christmas, the dining room was sealed off, the door from the hall and the sliding doors to the living room shut fast for secrecy. No one was allowed to enter. Meals were taken in the kitchen. And when it was finally time for the great unveiling, Maggie would call, "All right," and fling open the door with a great, dramatic gesture. "You can come in now." A second later, she'd slam the door in their faces, "No! Wait!" she'd call out. "Not yet." Then the door would open again. "All right, come in. Close your eyes." She'd turn off the chandelier, turn on the lights on the tree. "Open now." Every year it took his breath away.

Herb trailed the row of Park Avenue pyramids with his eyes, watching the trees descend, diminishing in size, block by block, all the way down to Grand Central. There the row disappeared, double tunnels through that glorious building sucking it along with two entire lanes of traffic out of sight. He remembered Grand Central without MetLife on top, without even Pan Am. He thought about that for a minute, the passage of time, his whole life in this town, then the light changed and he walked on.

Midway up the block, on the north side of the street between Park and Madison, a small junior college was nestled in among the brownstones. Herb didn't know the name of it, but he passed it every night on his way home from work. "Why can't you go there?" he'd asked Phoebe more than once, for the college was just around the corner from where they lived. "Afraid to make me happy?" "It's for special students, Dad," she told him. "Well, you're special," he answered, and she gave him a look that divided generations. "Not special like that." But no, it would have killed her to go to that school. She could have fallen out of bed into class.

Pulling up his coat collar, Herb rounded the corner onto Madison Avenue and saw their doorman Fred standing tall and lean, a sentinel at his post, with one hand already on the handle of the building's heavy glass-fronted, iron-framed front door. Another man, thought Herb, whose occupation kept him out in the cold. At least Fred had a hat.

"Evening, sir." Fred raised a white-gloved hand to the shiny leather brim of his green wool cap. "Everything all right?"

"Getting a little cold."

"I meant the time. You're late tonight."

"It's okay, Fred. Stopped off to do some shopping is all."

Fred threw him a look of surprise and pulled open the door.

"You keep warm now," Herb said, and passed on through into the lobby. It could stand a few strong lights, he thought, as he'd thought every night for twenty-two years, upon entering this lugubrious, marbled expanse, but Maggie claimed the lobby's dimness added to its old-world charm. He'd trade charm for decent lighting in a heartbeat. Maggie found the elevator charming, too. Shaped like a birdcage, fronted by a collapsible metal gate, and operated by old-fashioned brass controls, it went from floor to floor, stubbornly maintaining a pace even a snail could overtake. Centered above the elevator on the ground floor, a large wooden dial with brass numerals and arrow instead of a modern digital display told you what floor it was on.

Third, Herb saw now, glancing up at the dial. Then, an eternity later, two. He knocked the sides of his shoes together, dislodging some snow, tapped the tube of newspaper against his leg, checked in his pocket for his keys, adjusted his hat, unfurled the newspaper, read half of the *Post*'s front-page story about a double murder in the Bronx, and the elevator was on the ground. Empty, he saw.

"Evening, sir." Jimmy pulled open the gate.

"Shopping," said Herb. "Don't ask."

"I wondered what it was. Shopping, you say? I haven't started yet."

"Better get a move on."

"You're telling me. Five days to go."

"Got plans, Jimmy?"

"Wife, kid, the usual. You?"

"Same here."

"Think we're in for more snow?"

"Could be. Wind's picking up."

"I don't mind snow this time of year. It goes with the holiday."

"I don't mind it either, Jimmy."

On the fifth floor, Jimmy pulled the elevator to a halt, lining up the elevator floor precisely with the vestibule landing at the exact moment he released the brass controls. No matter how many times Herb saw that move, he was struck by the deftness of it, the synchronization, the amazing coordination it took to put all those steps together—lining up the two floors, releasing the controls, pulling back the gate—and make them come out even. Jimmy's hands and feet working the elevator, guiding the brass handle, bringing it up slowly, slowly, his eye, his expert eye, judging distances, lining up planes, matching floor to floor, the fingers of his other hand on the gate, tightening, tightening, then gripping and pulling back, the floors exactly aligned, the controls released, the gate opened. Like a goddamned ballet.

"Here you are," Jimmy said, pulling back the gate. "Safe and sound."

"Thanks, Jimmy."

"Ring when you're ready."

"Will do."

The building had two apartments only on each floor. They faced one another across a narrow, black-and-white-marbled-floor vestibule. Herb's apartment was directly opposite Wallace Kroenberg's, but they rarely saw their neighbor these days. He'd settled progressively deeper into the seclusion of alcoholism over the years and now, living with a caretaker, found little reason to go out. When Phoebe was younger, Herb used to worry about her meeting Kroenberg alone on the landing, but he gathered from what she said that whenever that happened, the man was never anything but a gentleman to her.

Kroenberg's apartment was to the left of the elevator, his own to the right, a small stained-glass window that opened onto a shaft between. Herb walked to the right now, put his key in the lock, gave it the one sharp turn that was all it required, also to the right, and pushed open his front door. Instantly, his steps, so quick and confident on the street, turned tentative. Here, in his own house, he tread lightly, habitually walking through the rooms in small, cautious steps with two primary, interconnected worries on his mind: waking Maggie, should she be taking a nap, and making some clumsy move that would knock a fragile, expensive object off a shelf.

Tonight, before he even had time to walk down the hall and hang up his hat and coat in the closet, Maggie called.

"My Iron Henry's home."

Her voice came from the piano room, the first room off the hall, to the left of the front door. Herb looked in. Lilac draperies at the windows, an oriental rug, a baby grand piano no one in the house knew how to play. Maggie was sitting naked on the floor.

"What's this?" he asked. "Pipes overheat?"

She looked up at him from where she sat but didn't reply.

"We got a policy for that," he told her and tried to smile.

She was sitting with her back against the wall, her knees pulled up to her chest. She stared at him a moment more then asked, "Have a nice day? Work hard?"

"No kidding, Maggie," he said. "What's going on?"

A six-inch strip of bare wood bordered the rug on all sides. Maggie was sitting directly on that strip of wood, leaning against the wall. She was almost exactly in the middle of the room, the piano down at one end of it, the door at the other end.

"Of course you worked hard," she said. "That's a silly question, isn't it? You wouldn't know what to do if you didn't work hard."

Herb tried to take this in. Lilac draperies at the window. A piano against one wall, his wife against another. Her bare buttocks on a hard wood floor.

"Why so quiet, Herb?"

Her hair fell in damp, unruly tangles about her face. The makeup around her eyes was smudged. He couldn't make sense of it. Maggie, his wife, sitting naked on the floor.

"Cat got your tongue?"

"Where are your clothes?"

"No, not the cat," she said. "Cats don't talk. Money does. Isn't that what they say?"

"What is this, Maggie?"

"I worked hard today, too."

"What are you doing there?"

"I've been working on the tree," she told him. "Like it?"

She gestured toward the dining room. It was two rooms away but in his direct line of sight from the piano room, through the living room and through the open connecting doors.

"Get up, Maggie. You must be cold."

"Look at the tree."

"Where are your clothes?"

"Look at it, damn you!"

Herb wasn't a religious man, but when Maggie's Christmas tree went up at home, he found himself giving thanks. Even now, with her on the floor like that, he couldn't help but turn his head and look.

"It's not quite finished yet," she said.

It stood in its place in the corner by the window, full and green, the top nearly grazing the twelve-foot ceiling. Bluebirds with spun-glass tails and crystal eyes perched on its branches. Silver bells and multicolored prisms dangled at carefully selected intervals. Red and gold and green glass globes caught the light from the chandelier, sending flashes like fire through the Scotch pine needles. Bare spots stood out here and there and the lights and tinsel had yet to be added, but yesterday she had placed a single bulb only. And today—Herb couldn't believe it. She had even finished decorating the floor. The wide bands of cotton had been laid down and the crèche positioned to one side in its special section of the cotton. Off to the left, the figures of the three Wise Men were poised to present their gifts. And just behind the Wise Men, his favorite scene was taking shape: twelve glass reindeer arranged on mirrors in two straight lines with long red silk ribbons looped around their necks and tied to a miniature of Santa's sleigh. Maggie hadn't yet looped the ribbons or placed the sleigh, but there were the reindeer, standing tall on fragile legs and beneath them, the mirrors, their frames cunningly concealed in the cotton, simulating silver lakes in a virgin snowfield. Maggie put her whole soul into that tree. Even now, half finished, it took his breath away.

"Gorgeous," he said.

"Really, Herb? You really like it? You're not just saying that?"

"It's out of this world."

"As nice as last year's?"

"Nicer. Now how about getting dressed?"

"Wasn't last year's taller? Fuller, maybe? A better shape?"

"Honest, Maggie, it's a peach."

She angled her head and looked at him from where she sat. "I can still do it, can't I? I can still make your eyes light up."

"You know you can. Now please get up. I hate to see you on the floor."

"Why, Herb? Does it hurt your eyes to look?"

"For Pete's sake, Maggie."

"Your big, brown, sad eyes, so sensitive to light and pain."

He bent down to lift her up. A sour smell rose from her body.

"Your eyes are like glass," she said, and recoiled from his touch. "Sight bounces off them like rain."

"Okay," he said, standing up. "Stay there. I'll get your clothes."

"Once upon a time I made a wish on your eyes."

Her arms were wrapped around her legs. Her breasts were crushed against her knees. Her beautiful breasts, flattened and crushed. Herb longed to cup them in his hands and restore their lovely shape. "Maggie," he said. "What is it? What's wrong?"

She leaned her head against the wall and let her legs fall open.

He opened his newspaper and spread it across her lap.

She plucked the paper from her body and tossed it aside.

"'If wishes were horses, then beggars would ride.'"

"Here." Herb held out his hand. "Let me help you up."

She took his hand between both of hers. Her skin was so cold he gasped in surprise. She held his hand tight a moment, then turned it over and examined it carefully, front and back.

"So small a hand to wield such power," she said. "A figure on Wall Street to make them sit up and take notice."

Herb didn't know what she was driving at.

"A veritable business tycoon."

"I don't get you, Maggie."

"And a naked woman scares you to death." She dropped his hand. "Don't I please you, dear?"

"You must be hungry."

"Don't you like to look at me?"

"I'll bet you haven't eaten all day."

"Or are you afraid to look?"

"Come on, get up. I'll take you to dinner."

"To Manny's, you mean?"

"Anywhere you say."

"You walk me in that place like a statue on your arm. Like something that isn't alive."

"You name the place, we'll go."

"Your friends watch my every move. Their eyes sting my flesh like nettles."

"Anywhere you want, we'll go, okay? Just, please, get up, get dressed."

"At least they see me, Herb."

"Maggie, Christ."

"Even naked, you don't see me."

"Get up."

"Take off your hat." She patted the floor. "Have a seat." She moved over to make room for him, as if there were a dozen people sitting next to her and she had to move to make room. Herb couldn't make sense of this. How had he come to have a wife who sat naked on the piano-room floor?

She lifted an arm, held her hand out to him, palm up.

"That's how you show an animal you mean him no harm. You let him sniff your palm. Sniff it, Herb. Don't be afraid. Don't back away. I'd never hurt you, don't you know that? Don't you know who I am? I'm not a statue, Herb, or some wild creature, either. But you tiptoe around me as if I were. As if I'm some dangerous animal you know nothing about. Not the first thing. Not the species I belong to or the country I come from, or the foods I like to eat."

"I don't understand what you mean when you talk like that."

"Damn it, Herb!" she shouted. "It's English. I'm speaking English. You understand English, don't you?"

He stepped back as she spoke, and she pressed her hand to her mouth.

"Oh, there. I've done it again. I've frightened you. I'm sorry, I didn't mean to shout. You flinch when I shout. Did you know that, Herb? Did you know you flinch?"

He said that he didn't.

"Well, you do. And every time I see it it's like a razor through my heart. But I have to shout to make you hear. I have to grab your head and hold it still to make you see."

"What do you want from me, Maggie?"

"I want you to see."

"See what?"

"Get out!"

He held his ground. He couldn't think of a thing to do to help her. Nothing in all his experience had prepared him for this. He had married a little late in life. Too late, maybe. Maybe there was a window of opportunity when you could jump into marriage and make it your life and maybe, if you waited too long, you missed the jump or landed wrong. An insult, maybe life considered it. And if you hadn't learned or weren't prepared, it fought you back. Maybe that's what was happening now. Life fighting him back. He unbuttoned his coat.

"Don't go," she cried.

"I wasn't going."

"Don't leave me, Herb."

"I'm right here."

She gazed up at him from the floor. "And looking awfully spiffy tonight, if you don't mind my saying so. But then you always do. Three-piece suits and Sulka ties. The ubiquitous hat. Felt in winter. Straw in summer. You'd be naked without your hat, wouldn't you, dear?" She laughed. "That's all it takes for you. Me, I have to strip."

"What's this all about? What's going on?"

"Show me your soul."

She scooted toward him like a crab across the floor. "You're such a tidy ship," she said, arriving at his ankles. "All battened down and buttoned up." She ran her hand along the seam of his trousers. "Nothing hanging loose, no demons flying free." She reached for his fly. "What if I undid this zipper here? Would something pop out? Would I see your joy?"

Gently, Herb brushed her hand away.

"I do bring you joy, don't I, Herb?"

"Oh, Maggie, please."

"I am your sunshine?"

"You know you are."

"And your moon and your stars?"

"Those too."

"One cross word from me and your world goes dark?"

"Here, take my hand."

"Always the gentleman."

"Please, get up."

She waved his hand away.

"Show me where you keep your joy."

"Get your clothes."

"Show it to me, damn you! Show me!"

"Get off the floor."

She moved back against the wall.

"I better not, Herb, and I'll tell you why. If I get up, I might do you harm."

"Sweetheart, no."

"I wouldn't want to, but I might not be able to stop myself. I might open your chest with a hammer to find your hiding place."

"Don't talk like that."

"I might pluck out your heart and wring it in my hands to feel what you feel."

"Stop it, Maggie, please."

"I might gouge out your eyes and hold them up to mine to see what you see."

"That's crazy talk. I'll get your clothes." He turned around and headed for the door.

"Don't go!" she cried again. "Please! Don't go."

He turned at her cry.

"I'd give them back, I promise I would. I'd fill your eyes with beauty and give them right back."

He turned away and walked out the door. He walked down the long white-tiled hall past the grandfather clock, past the closet, past the living room, past the dining room, past the cutoff to the kitchen and the den, past the library, past Phoebe's old room on the left, past the bathroom she shared with Maggie on the right, and on down to the end of the hall and the bedroom he and Maggie shared, over-looking the brownstones in the courtyard below. He walked into the bedroom and over to the bed. He pulled a white woolen blanket off the foot of the bed, draped it over his arm, and carried it with him out into the hall again. He walked down the hall past Phoebe and Maggie's bathroom, past Phoebe's old room, past the library, past the cutoff to the kitchen and the den, past the dining room and the living room, past the closet and the grandfather clock and into the piano room again and over to the spot where Maggie sat on the floor.

"My Iron Henry's back."

He gave the blanket a shake. He watched it rise, catching the air like a net and fanning out, fluttering and white before his eyes, obscuring her for a moment entirely from his sight, then settling down over her body to rest lightly in place.

"Come to bury me once and for all."

"Don't talk like that."

"I see rainbows in your eyes." She reached for his face.

"Oh, Maggie." He turned his head aside. "How much do you think I can take?"

"How much, Herb? You can't ever stop, don't you see, my dear? It's your nature to go on and on. And I know about nature. I was raised on a farm, remember?"

She grabbed his hand and pulled him to his knees.

"I only want to make you happy." She threw the blanket off and pressed the flat of his hand to her breast. "Does this make you happy, Herb? Does this please you? Or does it disgust you? How am I to know? You stand me on a pedestal and back away. 'Gorgeous,' you say, stepping back. 'Like a million bucks,' you tell me, looking on from across the room. And up close, Herb? Inside? What do you know of that?"

Herb pulled his hand away. "Come on," he said. "Get dressed. Have dinner with me."

She held her hand to his cheek. "Big, brown, sad eyes. Rainbows inside. Broken crystals glittering. No wonder you can't see. Never mind," she said. She caressed his cheek. "It's not your fault. You're a good man, your heart is made of gold. And your eyes of glass. Imagine that. But it's all right, Herb. I'm not even sad, see?" She flashed him a smile, a radiant smile, and for an instant he thought there was nothing to worry about.

"Maggie," he said. "Why can't you be like other women?"

"But that's just it!" she cried. "If I were, you wouldn't love me. And you do love me, don't you, Herb?"

"You know I do."

"Then everything's all right."

"It is?" He would give his life to have it so. "Everything's all right? You mean it?"

"Of course, dear. Of course I mean it. Go on now, go to Manny's."

"I don't have to go."

"Yes, you do."

He bent down and took his time arranging the blanket about her. He pulled it up to her chin and opened it wide to cover her shoulders. He pulled it down over her feet, which were like ice to his touch, and gently tucked it in at her sides and under her legs. "Keep warm, Maggie."

She sat very still while he did it, allowing herself to be secured on all sides, and the instant he was finished, she jerked up her legs, kicked her feet free, and threw the blanket off.

"Just one thing before you go," she said, her body bared before him again. "Show me your hiding place. Do me that honor."

"What are you talking about?"

"Let me feel what you feel. Let me feel it here."

She lunged forward and grabbed his hand and forced it high between her legs.

He felt the moist heat rise from the bush of reddish-brown hair. His palm was on fire, his fingers felt scorched. He twisted his wrist free and pulled his hand away. "Don't be crazy, Maggie," he said. "For me, I'm asking."

"A man who asks so little for himself, asking that. I'm sorry, Herb. I know it hurts your eyes to look. Go on then. Go to your friends. I know they're your friends, I know they are. I'm sorry for what I said about them. I wouldn't hurt you for the world."

"I'll wait," he said. "You fix yourself up."

"No, dear."

"Pretty, the way you do."

"Not tonight."

"Please, Maggie."

She shook her head and said she preferred to stay where she was, and it made sense to him to go then, that minute, to be a man who had just come home from work and was going out now to have dinner with his friends. Manny would be there for sure. He was in, running things, every night, six nights a week. God only knew how his own marriage survived. Chuck would almost certainly turn up, and Eddie and Bill were strong possibilities. And tonight there'd be Pat. Oh, Christ. Pat? What the hell was he thinking? He'd meant to phone and call it off.

"Please, Maggie," he said again. "I'll wait. You get yourself dressed."

She lifted a hand to her lips and blew him a kiss off the tips of her fingers. "'Shoe a little horse,'" she said. "'Shoe a little mare. But let the little coltie go bare, bare, bare.'"

FOUR

HANDS THRUST DEEP into overcoat pockets, Herb paced the marbled stretch of floor between his front door and Wallace Kroenberg's apartment across the hall. What the hell was wrong with him? Why was his instinct always to flee? *Maggie naked on the floor.* Even the picture of it. The recollected image. To flee from his own mind.

There was something missing in him, or something added that shouldn't be there. Something that made him look for a way to skirt an issue rather than face it head-on. Not at the office, there he functioned as well as any man, but almost always at home, this thing or absent thing would swell in him until it threatened to burst and made him want to run. A raised voice, a cross word, the slightest hint of a domestic confrontation and he'd put on his hat and head for the door. Eddie, help me out here. Manny, what should I do? He had seen her there, not the terrible after-image before him now, but the actual, real, unbearable thing, and his mind had gone blank, his mouth dry, the blood backed up in his veins. In typical fashion, he turned useless and stupid. *Show me where you keep your joy.* Stymied and stupid. What should he say? What should he do? *Do the right thing.* Christ, Pops, that piece of facile advice never came close to covering a situation like this.

He raised a balled fist to Kroenberg's door. Look, man, he appealed to the closed door, you've lived a long time, over eighty years, in fact. You've seen a thing or two. Ever see anything like that? Got any idea what I should do? I've helped you out once or twice, leading you back into your apartment when you wandered out, dazed and disoriented, into the hall. Sometimes wearing only your pajamas, and some of those times, you'll pardon me for mentioning it,

61

only the top half. I don't mean to embarrass you, but I'm in a jam here. I'd never bring it up otherwise. Christ, she made a wish upon my eyes. Tell me how to handle this.

It was no good. Kroenberg's door didn't open, the man didn't appear, offering solace and neighborly advice. The guys at Manny's remained silent. Herb was in over his head. He could feel the waters closing, briny and deep, about his ears, seeping in through his mouth and nostrils, filling up his lungs. He stumbled over to the staircase that spiraled around behind the elevator from floor to floor. He sat on the top step and put his head in his hands. He lifted his hat and raked his fingers through his hair, or what remained of it. The step on which he sat in a heavy coat and hat was two feet from his front door, behind which Maggie sat naked on the floor.

He stayed where he was on that step without moving, holding his head in his hands, and after a while, how long a while he couldn't say for sure, that other part inside him, that part that was not him exactly but a shadow part of him, stood up and roused the first to action. The two parts stood and did an animated little turn around the vestibule, then the part that was not him walked through his front door, straight through without any need to open the door, and there was Maggie, off the floor. Up and dressed and ready for an evening out.

"Take my hand," he says, and she takes it. "I know what you need," he tells her. "Air, food. A walk down the street, a decent meal."

He knows. He functions. He is of use.

He walks her into a restaurant on his arm. Heads turn. Men stare. Envy flashes from their eyes. He reads the menu. He makes all the right choices. "No more sherry for you," he says. "A thick steak is what you need." She accepts his authority without question. The color returns to her cheeks. He tells her to see to her diet, get more exercise, rest when she's tired, and consult another doctor. She agrees to all his terms.

He would give her the world, he says, give it without condition.

Show me your joy.

That is his joy. That's it. All of it.

"Honest, Herb?"

He would lay all that he has before her. What else was he to do with it?

"But that was never why," she implores him to understand. "It was never the money. Is that what you think? Do you know me so little?"

He would open his veins before her, spilling blood like gold at her feet.

"My king in his counting house," she says. "My quiet king."

His Maggie.

"My quiet man."

He closes his eyes. A quiet man with a lifetime of devotion to offer.

She comes to him, says his name.

"Remember our first time, Herb? It might have been my first ever. I told you it was because it might as well have been. You ruined me for men that night."

His beautiful girl.

Her fingers are light on his face. She touches his eyelids, grazes his lips. It is more than enough.

Herb pulled his handkerchief from his pocket.

My bones are turning to chalk.

The big white cotton square opened like a scarf before him. He bunched it in his fists and pressed it to his eyes.

Are you blind, Herb? Are you blind?

He pushed himself up off the step and rang for the elevator.

I hear them crumbling.

The birdcage rose ghost-like through its shaft and stopped before him. The gate pulled back. Herb stepped inside.

"Evening, sir," Jimmy said, just as if he hadn't said exactly the same thing when he'd taken him up forty-five minutes earlier.

"Evening, Jimmy," Herb replied. And there's no reason for that look in your eye, he would remind his old friend.

Nothing strange is happening here. Everything's routine. I'm going out for dinner at Manny's just the way I do most nights. Who knows that better than you? You take me up around five-thirty, down around eight, up again around midnight. Tonight is no different from any other night, except that maybe I came in an hour or so later and am leaving an hour or so earlier, but that's a variation on the routine, not a change in the routine itself, and certainly nothing peculiar enough to warrant that look in your eye.

But there was no look, Herb knew, and it was not in Jimmy's eye that something strange was happening.

As the elevator descended, a slow tearing away of fiber from bone, a gradual ripping of tissue from tissue accompanied the car from floor to floor.

"Here you are," Jimmy said, pulling back the gate at the lobby. "Safe and sound."

If only that were so. "Thanks, Jimmy," Herb replied.

He stepped out of the elevator and walked across the lobby that seemed to him darker than usual tonight. He wanted to turn back but something prevented it. Some unseen barrier or maybe a bulb that had burned out or a piece of furniture that had been moved. He took another step and found nothing in his way, no chair or table or obstacle of any kind to prevent him from turning around, telling Jimmy he had forgotten something—for he would, of course, have to offer the man some excuse and apologize for the trouble he knew it would cause him—and getting back in the elevator and going upstairs again. He could do it if he liked. He was a tenant share-owner with unanimous board approval. No one could stop him. But he didn't turn around. He didn't walk back across the lobby. He didn't tell Jimmy he had forgotten anything or offer him any excuse or apologize to him for this troublesome last-minute change in plans or ask him to let him back in his elevator and take him upstairs again. He buttoned his overcoat, tugged on his hat and walked across the lobby straight to the front door.

"Have a good evening, sir," Fred said with a smile, pulling open the heavy, iron-trimmed door, and Herb almost asked him what the hell he meant by that.

Maggie, naked on the floor?

Skin pale as plaster, breasts crushed against her knees. The images swirled about in the wind and snow that blew up Madison Avenue and hit Herb in the face the moment he stepped out the front door.

Maggie's bare buttocks on the hard wood floor?

He raised his collar, secured his hat with his hand, and glanced at the sky. Black but clear. A few stars visible between building tops. Snow now seemed unlikely.

Herb walked to the corner, feeling more convinced with each step he took away from his apartment building that he was doing the right thing. Maggie needed time to pull herself together. She'd soak in a hot tub, take a pill, an aspirin, or something one of those doctors she said never did her any good had prescribed, have a glass of wine, maybe a nap, and by the time he came home, she'd be her old self again. Restored, calm, filled with confidence about the future. Or deeply asleep. He had seen it before. Things settled down within her when he left her on her own. It was her pattern, her need. It was the way she functioned, and he respected that.

He turned the corner and headed east, straight into the wind. At the mid-block recess that opened onto the oval courtyard before that junior college Phoebe wouldn't go to, the wind became a boomerang. It darted in one end of the courtyard, crashed crazily around the building's glass and concrete facade, and shot back out the other end and onto the street again. Nearly losing his hat to a strong gust of wind, Herb was filled with a sense of dread. *Not special like that, Dad. Special.*

Pitting the strength of his body against the strength of the elements, Herb continued down the street. Now and then he was forced to yield to the greater power of the wind and staggering then like a drunk, was bandied toward the curb and bandied back again toward the building line, reduced to taking small, faltering side steps, as if he were uncertain of the street beneath him, as if these weren't his streets, streets he knew as well as he knew his own name, streets he had known all his life.

The subway was ahead of him, due east, and Manny's was west. Regaining his footing, he ran to beat the light and crossing Park, thought about the absurdity of that, of walking east to get west. In the old days, when he'd lived on the second floor of that westside hotel, all he'd had to do to get to Manny's was walk out the door, head over to Broadway and saunter on south eight blocks from there. Things were simpler then. Now it was a walk east to get west, the Lexington Avenue local to Grand Central, the Shuttle to Times Square, and then another walk, north this time, along Broadway to 46th and his desired destination.

Tonight the absurdity of the route distracted him. He walked past Rami's stand without stopping, despite the sudden emptiness he felt beneath his arm and within that emptiness, the realization that he'd left his newspaper somewhere, and within that realization, the dreadful recollection of where he'd left it. Too shamed to turn or even shout a reply when he heard Rami call, he ducked his head like a thief and kept on walking.

"Mr. Larrimore! Mr. Larrimore!" The man's frantic cries followed him to the end of the block. "What has transpired? The hour is too soon. Is something amiss?"

At the corner, Herb crossed to the south side of the street and took the steps to the subway double-time. Rami would be ashamed of him if he knew what he'd done. Rami would think he was less than a man.

At the bottom of the stairs, a large clapboard sign imprinted with bold black letters stood raised on a three-legged, easel-like structure. The sign was positioned outward so the people walking down the stairs couldn't possibly miss it: *Please don't eat or drink in the station or on the trains.* An "awareness campaign" the Transit Authority called it. Who were they kidding? These were New Yorkers they were talking to. Herb gave the sign a shove as he passed, knocking it off its perch. Awareness? That meant there was no law against it, so good luck enforcing it. And how could there be any law when food and drink were sold at nearly every major subway station in the city? Did they think the people in this town were fools enough to follow whatever condescending instructions were put in front of them? Hadn't they learned anything from the "politeness campaign" they'd tried a while back? *Please step aside*, those signs had read. *Let the passengers off first.* Christ! They'd even gone as far as to paint lines and arrows on the floor of some of the platforms, indicating where boarding and de-boarding passengers should walk, and that campaign had lasted . . . what? a month? three weeks? Didn't they get it? It wouldn't work. Not in this town. Not with the people in his city. Not ever.

I might open your chest with a hammer.

A better man would turn around, take the stairs in reverse, go home. But he had pulled his MetroCard from his pocket. He was sliding it through the slot.

I might pluck out your eyes and hold them up to mine.

He could see the lights of the Number 6 already streaming into the station.

To see what you see.

Oh, Maggie. Oh, God.

He got the green "Go" signal, gave the metal bar a shove, crossed the platform, entered the car, let the doors slide shut behind him, and was away, scot-free.

Maggie would want it this way. She needed time and privacy. *Go on, Herb. Go to Manny's.* She'd pull herself together. *Go on, get out.* How many times had she said it? *Leave me alone. Just go.* And he'd be home before she knew it. Midnight at the latest. Dinner with a friend. She didn't need to know who. Why upset her by dropping a name? What would be the point of that? A harmless dinner with an old friend. Christ, it would be good to see her.

Herb took up his favorite place to stand on the trains— at the end of the seats, near the door, facing the last window in the row. He planted his feet firmly, grabbed the overhead rod, and readied his knees for the takeoff lurch.

Maybe he was wrong not to have told Maggie about Pat. Maybe honesty was the best policy, even in a situation like this. But he thought there was more than honesty involved here. There was a whole world of possible misunderstanding and almost-certain complication, and it wasn't as if he were having an affair.

Affair. Affair. The rhythm of the train gathering speed picked up the word and repeated it over and over in his ear. *Affair, affair.* With each revolution of the wheels the word was driven deeper into his brain. *Affair, affair.* In the easy give and take of the steel suspension springs . . . *affair, affair.* In the steady rumble of the rails . . . *affair, affair.* The full composition of the train, its seats and windows and overhead rods, the wheels and rails it ran on, the entire underground system of the city where he had been born and lived all his life was berating him for a past indiscretion. *Affair, affair.* But what he'd had with Pat hadn't been an affair. Or it had, but one so brief it hardly counted as such. Not that he discounted it, he didn't mean that. He valued it, cherished it. He cherished her. But it had nothing to do with his life with Maggie. It had ended before that had properly begun, before they were married, certainly, and since then, he'd never strayed, never once. He was a faithful man. A faithful family man.

Show me where you keep your joy.

Oh, Christ, Maggie. Naked on the wooden floor?

At 68th Street, it wasn't college kids who got on this time, but businessmen, three of them with briefcases in hand. Colleagues, Herb figured, who maybe had been working late, then gone for a couple before heading home, judging from the way they were talking louder than they needed to and jostling one another as they came aboard. A bunch of Christmas shoppers crowded in behind the three men. Then two Eastside couples, dressed for dinner or the theater, who rolled their eyes, whether over the loudness of the businessmen or the packed condition of the train was a toss-up, but this was a New York City subway, for Christ's sake, Herb would like to remind them. What the hell did they expect? Just as the doors at the far end of the car were closing, a homeless man squeezed through, holding out a metal cup and sending the stench of flesh that had nowhere to get cleaned and clothes that came into regular contact with city pavements and grates through the car. The two well-dressed couples fell all over themselves to get out of his way. As soon as the train started rolling again, the man rattled the coins in his cup and began pleading his case.

"I ain't robbin', I ain't stealin'," he told the passengers who did their best to pretend he wasn't there. "I'm homeless and hungry and askin' you kindly. Whatever you can spare . . . a nickel, a dime. I'd be much obliged."

He waited a moment and attracting no takers, slowly made his way toward Herb's end of the car, repeating his appeal word for word and shaking his cup before him. The few coins he'd left in it just for this purpose made hollow, lonely sounds as he approached. His stench, as powerful as steel spreaders, parted the crowds before him, giving him almost unobstructed passage through the train.

Most people looked away, staring down at the floor or at their laps or up at suddenly riveting advertisements overhead as the man approached, conferring instant invisibility upon him and leaving him free, therefore, to carry on as he pleased. Subways did that to people. They created spaces inside of which commuters could conduct any private act, short of a criminal one, with absolute impunity. New York City subways operated according to strict but unwritten rules of behavior: no eye contact, no touching (other than motion-induced) or talking to strangers, no manifest acknowledgment of another's existence, no spoken interpretation or overt signs to indicate judgment of another's behavior. Speed and noise sealed the agreement. People rode these cars as if alone on them. The arrangement had always appealed to Herb. Forced into the closest proximity with perfect strangers, feeling a stranger's elbow in his ribs or between his shoulder blades, having a stranger's sleeve brush his face or fingers cover his own as he struggled for purchase on the bar, feeling a stranger's breath on his neck, feet trampling his shoes, hips grinding against his as the train pulled to a stop, he felt his privacy preserved. And others did as well. He knew it from watching them. Crammed in side by side, flesh to flesh, people on subways felt free to perform acts of a personal nature they would normally perform only if alone. They changed their shoes and socks, picked their teeth and noses, filed their nails, combed their hair, ate entire meals, engaged in domestic arguments of the most intimate sort and acts that fell just short of being sexual.

Once, on his way to work, Herb had seen a woman, fortunate enough to have found a seat and oblivious to the morning rush-hour crowds around her, put on her makeup from scratch. With an aplomb she might have exhibited standing unobserved before her bathroom mirror, she pulled a succession of jars, bottles and creams, pencils, brushes and powders, tubes of color and small, strange tools from an oversized bag. She set up a mirror the size of a baseball mitt on little metal supports in her lap and, despite the pitching and swerving of the train and through four consecutive station stops and starts, applied the creams and colors to her cheeks, the pencils and brushes to her eyes, without, so far as Herb could tell, leaving a line, mark or spot she didn't intend to leave. She shaped, contoured, highlighted and shadowed. She enhanced her lashes, rouged her cheeks, carefully outlined and painted her lips. She clamped what looked to Herb like an instrument of torture onto her greatly thickened lashes, then finished them off with several deft strokes of a brush that seemed to have tarantulas crawling out of it. People all around threw surreptitious looks her way, then quickly looked away. They watched as New Yorkers watch, seeing everything at once and nothing at all. It was what Herb liked best about the trains—they crowded you in and in the crush, left you alone.

But what did he care about that woman and her bag of cosmetic tricks? A woman he didn't know and didn't love? The woman he cared about, the one he loved and should be thinking of, the one who should be here, standing next to him on this train, was Maggie. He shouldn't have left her at home. Maggie should be with him now, on her way to dinner at Manny's.

There was a time when she had gone with him willingly. Not often, but once in a while. And she had enjoyed herself.

Or sometimes she had. Provided nothing happened to upset her.

"Comfortable, dear?" He pulls in her chair.

"You're happy here, aren't you," she asks him. "Happier than you ever are at home."

"I wouldn't say that," he replies.

"I would," she responds and scans the mirrors around her. "Who's that man at the bar?"

Herb turns to look. "Which man?"

"Don't stare," she tells him. "Black shirt, pink tie. You can see him in the mirrors."

"Oh, him." Herb checks the reflected image in the glass. "Jerry Parker. He's a bookie."

Maggie smiles a smile that rocks him in his seat. "Bookie? That's like a Broadway stockbroker, isn't it?"

"You got it, sweetheart."

"And him?" she says, lifting her eyes to the mirrors again, and giving her head a toss. Crimson flares light up the room. Golden-red sparklers go off. "With the broken nose and mashed ear. Another friend of yours?"

"That's Angel," Herb replies. "You know Angel. Used to be a prizefighter."

"Call them over, why don't you? I know you want to."

"Not tonight."

"You love these men, I know you do. If I weren't here, they'd be over in a flash."

"Tonight I'm with you."

But she's right. He sees Eddie Taylor at a table, Manny keeping his distance. The room's spatial boundaries draw tighter, its tension increases when Maggie's along.

Suddenly Maggie lurches toward him across the table. She looks stricken, abruptly taken ill. "Oh, no!" she cries. "It can't be."

"What?" he says. "What is it?"

"Tell me I don't see what I think I see."

She reaches out, grabs him by the lapel, pulls him over into the light. "Oh, Herb." She presses the lapel of his jacket flush against his vest. "Oh, God. It's true."

"What?" he asks. "A stain?"

"Not a stain! Not a stain!" She releases his vest and shoves him back into his chair. "It doesn't match!"

"What doesn't match?"

"Your vest, Herb. It doesn't match your suit."

Her beautiful eyes are filling with tears. Tears! He feels a moment's panic. Tears in here? In Manny's place? Where his friends might see?

"It's the wrong vest, Herb," she tells him. "It doesn't go."

He was afraid of this. "Take it easy, Maggie," he says.

"It's the wrong blue," she says. "You look like a derelict." Her eyes are brimming over. "Like no one cares. How could you, Herb? How could you?"

"It doesn't matter," he replies.

"Of course it matters!" she shouts. "Don't you look when you take something out of the closet? Do you just grab the first thing you lay your hands on?"

He wants to help her, to calm her fears. "It's not important," he says and pats her hand. "Don't give it another thought."

"It is important!" she cries. "How can you say it's not? It matters how you look. That's the wrong vest. Don't you know that? It goes with your other blue suit."

"Yes," he answers.

"Yes? Yes what?"

"Yes, I know." He says it quietly.

Her reply is heard throughout the room. "You *know*?"

She starts to sob. Manny is looking over. Eddie glances up from his table. "Hush, Maggie. People are watching."

"You know? What do you mean you know? And don't hush me! You mean you did it on purpose? Deliberately put on the wrong vest? Why would you do a thing like that? Wore it out? To the office? Why, Herb? Why?"

Chuck Zimmer walks in the door, sees Herb, starts over, sees Maggie, detours to Eddie's table.

"I asked you a question, Herb. Why?"

"I had to."

"Had to? Why? Why couldn't you wear the right vest?"

72

"I couldn't find it."

"What?"

"It's missing."

"What do you mean, missing?"

"The cleaners must have lost it."

"The cleaners lost your vest?"

"That's all I could figure."

"The cleaners lost the vest that goes with that suit?"

Great, round tears are trickling down her cheeks. Herb wants to catch them in his hands, return them to their place of origin.

"And a couple of others," he admits and instantly regrets it.

"*Others*?" she cries.

He takes her hand. She throws him off.

"You've done this before?"

"Once or twice."

"But how——?"

"I just pick out the ones that go best."

"Oh, Herb."

She's crying hard now. "Aw, Maggie, don't. I hate to see that."

"And nobody noticed?"

He wants to see her smile, make her laugh. "This one's pretty close, don't you think?"

"Ethel never noticed? *I* never noticed? How is that possible?"

"Now don't get all upset."

"Of course I'm upset!"

Her voice ricochets off the glass. Manny and Chuck and Eddie are looking their way. Herb's heart is beating rapidly.

"Why shouldn't I be upset?" Maggie demands. "When did this happen? When did the cleaners lose your vests?"

"A while ago," he confesses.

"How long ago?"

"Not long."

"How long?"

"A few weeks, I guess."

"Weeks! And you didn't tell me?"

"I didn't think you'd——"

"What? Care? You didn't think I'd care?"

"No, Maggie. I thought you'd be mad."

"Of course I'm mad. I'm furious."

The tears give way to rage.

"I won't have you walking around like that. It's not right. You're too good. I'll talk to them. I'll go to the cleaners in the morning and get your vests back. You'll see, Herb. I'll get every last one back."

"Thanks, Maggie."

"Don't do that! Don't thank me." She holds her hand across her mouth. Her eyes fill with tears again. For a moment she cannot speak. "It kills me when you thank me. It's like you think you don't deserve it . . . that you don't have a right to have me . . . your wife . . . do something for you without thanks. You do deserve it, Herb. You have a right. I care how you look. I care what people think."

"I know you do."

"And to think of you going out like that——"

"Oh, Maggie. Please."

"Going to the office——"

"Hush, sweetheart."

"What must people think? Oh, God. Reilly!" She hails a waiter. "Come over here. What do you think of this?" She grabs the man's hand.

"Oh, no. Let him go," Herb says. He can't stand this. His ears are burning with shame. "That's Red," he tells her. "Reilly's off tonight."

"Red, all right. I beg your pardon. Red, tell me . . ." She's pumping his hand. "What do you think of a man who goes out wearing a vest that doesn't match his suit?"

Guessing, maybe, it's a quiz, Red looks to Herb for the answer.

"Doesn't it make your heart break?" Maggie says. "It does mine, I'll tell you that. It breaks it right in two."

She releases Red's hand and the man ducks into the kitchen.

Herb sees Bill Schummacher walk through the door, start for his table, see what's happening, and look around like he's lost. Spying Eddie and Chuck, he walks toward them like he's been reprieved.

"For weeks, Herb?" Maggie says again. "Going to the office in vests that don't match? Taking people to lunch?" Tears are streaming freely down her cheeks. She lets out a sob. "For weeks?"

"Don't do that, honey. Don't cry, please." Herb whips his handkerchief out of his pocket, unfurls the great white cloth. It waves on the air like a signal for help. "Take this, please. Oh, please, don't cry."

"You can't let people treat you like that," she tells him and snatches up the handkerchief. "You can't let them walk all over you. Why didn't you tell me about it?"

Herb looks at Eddie's table. Eddie looks sick. Bill and Chuck have their hands up to their foreheads, shading their eyes. Manny is with a customer, but every now and then glances his way.

"Why didn't you tell me, Herb? Why didn't you?"

"Aw, Maggie, please. It's all right. Stop, now, please. You know I hate to see that." He pats her hand, squeezes her wrist.

She looks straight into his eyes. Her face is different.

"They're only tears, Herb."

"What?"

"They're only tears. Not explosives. Not bombs to blow up your friends."

"Okay."

"Your friends won't die to see this. You won't die."

"I know—"

"You don't know. You think this will kill them."

"I— No, I don't— I— Maybe you'd better go upstairs and—"

"What? Hide in the ladies room? Is that what you mean?"

"No, I—"

"All right. Fine." She hurls the handkerchief onto the

table and pushes back her chair. "If it will make you feel better, I'll go."

"I didn't mean that, Maggie. I—"

But she didn't turn around. She held herself straight as a queen and walked across the room, passing Manny without a word, passing Chuck and Bill and Eddie at their table, walking across the room with Angel and everyone staring after her, with Stan and Jerry looking on from the bar and the waiters and chefs peering through the glass partitioning off the kitchen. She walked up the great marble central staircase that was hardly ever used these days because at its top were only a small dining room, reserved for private parties, and the ladies rest room.

For him. All for him. Carrying on in a public place, appealing to the waiter, for him. The sobs and streaming tears. For him.

"Wait up, pal." Herb hitched up his overcoat and called out to the homeless man who now had reached his end of the car.

Herb carried his money in his trouser pocket the way his father had carried his—singles on top, larger bills beneath, graduating to fifties and hundreds in the center, the whole folded over once and wrapped in a rubber band that was never changed until it broke. Naturally, after weeks or months of use, pulled off and on by fingers embedded with newsprint and city grime, that piece of rubber got pretty rank. Maggie hated the very sight of it. "Oh, Herb!" she'd protest when, pulling out his money to pay a restaurant tab or taxi fare, he'd expose the grimy rubber band. "How can you use a thing like that?" He'd pull off the band and lick his thumb to peel back the bills. "Oh, no," she'd cry. "Touching a disgusting thing like that, then putting your fingers in your mouth!" Once, she had even leaned forward in a cab and tapped on the Plexiglas to get the driver's attention. "You see that, driver?" she demanded. "You see what he's doing?" Unfazed, the cabbie had raised his eyes to his rearview mirror for a look. "A man of his caliber using a rubber band for a money clip," Maggie said. "And licking his thumb to touch the filthy bills. Can you believe that? Carrying the germs from the money to his mouth!"

Maggie bought him any number of money clips over the years—gold-plated and sterling silver, fashioned in the shapes of oversized paper clips and dollar signs. Herb made her take them all back. "The rubber band's good enough for me," he said, but she wouldn't hear of it. "No, it's not, Herb. It's not," she replied every time, and once had even burst into tears while saying so. "You don't know your own worth," she told him, her eyes like violets swimming under water. "You don't realize how much you deserve in life."

"Here you go," Herb said now, rolling back the rubber band from his wad of bills. Freeing what he knew without looking was a dollar on top, he pulled it from his pocket and stuffed it into the homeless man's cup.

"Bless you, sir," the man replied, and Herb knew himself the least deserving of men for any man's blessing.

With a screech and a blast of hot air, the train came to a halt at 59th Street. This was his chance to get off. He could run up the stairs, take the overpass, run down the stairs on the other side, switch trains, head back uptown, do the right thing. He squeezed through the crowd in front of him, took a step toward the doors, but just as they opened a woman, weighing in the neighborhood of three hundred pounds, barreled her way onto the car. She forced Herb back, shoved the people nearest him aside, and stationed herself like an armored tank directly between him and the exit. There was no possibility of getting around her. The car was too crowded to make a move for the door at the opposite end with any hope of reaching it before the train took off again. So Herb stood where he was, gripping the rod and staring out through the window at the people standing on the platform, staring back at him. He should be out there among them. He should be off this train and on that platform, not waiting, as they were waiting, patient and staring, for a less crowded train to come along. He should be dashing up the stairs, racing across the overpass and down the other side, crossing the platform, and taking a northbound train, slipping aboard at the last possible moment just as the doors were closing, as he had seen kids do—black teenagers mostly, so quick and athletic—slipping through the doors just as they were sliding closed, timing it so exactly it seemed for a second that their bodies were bisected by the door, split cleanly from head to toe, half left outside on the platform, half leaping into the train, or their physical bodies flying through the door and, just as it closed, their shadow parts flying after. Get off, change trains, ride the northbound local home. That's what he should do. Then the doors shut and the subway lurched into motion and gradually picked up speed and the figures of the people standing on the platform slid past, falling away into darkness like people dropping one by one off the end of a dock, and then there was no platform left and no one standing anywhere and nothing at all before him but the blackness of the tunnel and the steady, comforting rumble of the rails.

I am your sunshine? Your moon and your stars?

He missed his paper. He would have held it up before his face. He heard the voices of the businessmen behind him, still loud but slower now, like they were running out of gas, and thought he was a guy like them, a working stiff, a man who led, or longed to lead, a simple life. He went to his office and did his job and came home to a wife and child and, like the men behind him and others, everywhere, he presumed, throughout this car and the other cars on the train, and other trains and elsewhere in the world, kept at it day after day, struggling to put a roof over their heads, food on their tables, and something away for a rainy day. But here, tonight, the resemblance between himself and other men ended. Tonight, his wife had sat before him, naked on a floor, and he had put his hat on his head and walked out the door.

Suddenly the northbound express overtook his train on the inside track and, looking out his window, Herb looked into the faces of the people standing at the windows of the car shooting past, holding the overhead bar and looking back. Then the express gave one long, high-pitched screech that might have been the voices of all those people staring out the windows raised in a single, deafening scream, and was gone.

FIVE

HERB GOT OFF the train at Grand Central. As he strode purposefully through to the Shuttle, his thoughts were drawn back to the newsreel theater that had been here in the station many years ago. His father sometimes dropped in after lunch. One day when he failed to return to the office, Herb had sent Ethel, a very young but remarkably efficient secretary even then, to look for him. Having an inkling that his father might be catching up on world events in Grand Central's newsreel theater, he'd given Ethel instructions to search it carefully. Ethel did as she was told and spotted the old man in a back row in the dark, eyes glued to the flickering screen. When she had made her way over to him and tried to persuade him to come back to the office with her, he claimed not to know who she was. "Get away from me!" he cried, rearing back in fright. "Leave me alone. What do you want?" She gently took his arm, and his father shouted, "Take your hands off me! I don't know you. I don't want to go with you. I'm staying here." Young as she was, Ethel had somehow calmed his fears and convinced him to get up from his seat and leave the theater and return to the office with her. By the end of that day, Herb had believed his father to be his old self again, for he even gave him the familiar raised eyebrow look of expectation when he walked into his office. Two days later, he died at his desk.

Herb took the Shuttle to Times Square, bought another *Post* at a stand on the corner to replace the one he'd left at home, and gave a fistful of change to a man he saw walking down the street wearing nothing, despite the cold, but shorts and an undershirt. Then he crossed to the west side of Broadway and proceeded north to 46th. On the south side of 46th, he made a sharp left, walked in less than half a block, and there he was, facing the big, welcoming, double-fronted glass doors of Manny's. His hangout, he called it. Just seeing those doors before him filled him with joy. And the moment he put the flat of his hand over the elegantly carved M.G.—his friend Manny Green's initials—etched deep in the glass, and gave the doors a shove, he became a different man. Or not a different man exactly but, and for this he asked forgiveness, an undeniably happier one. He pushed the doors open, crossed the threshold as into another life, waved to Stan behind the bar and felt a loosening begin in his body. Starting with a point between his shoulder blades, it traveled down his spine to his hips, then dropped to his knees and ankles, freeing his joints as it went. Stan waved back, and the tightness in Herb's chest dissolved. As Herb walked across the floor, his throat opened up and the tenseness in his arms evaporated. He took in the gleaming marble floor, the shiny brass rail along the great oak bar, the starched white linen on the big, round tables, the bright lights and chrome fixtures, the polished mirrors on the walls and standing pillars—precisely the sort of details he'd be oblivious to at home—and felt himself truly at home.

The waiters working the room nodded to him as he crossed their path. The tangy smells and warmth emanating from the glassed-in kitchen in the rear seemed its own personal greeting. In a minute he'd be sitting at his table in front of that kitchen, white-coated waiters scurrying at his beck and call, his newspaper spread before him, a drink in his hand, a good meal coming his way. Manny would stop by later for a chat and his friends, coming in, would know just where to find him. One by one, they'd push open those glass front doors, give the place the once-over, zero in on his table, see him sitting there and saunter over; they'd slap him on the back, pull out their chairs, take a load off, order up their beers, light up their cigars, and for the next few hours all would be right with the world. It was his place. His hangout. His joint. It was a club to him. A man's club. Women were tolerated but not sought after, and that suited Herb just fine, as politically incorrect as that opinion might be in this day and age.

"Hi ya, Herb!" Manny called out the minute he spotted

him, his great booming voice the vocal equivalent of the man's considerable girth. "How ya doing tonight?"

"Can't complain. Yourself?"

"Business a little slow. Me, I'm perking."

"That's what counts."

"When you're right, Herb, you're right."

Manny placed a massive arm about Herb's shoulders and walked him the rest of the way to the cloakroom. There Maisie, standing behind her little half-door, arms already thrown out in wide affection over its shelf, was waiting to receive his hat and coat. As Herb approached, she turned her head and lifted her chin, presenting one cheek, shiny and polished as an apple, for his kiss. Herb obliged with not one kiss but two, one for each glossy cheek. Then he removed his coat, took off his hat, and entrusted the garments to Maisie's care.

Maisie's cloakroom was separated from the restaurant at large and set back in an alcove, which all the regulars referred to as "Maisie's empire." She guarded it fiercely, having been with Manny since he opened for business just before Christmas in 1964 and having exercised strict control over all the hats and coats, gloves and scarves, canes and umbrellas, packages and briefcases that came her way in all the years since. Maisie, Herb noted, was as much a fixture in the place as the fixtures themselves, or as himself, for that matter.

"What's the occasion?" Maisie asked, throwing back Herb's coat, which was draped over her arm on its way to being hung on the revolving circular rack behind her, to check her watch. "It's seven-twenty, Herb. We never see you before eight."

"You, doll," Herb answered. "You're the occasion. I rushed in early for a sneak preview of that gorgeous face."

He planted another kiss on her cheek, then turned to Manny who took his arm and walked him down the generous center aisle toward his table. Proprietor and friend, they strode across the large, brightly lighted room like a couple of well-heeled land purveyors overseeing their territory. People waved and called out to them from tables on both sides of the aisle as they passed. "Hello, Herb." "Good to see you." "Great meal, Manny." "Chef's really cooking tonight." Herb and Manny nodded and waved in reply, exchanging greetings and pleasantries with the evening's customers—long-term habitués, mostly, and friends from way back—as they made their way to Herb's table by the open kitchen in the rear.

Herb loved that table. It put him near enough to the kitchen to be suffused by the rich aromas of the special spices and sauces Manny's was justly famous for, and to sense the rhythms, like it was his own personal chorus line, of the chefs' tall white hats moving to the beat of their spoons going round and round in their oversized brass pots. That table got him close enough to the overhanging television set for a front-row view of whatever fight or game was on that night and worth laying down a friendly wager with the gang. Four nights a week on average, Herb sat at that table, where he'd been sitting, night after night, week after week, year after year, since Manny opened his doors to the public, thirty-five years ago this month. Manny kept the table tacitly reserved for him every night until nine. If Herb hadn't come in by then, he was free to release it to somebody else. "But it never seems right," Manny sometimes said to Herb when in a rare sentimental mood, "seeing anybody but you at that table."

"In early tonight," Manny said to him now.

"Meeting a friend."

"That so? Mind if I sit?"

"You gotta ask?"

Manny pulled out a chair and Herb slapped his newspaper down on the table and off to his left as was his habit. It was an automatic thing, born of the many nights he came in alone and sat here at this table, waiting for Eddie or Chuck or Bill or one of the others to drop by. The paper remained untouched at his left until a tall Dewar's-and-water appeared at his right (an event that never took long to occur, for Red or Reilly signaled the order to Stan the second they saw Herb walk through the door), then Herb would pick up the paper in one hand, the drink in the other, and slowly, leisurely sift through the evening's news while savoring his Scotch.

Now Manny leaned a hefty forearm on the table and turned himself sideways in his chair to face Herb. Being a heavyset man, Manny found the position comfortable for it allowed the weight of his voluminous hips to spill off the seat on one side of the chair while providing him support from its back on the other. But the position, Herb understood, served his friend in another way as well. By seating himself sideways at a table, Manny, the most discreet of men and one who never would dream of intruding on the privacy of a paying customer, indicated that he wasn't staying long and had only taken the seat to pay a courtesy call, ask after a customer's health, the health of his family, catch up with a business acquaintance or old friend, and would soon be off. Only in the early morning hours, when all but the most recalcitrant stragglers had gone home, say around one or two (hours which Herb saw fewer and fewer of as the years went by), would Manny loosen his belt, pull up a chair, and sit in it facing forward like a regular guy.

"Haven't seen Maggie in a while," Manny said to him now, leaning in close over his forearm.

"Guess it's been that."

"How's she doing?"

Where do you keep your joy?

"Fine, just fine."

I might open your chest with a hammer to find your hiding place.

"Glad to hear it. Thought I heard she was a little under the weather."

"No, nothing like that."

"Sure, Herb, not like that."

I might hold your eyes up to mine to see what you see.

"Just under it, that's all. That's what I heard."

"Who from?"

"The guys. Around."

84

"The guys got it wrong."

"Whatever you say. Red get your drink?"

"On its way."

"Oughta give that guy a raise."

"What, and break your record for Depression-era wages? Meantime, my friend comes in, you show her over."

"Done." Manny heaved himself forward, pressing down on the table with his arm and using it like a lever to lift himself out of his chair.

"It's Pat."

"Pat?" Manny stopped in mid-elevation.

"From the old days, remember?"

"Pat? *That* Pat? Well, what do you know?" He finished the rise. "She back in town?"

"Couple of days. Holed up at the Sheraton."

"What brings her here?"

"Shopping, I'd say. The holidays, you know."

Manny's big round face went solemn. "I heard her dad took sick a while back. She moved home to nurse him. Chicago, I got that right?"

"You do. Had to put him in a home, she said."

"You don't say? That's sure a shame. Swell guy, he was. A real fixture around here. Now there's you, me, Maisie, one or two originals, and the brass rail along the bar." Manny squeezed his shoulder hard. "But long as you keep coming in I know which way is up." He stepped back as Red approached with his tray. "Well, here's your drink. Enjoy. Give Maggie my best."

"Thanks, Manny. Will do."

Red slapped a cocktail napkin down on the tabletop, angled it smartly toward Herb, and placed a tall glass of Dewar's-and-water dead in its center.

"Nicely done, Red. There'll be two of us tonight."

Red and Reilly were the best waiters in the place. When one was off, the other took Herb's station. They kept the food and drink coming without wasting time taking any orders. A Dewar's-and-water before dinner, Miller's with, another Dewar's afterward, that was it for him if he was in alone, they didn't have to ask. They'd clear the table the minute he finished eating, taking off the salt and pepper shakers, the bread, the mustard and ketchup pots, any extraneous utensils and plates, like that little white dish with green trim that held the cold beets Herb never touched but Manny insisted on placing unrequested at every table, his included, whether the beets were eaten or not—"My trademark," he called it—everything would go, except his Scotch. They knew not to touch that. Or his paper either. Then they'd leave him alone and not come back, understanding how he liked to read his paper and sip his drink in peace, but if the guys came over, it was a whole different story. They'd be back in a flash, laying down ashtrays, lighting up cigars, joining in on a joke now and then, and keeping the nightcaps flowing.

Herb looked down at his paper now, appreciating the generous way the light fell across the page. He came to Manny's as much for the lighting as for the food and the company. There wasn't a bulb at home bright enough to comfortably read a billboard by, let alone a newspaper, for Maggie had an abiding preference for rooms that had to be negotiated in almost perfect darkness.

Oh Christ, Maggie. Naked on the floor?

Had he really left her there? What kind of a thing was that to do? He'd asked her to come along, several times in fact, he was certain of that, although much of the rest of that encounter was more like a dream now, or something glimpsed under water and growing fainter and fainter with each passing hour. But he'd asked her to come with him for dinner, he was clear on that. He could have fixed something up with Pat . . . she was always quick to get his meaning . . . made it look like her walking in was a total surprise, but Maggie had summarily declined his invitation, adding that comment about his friends. *Their eyes sting my flesh like nettles.* What the hell was that supposed to mean? No point in dwelling on it, he told himself, for Maggie was a hope, an aspiration, he'd always believed, not a woman meant to be captured or comprehended, especially not by a guy like him.

He should get up right now, make some excuse to Manny, leave a message for Pat, and take a cab home.

"Well, well, well." Manny's voice resonated like a bass drum from the center of the room, causing heads to turn and those who turned to see him striding down the aisle with a grin on his face and Pat under his arm. "Look who I got here."

Dwarfed by Manny's mammoth shoulders and torso, Pat looked like a kid caught in the folds of a voluminous tent. She gave a shy little wave upon seeing Herb, and he stood up to greet her.

"Hello, Pat."

"Hello, Herb."

Manny enfolded Pat in a quick bear hug, temporarily deleting her from view, before reluctantly releasing her to Herb. "Great to see you, kid," he said. "We've missed you around here," he told her and, ever the proper host, held her chair steady while she daintily lowered herself into it.

"Thanks, Manny," Pat said. She placed her handbag on the floor and pulled in her skirt and lifted herself up a bit as Manny gave the chair a couple of last minute professional adjustments beneath her. "I'm not in town much these days," she explained. "I got obligations."

"So I heard." Manny stood by her side, attempting to clasp his hands behind his back as he had done in the days when he was forty pounds lighter and that particular maneuver came easily to him. Herb recalled Manny standing by a customer's chair, leaning down to explicate some item on the menu or to hear a confidence only he was privy to, hands clasped naturally, yet respectfully behind his back. A considerate pose, Herb had always thought it, as if his friend's hands were waiting patiently back there for the moment they would be needed, and when that moment came, as invariably it did, he'd unclasp his hands, bring them forth and pat the customer on the back to offer congratulations or sympathy, as the confidence dictated, or maybe only to show solidarity with the choice of entree, then quietly slip away. Finding the reach beyond him now,

Manny let his hands drop to his sides and asked, "How's he doing, your dad?"

"Up one day, down the next," Pat replied. "His mind's none too sharp."

"Whose is at our age?" Manny laughed. "You give him my best now, you hear?" He squeezed her shoulder. "Take care, Pat, and don't be a stranger."

"I'll try."

I try to keep them, Herb. Honest I do. I try so hard. I'm always trying.

Herb sat down again as Manny walked away. "Thanks for coming, Pat," he said.

"You called," she answered. She looked him in the eye a moment, then looked away. Leaning back in her chair, she let her eyes travel at their leisure about the room. A slight smile appeared on her face as she took it in. "I always liked this place," she said.

Herb could have jumped up and cheered. Any woman who felt that way about Manny's was okay in his book.

"You're sure looking great," he told her, and that was no lie. Shiny, blond hair cut in a bob that flew away from her scalp and swirled like silk when she turned her head. Red saucy mouth. Bright blue eyes. A very classy lady. "What's your pleasure?" he asked, and motioned to Red, who was by his side in two seconds flat.

"Scotch Sour, please."

"Scotch Sour for the lady," Herb instructed. "And have Stan make it with my Scotch."

Red gave an almost imperceptible nod, all that was needed to convey he had registered the importance of the instruction, and headed for the bar. Herb watched him go. The swing of his arm, the hang of the white linen towel artfully arranged over his white sleeve, the turn of his head and stretch of his leg—all meticulously picked up and multiplied to infinity by the mirrors lining Manny's walls and by those on the free-standing pillars positioned at intervals about the room. Manny's wasn't a place where you could get away with anything. Not that he was trying.

"I appreciate this," he said, leaning toward Pat. Her hand rested on the clean white tablecloth. He placed his own over it. She left hers where it was.

"My pleasure." She smiled.

It came at him like a kid's, that smile—quick and ready and open, her lips pulling back without embarrassment to reveal that little gap between her two front teeth that Herb had always been partial to. A smile to die for. Pat had been a hatcheck girl at the Copa when Herb first met her. She'd had a station like Maisie's, only bigger. Herb still kept a picture of her in his mind from those days, leaning over the glossy white half-door in that white ruffled blouse management made her wear that came down low off her shoulders and had shiny blue ribbons running through the ruffles. He remembered how she'd take his hat and coat and throw him her sensational smile in exchange, real fast, like she'd just done, and how her lips would pull way back to reveal that enchanting gap between her teeth. A special part of her, he liked to think of it, exposed for his eyes alone. A quarter century ago that was now, and she hadn't changed a bit.

"How's the city looking to you, Pat?"

"I've thought about you, Herb."

"Me too."

"No, I have."

"Same here."

"I mean it. A lot."

Herb never thought hanging up other people's coats was anything a kid like Pat ought to be doing, same as he later came to think about Maggie's job at Jake's. It turned out, as fate would have it, the two of them knew each other before he and Maggie ever met. They took acting classes together, or singing or dancing classes, some kind of classes anyway. They weren't exactly friends, but if they chanced to meet at an audition, which happened fairly frequently, according to Pat, they'd go for coffee afterward and exchange notes on the business. "Who she knew, who I knew, you know? Who was doing what. Casting, looking. That's important. It keeps you current." They even got together once in a while, though not for long, after Maggie had stopped dancing at Jake's and all other clubs and married him. Pat went on to night school, using some of the money, Herb hoped, that he'd made her take when they stopped going out. "I can't take that, Herb," she'd protested at first. "For a rainy day," he told her. "Or a sunny one if you need it." "I'll pay you back," she promised, but he wouldn't hear of it. "It's not a loan, Pat," he told her. Eventually, he heard through the grapevine, she got herself a regular paralegal job, pulling in the kind of decent wage he always thought she deserved. Then he lost track. Didn't hear zilch about her for years. It was Eddie Taylor who had an uncle in Chicago he visited every now and then who told him she had moved back home to care for her ailing father. And the next thing he knows, he's bumping into her on the street.

"So," he said, and gave her hand a squeeze. "What you been up to?"

"The usual. Back and forth between my job and the nursing home. If the shuttle bus ever quits, I'm a natural human replacement."

They both laughed at that and again it came back to Herb how easy laughter had always been between them. They never lacked for some little joke to exchange or incident to kid about when he was turning over or picking up his hat and coat from her at the Copa. And at the end of her shift, when he'd pick her up after Manny's and take her to his favorite all-night diner on Eighth and 43rd to make certain she got a decent meal, they'd sit scrunched way down in a maroon-colored booth, the vinyl peeling on the seams beneath them, and, late as it was, start in on a story. It didn't matter what the subject was or who was the first to begin, but halfway in, they'd find themselves laughing like a couple of loons. It came naturally with Pat. And for him, too, in those days. Maybe laughing's what got them started in the first place, but they stopped for good the minute he laid eyes on Maggie.

"What's the latest with your dad?" Herb inquired.

"Last visit, he thinks I'm the Queen of England." Pat looked up at him and smiled her million-dollar smile.

"Makes everybody in the home run around, searching for a footstool, saying my feet are too good to touch the floor."

"He's got something there," Herb began, and Pat pulled her hand from under his as Red came over with her drink. Displaying a formality that might truly befit a queen, Red bent at the waist, took a scalloped-edged paper napkin off his tray with a flourish, arranged it at the point of Pat's knife, lifted her drink from his tray, and centered it carefully on the napkin. He placed a menu to her right, leaving it discreetly off to one side so as not to be intrusive, but close enough to reach the instant she felt an urge to order. Then he snapped to attention, made a sharp U-turn, and walked away, knowing a menu for Herb was superfluous.

"Old times," Herb said, raising his glass.

"Old times," Pat replied, clinking her glass against his. She held his eyes with hers a moment, then took a sip.

Herb sipped his drink as well, hardly believing his luck in being here, seated across the table from her, then asked, "How's your job?"

"The pay's good and I can choose my own hours. Leaves me free for Dad."

"What's the outlook there?"

"Not promising." Pat looked him straight in the eye as she said it. "But he doesn't know the extent."

"You never married?"

She shook her head, but held her gaze.

"Never found the right guy?"

"I found him."

The blue of her eyes swelled like a sea and swallowed whatever words Herb might have been planning to say next.

"How's Maggie?" Pat took up the slack.

"Fine. Just fine." *Show me your hiding place. Let me see what you see.* "Hungry?"

"Starved."

He laughed. "You always had a healthy appetite as I recall."

"You never let me go hungry." She held his eyes a moment longer then picked up her menu. "What are you having?"

"What day is it?"

"Tuesday. Why?"

"Tuesday?"

"All day, Herb." Her lips parted quickly and the little gap between her two front teeth flashed before him.

"Then I'm having the Tuesday special."

"Which is?"

"Beats me."

"So how do you know you'll like it?"

"Red knows. Or Reilly. If it's Tuesday, they bring it."

"And if it's Monday?"

"They bring the Monday special."

"And Friday? And Wednesday?"

"You got it. They see me coming, they prepare the daily special."

Pat threw back her head and laughed. It was like bells ringing. Maggie once had a laugh like that. It rang down the long white-tiled hall and through every room in the house. *I'd fill your eyes with beauty and give them right back.*

"I'll have the Tuesday special, too," Pat said, and Herb motioned for Red.

Two fingers off the tablecloth was all it took. A barely perceptible signal, and, without a word exchanged, Red disappeared into the kitchen beyond.

"So," said Pat. "Maggie's doing well?"

"She is."

"Your eyes still light up at her name."

Herb looked down into his drink.

"She always had the dazzle," Pat said softly.

The Scotch-and-water did a little dance inside his glass.

"I couldn't hold a candle."

"I wouldn't say that. Look, Pat, I gotta be honest with you."

"You never were anything but."

Herb lifted his glass to his lips. "You're a hell of a gal."

"You don't have to say that."

"I'm not saying it, you are. You don't know the half of it."

92

"Don't, Herb."

"What you meant to me— What we had—"

"Please, don't."

"I'm honored. You did me an honor. Any guy gets you ought to know how lucky he is. The truth is, bumping into you like that the other day . . . well, it brought things back."

"For me, too."

"And it crossed my mind, though I realize I got no right thinking along those lines . . . none at all . . . still, in all honesty, I gotta say it occurred to me we might resume an old acquaintance. I wanted you to know that. Didn't want you thinking I didn't think about it when I did. But I can't, Pat. It was never exactly a habit with me."

"I know that, Herb."

"And since I'm married, never once in all those years."

"I know that, too."

"You're something special, you are. And it's not that I wouldn't like to, you have to know that—"

"It's all right, Herb. You don't have to say any more."

"But I'm an old-fashioned guy and it doesn't sit right with me. That's me, Pat. Nothing to do with you. Honest."

"You better stop now."

"I didn't want you thinking I got you here under any false pretenses."

"Really, you better."

"Hell, Pat, I'm no good at this. But I wanted you to know . . . you really are special, and what we had, what I felt for you— Oh, here." He had his hand in his pocket before he knew what he was doing. "I want you to have it." He had almost forgotten the package was there. "Old times." He brought it out from his jacket and held it before her.

"What's this?" She stared at the shiny white paper and curly red ribbons. "Still giving me gifts, Herb?"

"It would mean a lot to me if you'd take it."

"You know I can't do that."

"Go on. Make me happy."

"That always was my plan."

Herb placed the box on the table and edged it toward her, pushing it gently along with the back of his fingers. "It's nothing. A token."

"Honest, I can't."

"Please, Pat." He reached for her hand. "A token, that's all." He turned her palm up and pressed the little box into it. "Put it in your bag." He closed her fingers over the top. "Open it Christmas morning."

"A Christmas present?"

"From me to you."

"In that case, I accept. And with thanks. But you didn't have to, Herb, you know that."

"I wanted to."

"No need."

"Nothing about need, I wanted to."

"I appreciate that. I'll think of you Christmas." She looked directly into his eyes for what seemed a long moment, then picked up her bag from the floor and tucked the present inside. "So, everything's all right between you and Maggie?"

"Between us? Yes, sure. Between us, no problem. But on her side alone—"

"What do you mean?" She returned her bag to the floor. "You said she was fine."

"Oh, fine. Yes, she's fine. It's just—"

"Just what?"

"Well, to tell you the truth, she's been a little under the weather lately."

"I'm sorry to hear that, Herb."

"No, nothing like that. Just under it, is all. And if she ever got wind—"

"No way she could."

"The two of us having dinner like this, if it ever got back—"

"It won't."

"That's all it would take."

"It won't."

"She wouldn't need any more."

"It won't get back, Herb. How could it?"

"She takes things hard these days."

"I'm real sorry, Herb."

"No, not like that. Nerves is all. They make her kind of jumpy."

"She always was high-strung."

"High-strung. That's it exactly. I wouldn't want to add to that."

"Enough said."

"You're swell, you know."

"I'll always love you."

"Now cut that out." He took her hand. "You deserve somebody a whole lot better than me."

"Better than you, Herb? Not a lot of guys even come close."

He didn't know what to say to that. That kind of remark played havoc with his mind. It led him down unfamiliar streets and into neighborhoods where he had never spent much time, but thought he might get used to, given half a chance. Yet that opportunity had long since passed and there had never been a woman for him since Maggie. Maggie, oh, Maggie. *Does it hurt your eyes to look? Your big, brown, sad eyes, so sensitive to light and pain?*

"What is it, Herb?"

For a minute the possibility loomed—he could make a clean breast of it, spare no detail, lay it all out—and then it was gone. "It does my heart good to see you, Pat."

"Mine too," she replied. "Real good. What do you hear from Phoebe?"

"Doing great."

"First year in college, right?"

"How did you know?"

"I keep track."

"A college kid already, can you beat that?"

"You must miss her like hell."

"You can say that again."

The house wasn't the same without her. The two of them in the living room evenings, Phoebe on the sofa, her nose in a book, him in his chair by the window, reading his paper. They could sit like that for hours, not saying a word. And when it came time for him to leave for Manny's, he would toss the paper on the floor and go in to see if there was any chance Maggie might want to come along that night and if, like most nights, she said no when he asked, he'd wash and shave and put on a fresh white shirt, then walk back into the living room and kiss Phoebe, first on the right cheek, then on the left, as was their long-established practice, and not see anything in her eyes, anyway, that said he was doing something he ought to be sorry for.

"She always was the light of your life."

"No argument there."

His little girl.

"Where is she again?"

"Michigan. Wisconsin. Some place like that."

"She coming home for Christmas?"

"It'll break her mother's heart if she doesn't."

"Not just her mother's."

Herb thought he would risk it all at that minute, then Red arrived with the food.

The Tuesday special turned out to be roast baby chicken with rice and string beans. A small green salad with Manny's own dressing came along like a bonus, and Red had known without being told to substitute baby peas on Herb's plate for the string beans he'd never touch—it was the strings in them that bothered him. Red put a bottle of Miller's and an iced mug next to Herb's plate, picked up his empty Scotch glass, asked Pat what she'd like to drink, and went back to the bar for the glass of white wine she requested.

"Everything all right here?" Red asked a moment later, returning with the wine.

"Swell, Red. Thanks," Herb replied, then Red was gone, and he and Pat turned their attention to their meals.

"Empty-nest syndrome," Pat said after a while, her fork hovering inches from her mouth, a small piece of white chicken impaled on its tines.

"Say what?"

"What Maggie's maybe suffering from." She brought the fork to her mouth and chewed busily at the chicken a moment, lips closed, eyes fastened on Herb. "That's what they call it when a kid leaves home."

"No kidding?" said Herb, imagining those industrious red lips pressed to his, those deep blue eyes like pools close enough to jump into. "Well, that could be it, all right, I guess. Sometimes I'll catch her lying on Phoebe's bed . . . just lying there, staring at the ceiling."

"It must be hard."

"Awful, at first. For weeks she didn't leave the house."

"I meant for you."

Herb looked at Pat and knew a great many men would have no trouble at all walking out of here with her and going back to her hotel and seizing a moment of sweetness for themselves. Why couldn't he be that kind of man? Why shouldn't he have something normal and sweet in his life? *Does it hurt your eyes to look?* He thought of a life filled with easy laughter and gentle talk, not wild talk, not crazy talk . . . *I might pluck out your heart and squeeze it in my hand* . . . and imagined he would like to have a life like that . . . *to feel what you feel* . . . but somehow that life had always eluded him, as if it were on reserve for some other kind of man. *I might gouge out your eyes and hold them up to mine* . . . What kind of man might that be? . . . *to see what you see.* The kind who could pull out a present intended for one woman and hand it over to another? He could do that. He could be that kind of man. He had done it already, in fact. He had been him. And with an ease he'd never suspected he was capable of. An absolutely astonishing ease like it was the sort of thing he did every day of his life. But it couldn't have been him doing that. It must have been that other guy, the shadow man inside. That man must have stepped out from his usual hiding place and taken up another behind one of Manny's mirrored pillars, then stepped out from there and thrust his hand into Herb's pocket and pulled out a gift intended for Maggie and handed it over to Pat.

Maggie. Oh, Maggie. His beautiful girl. *I want to see your soul.* Talking like the circuits had blown inside her brain. *Take off your hat. Have a seat.* Patting the floor, moving over to make room for him to sit down. *Show me where you keep your joy.* Her beautiful buttocks bare against a hard, cold floor. *I want to see what you see.* Her lovely breasts crushed against her knees. *I want to feel what you feel.* Her legs opened wide. *I want to feel it here.*

Maggie! He nearly cried her name aloud, but Pat was there, her eyes on his, and Red was clearing the table now, removing the empty plates and glasses, the cutlery, snatching up in his efficient little gadget the crumbs from the tablecloth, turning his back, disappearing for a moment, reappearing the next, carrying coffee on a tray for him, which he knew was all he ever took after a meal, and a pot of tea with lemon for Pat, which was all she had said she wanted. Then Red was gone again and Herb raised his cup and looked over its rim at Pat.

"You ever sit naked on your floor?"

"Which floor?" she asked without a beat.

"Piano room."

"That's a room I don't have." She smiled. That smile again. "But the bathroom for sure. The bedroom maybe."

"You think that's a normal thing to do?"

"There's a whole range of normal, Herb."

"What if it's accompanied by crazy talk?"

"How crazy?"

"Comments about splitting open chests and gouging out eyes."

"What's been going on?"

"She says I'm blind." *Broken crystals glitter in your eyes.* "She says I don't see. Am I, Pat? Am I blind?"

"That's not for me to say."

"She scared me tonight."

"What happened exactly?"

He told her only the parts it didn't tear out his heart to repeat. *Let me feel it here.* "She said my eyes are made of glass. She said sight bounces off them like rain."

98

"Maybe it would be a good idea if you went home."

He gripped his cup in both his hands. He let the steam from his coffee rise up into his face. "She said I tiptoe around her like she's some kind of dangerous creature."

"Maybe you'd better go on home."

"She knows where I am. She said she'd be all right."

"All the same—"

"She will, Pat. She'll be all right. I've seen it before. She gets a little excited now and then. Mood swings is all."

"You're sure, Herb?"

"Sure I'm sure. She swings back."

He looked into the blue of Pat's questioning eyes and thought if only he could make the leap, he'd jump right in and never mind he couldn't swim.

"Sometimes she needs time alone to think," he said. "To pull herself together, you know? The next day she's fine. Or the day after. I swear, Pat. Out and about, shopping up a storm. You remember how she always loved to shop?"

"I do."

"Well that hasn't changed. And now she's fixing up the house for Christmas. She just got started on the tree." *Wasn't last year's taller? thicker?* "You ought to come over and see it when it's done." *Oh, do you mean it, Herb? Do you really mean it?* "It'll knock your eye out."

"I don't know about that, Herb."

"Oh, it will. Guaranteed. Maggie's Christmas tree is a work of art."

"I didn't mean that."

"What then?"

Pat leaned down and picked her bag up off the floor. "It's getting late," she said. "I better go."

"You're a peach, Pat."

Herb hailed her a cab. He held the door open for her when it pulled up to the curb, and thinking that he saw her hesitate, moved up close and kissed her cheek. She touched her hand to the spot where his lips had been and gave him a little smile and stepped into the cab. He watched her slim ankle and high heel take the step and disappear into the darkness where he imagined a world of soft voices and ringing laughter would open up for him, a sweet, easy world, which he might claim simply by letting that other man he sometimes went round and round with follow her inside. He gripped the handle of the cab for balance and felt a pressure like longing shoot up his forearm and pierce his brain. Then he shut the door, stepped back up onto the curb, and stood there, waving, until the cab was out of sight. He stayed where he was a moment more, his hand in the air, his eyes searching the long line of traffic for the glow of her cab's taillights, already lost in the night. Then he dropped his hand and headed instinctively for the subway. Before he had reached the end of the block, he turned and walked as if drawn by a magnet back down the street toward Manny's.

SIX

"WHAT'S THIS? A hallucination?" Manny met him at the door, a look of open astonishment on his face. "Never expect to see you twice in one night."

"Didn't mean to scare you, Manny," Herb said. "Just thought I'd have a nightcap."

"Sure, Herb. Sure. Whatever you need."

"Got a little something on my mind."

"Understood. You sit, think it out. Red." Raising one imposing arm above his head, Manny snapped his fingers in the air. "Bring Mr. Larrimore his usual to help him think."

With Red dispatched and Manny attending to other duties, Herb sat at his table alone, waiting for his drink. It was a little after nine and the place was nearly empty, the theater-goers having exchanged their seats in the restaurant for orchestra or balcony seats in neighboring Broadway theaters. Stan had three customers at the bar, none of whom Herb knew. Tourists, must be. Before he'd had time to wonder from where, Red arrived with his Dewar's-and-water.

"Here you go, sir."

"No sir here," Herb corrected. "Just a hallucination."

Red put the drink down on the table and ducked into the kitchen, as was his habit at this hour, to grab a bite before the after-theater crowd showed up and put him back to work. Herb looked around. Manny's was deep in its first lull of the evening—a pause in the proceedings Herb relished. With one group of patrons swept out the door, he had the place practically to himself before the next group would sweep in for dessert and drinks. A second and deeper lull would descend when that group left about two, not that Herb often stayed on any more that late into the morning (barring some major prizefight on TV that didn't begin until close to midnight, or some poker game that Eddie or Bill got him into and he couldn't extricate himself from without appearing rude). The second lull lasted roughly an hour and was broken up by pockets of drunken revelers, usually loud and obnoxious and none of them regulars or even people they were ever likely to see again, who wandered in, not caring where they were but intent only on doing their damnedest to make the night extend deep into the following day. The third and final lull settled in between three-thirty and four a.m. when Manny's belonged entirely to itself. At four, Manny shut down definitively, ushering everybody out the door, consistent with their wishes or not.

Herb had seen his share of those phase-three, pre-dawn lulls in the past—Manny sitting forward in a chair like everybody else, surveying his kingdom that had, for the night, been all but stripped of its inhabitants, himself sitting at his table chatting with one or two of the gang and nobody inclined to go anywhere any time soon. But of the three lulls his favorite was the first, this two-hour-or-so post-dinner, theater lull, and was the reason he made a point of coming in every night about eight. He'd arrive just as the place had cleared out, a huge roomful of tables having emptied at once as if a whistle had blown, and the former towering decibel level dropped to a hush. The only sounds then above the buzz of quiet talk at the few still-occupied tables might be ice rattling in a glass or the staccato click of high heels across the marble as a woman who'd spent too long in the powder room hastened to join her escort, waiting at the door, impatiently slapping theater tickets in his hand. Coming in at that hour, Herb could take his reserved place at his table, spread out his paper, sip his drink, and anticipate the pleasant prospect of consuming a meal in almost-perfect peace. Sitting there in the back, he could enjoy a nearly unobstructed view across a sea of round, white-clothed tables to the front doors and through the spotless glass on Manny's doors to the street beyond. It was the best of both worlds: the quiet of an almost-private room, the flurry of a city that didn't know the meaning of quiet.

And it was during that lull that his friends, if they were coming at all, would drop by. Herb would sit at his table, one eye on his paper, the other on the door, looking forward to the moment they'd saunter in, as at his personal invitation, and make their way toward him across the room. Waiting, he'd amuse himself by placing a private wager on who'd be first in that night. Almost always, Eddie got his bet, though it could as easily be Chuck or Bill. Johnny Reif and Kenny Blau were long shots. They'd all be by, the whole gang, sooner or later, if not that night, the next, for they came to Manny's, as did he, in honor of an old routine. It filled a need in him and in the men he knew, all roughly the same age and now in the same tax bracket, to wander in night after night, despite the wives and children they had at home, and find themselves finishing up the evening in a place they had known and in the company of friends they had had longer than they'd known or had those particular incomes or wives. Manny's was a hearth to them. Restricted, for all intents and purposes, to men only after dinner. They could gather round, loosen their ties, undo their belts, hoist a few, place their bets on a fight, haul out the cards and the tall tales, the taller the better, and not feel constrained to watch their language as they were inclined to feel they had to in the company of ladies.

Things were simpler with men. That was Manny's draw. The food, the talk, the male camaraderie. It pulled them in. And the glamour, too, of course, for this was Broadway, after all. No telling who might show. Since the day he opened, Manny got his share of the famous walking through his doors. From the very seat he now occupied, Herb had seen Muhammad Ali, Ed Sullivan, Phil Rizutto, Mickey Mantle, Joe DiMaggio, to mention only a few of the greats, plus big-time movie stars like Alec Baldwin and Kim Basinger, and old-timers, too, like Tony Bennett and Tony Randall, who knew Herb and his buddies on sight and never failed to give them a wave or a nod as they ambled in. Beef stew, American beer. Friendly faces, easy talk. A clap on the back, "How ya doing, Herb?" It was simpler, that's all. With women it was French champagne and complication. With Maggie, anyway. He didn't blame her for it, it was just how she was. But tonight, Christ, tonight, if he could bring himself to think of it, had gone well beyond complication. Tonight had scared the hell out of him.

And there, first in, his phantom bet paying off, was Eddie Taylor, preceded by a visible blast of wind, white and curling on the glass, coming through the doors. Herb's heart rose in his chest as if to meet him. He shoved his paper aside, indicating he was far from opposed to a visit, and anchored himself in readiness for the slap Eddie would deliver that, landing unawares, could knock him to the edge of his chair. Eddie came across the room in a sequence of actual three-dimensional motions and instant replays off the mirrors. Herb might be watching through a kaleidoscope: jagged salutes to Manny and Stan, the etched outline of the stop at Maisie's, a corner of Eddie's coat and hat handed over like a surrendering of arms, a peck on a polished cheek. Then a whole series of moves and gestures caught in the glass and bounced back his way during the pause for Eddie's recitation of biographical highlights since he'd last been in. It was an obligatory thing. Maisie demanded it from all of them. She was like a den mother in that, keeping tabs on the doings of "her boys," as she called them, between visits. "Give with the juicy bits," she'd command, and if they didn't have any factual ones to offer, they'd invent a few for her personal delectation.

Eddie must have come up with a whopper just then, for Maisie let out a peal of laughter that reverberated like violins across the nearly empty room. Then Eddie was strolling down the aisle, giving the thumbs-up to the waiters and other people he knew along the way, and then the slap, even anticipated, rocked Herb in his seat.

"Hi ya, Herb. How ya doing?"

"Not bad, Eddie. Yourself?"

Red arrived like clockwork with the drinks—rye for Eddie, another Scotch for him—the cigars came out, the spines slid down the backs of chairs, the legs shot out beneath the table, knees locking, toes coming up off the floor, ankles crossing, and the evening beginning in earnest.

Then a gap and time jumped forward, and Red was freshening his Dewar's and plunking down another rye for Eddie, and then, without meaning to say it, without even knowing for sure how the words got to the tip of his tongue, thinking they were safe way in the back of his mind and not in any danger of coming out into the open where they ran the risk of embarrassing a friend, Herb heard himself asking, "Ever do anything that shamed you, Eddie?"

Eddie's eyes went still and his mouth did that pursing thing that showed he was thinking.

"Got pretty stupid at the office Christmas party last Friday," he confessed after a moment.

Herb shook his head. Now that it was out, he might as well go the distance. "Worse than that."

"Four sheets to the wind," Eddie amplified. "Pitching around like a high school kid."

"Worse."

"Even put the moves on the boss' wife. How stupid is that? Scared shitless to go in Monday morning."

"Not stupid." It was like a compulsion now. "Shameful."

Eddie's eyes went still as glass. "Shameful?"

Herb nodded.

"Like how?"

"Like something that made you ashamed to be you."

"You did that, Herb?"

"I did."

"No way. Not you."

"I did, Eddie. If I'm lucky, she'll forgive me."

"Who?" Eddie's mouth pursed hard. "Maggie you mean? Forgive you? Oh, sure she will. Maggie? You? Sure. No question."

Then Red was back, pouring beers into chilled mugs, and Chuck Zimmer was on his right and an instant later Bill Schummacher was sitting across the table between Chuck and Eddie.

"How's it going?"

"Good. With you?"

"Swell."

"How's the wife?"

"Swell."

"The kid?"

"Swell. Yours?"

"Swell."

The questions and answers, the slaps on the backs and punches on the shoulders made the rounds and a little later, when the subject of wives came up again, Herb considered coming clean. If he couldn't do it here, surrounded by the best friends he had in the world, where in the world could he do it? But he ruled it out fast. It would only throw a monkey wrench into the evening's proceedings, ruining the talk, breaking the rhythms, and breaching the statute of limitations on confessions they'd tacitly established years ago. Unspoken rules governing personal revelation by any single member of the gang, out of consideration for the comfort of all the others, had been laid so deep and so long ago now it seemed those rules hadn't been laid by them at all, but by some ancient religion or mysterious sect that to this day had final authority over their conduct and demeanor. Consequently, when the question of wives again made the rounds and stopped at Herb's chair, all he said was, "Fine. Just fine, thanks."

"And Phoebe?"

When it came to kids, more leeway was permitted.

"Beats me." Herb shrugged. "Fancy college kid too busy to write."

"They do that." Bill nodded in profound commiseration. "They grow up and it's like you never existed."

"Not only that," Chuck said. "They get these lives of their own. Crazy lives. Lives you'd never think. Weird cliques and things. Get this, for instance . . . . My kid's twelve—"

"Don't give me that," Eddie interrupted. "Not twelve."

"Yeah, twelve. Don't ask. Who needs twelve? Thing is," Chuck went on, "she's the only girl in her class not on some crazy diet. Everybody else is stuffing and purging and she eats and keeps it down. Her best friends hate her for it."

"Hate's pretty strong," Bill interjected.

"Bill's right," Eddie agreed. "Not hate."

"Hate, Eddie," Chuck replied. "Pure and simple. Hate." He hit the word hard. "They call her gross. Gross, for God's sake. She's five-three, ninety pounds soaking wet."

They all shook their heads, considering that.

"Nothing crueler than a kid," Bill said.

"Nothing." Eddie nodded in agreement.

"You can say that again," said Chuck.

Herb thought there was. It swirled around in his head with his swallow of Scotch. Something a whole lot crueler than a kid.

"Unless it's a partner," Bill said, reconsidering. "A partner and friend for seventeen years skimming a layer off the top."

A thing they'd long suspected.

"You got proof?" Eddie inquired.

"Beyond reasonable doubt."

"Sorry to hear that, Bill," Herb said.

"Me too," offered Eddie.

"Partner or not . . .," said Chuck.

The penalty was clear. They'd voted on it many times, but Bill couldn't bring himself to carry it out.

"You know what you gotta do," Chuck told him.

"You gotta dump him." Eddie said it straight out.

"Seventeen years, Eddie."

"Don't make no difference."

"Not just partners, friends."

"Not after what he done," Chuck insisted.

"Seventeen years," Bill said again.

"What are you going to do?" Herb asked.

Bill shrugged and studied his beer.

Down to a man, they knew discrepancies in Bill's clothing business had been showing up for some time now. The prime suspect in all their minds was Bill's friend and business partner, Joe Meeks, but nobody wanted to come right out and say so.

"Need anything, Bill?" Herb asked.

"No, Herb. But, thanks. Appreciate that."

"Just a little something to tide you over?"

"Thanks, that's swell, but I'll make it up."

"You sure?"

"Sure. Everybody needs clothes for the holidays, don't they?"

They all went silent then and attended to their drinks.

After what seemed a very long while, Chuck leaned forward. He raised his head and looked at each of them and they all leaned forward, too.

"Joanne's added a new item to her list of ways I drive her up the wall," Chuck said. "It's like a cell that list. I do one thing to piss her off, it splits in half, now we got two, then those two split and we got four. Four make eight, and on and on until we're into millions. And petty! You wouldn't believe it. But does she quit? No way." He slammed the table hard. "And now she's down to—this beats all—flecks!"

"Flecks?" Herb drew a blank.

Chuck nodded solemnly. "Flecks."

They all sat back in their chairs.

"I don't get you," Herb confessed and looked at Eddie. Eddie shrugged and looked at Bill. Bill shrugged and it was back to Herb again: "What flecks?"

"Toothpaste. Little spots of toothpaste." Chuck raised his glass to his companions. "That, gentlemen, is my crime. They fly out of my mouth and stick on the bathroom mirror. She sees them in the morning and goes bananas. Still fuming when I get home. My face comes through the door, she blows like Vesuvius."

Herb was still uncertain. "Toothpaste?"

So, apparently, was Bill. "Flecks on the mirror?"

Eddie, too. "We're talking spots?"

"Yeah, you guys. Spots. Flecks. You know, when you're standing at the sink, brushing your teeth and you got your mouth open and those little bits fly out and hit the mirror?" Chuck made the rounds of their eyes, seeking understanding. "Everybody does it. It can't be helped. It's the human condition. You know what I'm talking about now?"

"Flecks," said Herb.

"On the glass when you brush your teeth," Bill agreed.

"If you say so, Chuck," Eddie threw in magnanimously.

"There! You see?" Chuck tossed a look of triumph around the table. "You all do it. Even Herb." He did a double take then, back at Herb, disbelieving. "And Maggie doesn't complain?"

The three of them turned to him as one, the question of Maggie's response to the flecks burning in their eyes. *Maggie.* Oh, Christ, what was he doing here?

"Sorry, guys," Herb said. "I gotta go."

"What, now?"

"You kidding, Herb?"

"We just got here."

"Sorry, fellas." He stood up.

"Not so fast."

He allowed himself to be pulled back down into his chair.

"Not till you tell us how you hide them from Maggie."

"Hide what?"

"The flecks on the mirror."

For a second Herb was stymied. The guys were right. No way on earth he could hide a thing like that from her. She'd see it, blow her stack. Then Red appeared with another round and the answer came clear as day. "We got separate bathrooms," Herb announced to the table.

The relief all around was palpable.

Eddie let out a sigh. "So, no wonder."

Chuck slapped the table with the flat of his hand. "That's it. That's what I gotta do. Gotta get myself a separate bathroom."

Only Bill was still struggling with the original proposition. "I never noticed no flecks."

"Trust me," Chuck told him. "They're there. You leave them. Everybody does. Your Amy's saint enough to clean them up without a fuss, but Joanne won't let nothing go. Claims she can't see her face through the mess on the mirror. This morning she threatens to rip the thing off its hinges, bring it downtown to my office, and smash it across my desk. Can you believe that? Can you imagine wasting even a scintilla of brain power dreaming up a scenario like that? I wouldn't put it past her, though. I get this mental image . . . Joanne in my office, that maniacal look she gets on her face when something's got her complete attention . . . the goddamned bathroom mirror in her hands."

"You think Amy's a saint?" Bill seemed beached solid on that one.

Chuck dropped his voice. "No question about it."

"You think she's been cleaning flecks off the mirror all these years without a word of complaint?" Bill asked, visibly dazed by the possibility.

"If anyone would," Chuck told him, "it's Amy. A saint, that's what she is."

"I gotta ask her."

"Bad idea," Herb quickly intervened.

Chuck concurred. "I wouldn't if I were you. Next thing you know you'll have a friggin' mirror smashed across your desk."

Before Herb knew it, a couple of hours must have passed, more rounds coming and going, unperceived and unprotested, theaters breaking without his notice, people streaming out onto the sidewalks, spilling off the curbs and into the streets, looking for cabs where they saw vacancy lights snuffed in the night like matches in the wind, and thinking they'd wait it out, have a drink, a bite maybe, for Manny's was filling up again.

"Christ, look at that." He checked his watch. "I gotta get out of here."

"What's your hurry, Herb?"

"Gotta get home."

"Not so soon."

"We just got started."

"Shank of the evening, old man."

Chuck and Eddie each had him by an arm.

"Stay put, will you?" Bill was leaning across the table and tugging on his jacket. "I haven't seen you in an age."

The sound of laughter filled the room. People were streaming through the doors, separating and merging and pouring like bright water down the aisles. They called out to Manny, and Manny called back, gesturing for parties to be seated and orders taken. His silver-gray hair, shiny as a newly minted quarter, flashed in the mirrors as he made his way from table to table, paying courtesy calls, checking to see that all was in order. White-coated waiters moving into high gear with trays held aloft, free arms motioning for space and swinging for balance, plied their way from kitchen to station and back. Laughter broke, shoes and chairs scraped the marble, crystal clinked. The glitter of jewelry and flash of cutlery ricocheted off the glass. And in the center of it all, Herb sat with his friends, the bustle and commotion, the clatter of an occasional fork or knife on the floor, a chorus of voices rising and falling, holy music to his ears.

Yet something weighed on his mind. There was something he knew he ought to get up and do. Or something he'd done that he ought not to have done. Or both. Both seemed likely. Then another round was delivered to the table without anybody anyone could remember having asked for it, and then another, and after that the rounds kept coming like a standing order, and with each round whatever was weighing on his mind weighed less and less. Soon, it was down to practically nothing. Still, Herb did or thought he did all he could to get out of there. He stood up and was pulled back into his chair. He protested and was shouted down. He made serious, repeated attempts to leave, he was certain he had. The guys took him by the arms. They yanked on his jacket, they begged him to stay. It would hardly be polite to go against the wishes of his friends. Then Red was picking up the dirty ashtrays and in a single, graceful motion, like an art, Herb had always thought it, flipping them over to empty out and laying down clean ones. Then another round was topping Red's tray, and fresh slaps were landing on Herb's back and people he hadn't seen in weeks or months, and others he saw every night, were coming over to exchange a word.

111

He seemed to recall making a great many toasts to the health of a great many friends, and when he looked up again the place had emptied out for the second time that night, a post-midnight tide having swept woozy customers out the door and swept a current of tranquillity back in to cover their traces. In the momentary stillness, Herb wondered how he could have missed it. Was he blind? Did sight, as Maggie said, bounce off his eyes like rain? He needed the gang's opinion on that.

"Hey," he said, his voice loud on the quiet room. "You think it's true?"

"What's true, Herb?"

All of a sudden he had no idea.

"True blue."

"True to the end."

"True to you always in my fashion."

And whatever truth he had been after merged with a thousand others. He saw a big, empty room with round tables like kettle drums covered by clean white cloths and flashes of lights going off like sparklers in the mirrors and that room merged with another, just seemed to get up, all four corners curling back, the room rising, taking the tables and chairs and the people in the chairs with it as it rose, and passing through the mirrors on the walls and coming out the other side and turning into a totally different room, smaller and without all the people, but also with a table, though just one, not the dozens here at Manny's, and not round like his, but long in shape, shiny and narrow, and that table, too, covered by a clean white cloth and laid with special care.

Long-stemmed crystal goblets stand at the points of sterling silver knives. A Venetian chandelier hangs overhead, a scattering of pink and gold reflections flitter through the room.

"What's this?"

"Dinner for two," Maggie replies and flashes a dazzling smile.

"Phoebe's not eating?"

"Phoebe's not home, Herb. She hasn't been home all evening. Didn't you notice?" Maggie runs her fingers through his hair. "She's having a sleep-over at a friend's." She presses her hip to his and drapes her arm about his shoulder. "I've had Josephine cook us a special meal." She takes his hand and leads him to the table. She pulls out his chair.

Their chairs are placed side by side tonight and not, in the usual arrangement, with his at one end of the table and hers at the other. Herb feels the awkwardness of the new positioning the moment he sits down. This side-by-side seating is something he'd expect to find in one of the restaurants Maggie favors that goes in for things they call banquettes instead of chairs, meaning you have to turn your head ninety degrees one way or the other to look at the person next to you and makes eating and conversing things you can't do at the same time.

Pink and white roses on stems straight as sticks protrude from a vase in the middle of the table. Tapering white candles flicker on each side of the vase.

"What's the occasion?"

"No occasion."

Maggie walks behind him, trailing a finger along the back of his neck. "How smart you look this evening." She stoops to kiss the top of his head. "Clean shave, fresh shirt. You even changed your tie." She pulls her chair close to his.

"I'm having dinner with a lady."

"Why, Herb. What a sweet thing to say. And I bought a new dress just for you. Like it?" She stands up again, puts her hands on her hips, swivels them smartly, and tosses her hair from side to side. Through a slit in her skirt, Herb admires her leg.

"No touching," she admonishes, and slaps at his wrist as he reaches out to do just that. She sits down again and delicately wipes at a corner of her mouth with her napkin, although she's had nothing at all as yet to eat or drink.

"Now tell me," she begins. Her voice is low. "What kind of day did you have today?"

"Busy," Herb replies. "Clients all morning and afternoon. Tailored policies, reviewed claims."

"Poor dear." She pats his hand. "So many people making so many claims on you. What were they after today?"

"The usual. Recovery for lost or stolen property, weather damage, burst pipes."

"You really are a funny man." She tosses her hair and laughs her golden laugh. "Paying out claims seems to make you happy."

"I don't mind," he says, as Josephine comes in with the soup. "Long as they're legitimate."

With the great china tureen balanced carefully on her tray, Josephine ladles a portion of the steaming soup into Maggie's plate. Then she comes around to Herb's side and ladles a portion into his own. Herb admires the skill with which she does it, not spilling a drop on the tray or on the tablecloth, not letting the soup drip off the ladle and back into the tureen. She's an expert at her job.

"Thanks, Josephine," he says, grateful to Maggie for having earlier supplied the woman's name.

"Are we insured, Herb?" Maggie asks, when Josephine has left the room.

"You better believe it," he replies. "Fire, theft, water damage, personal injury. You name it, we got it."

"I mean us," Maggie tells him. "Our lives, our future. Are those insured?"

"Taken care of," he assures her. "Whole term and life. Not to mention your common, garden-variety household accident. If, for instance . . . " He scans the room for an apt example. "That pitcher there . . . ," he points to an object on the shelf, "topples off its perch and whacks somebody on the head, we're covered."

"That pitcher, as you call it," Maggie replies, "happens to be an exact replica of an eighteenth-century Ch'ing Dynasty vase."

"You don't say."

"I do. The precise hues you see there, that deep red enamel and bluish-white interior, are almost impossible to replicate."

"No kidding," Herb replies, and sips his soup.

114

"Don't slurp."

"Sorry, Maggie. Soup's good. You ought to try and keep this cook."

"I do try!" she shouts. Her body shoots toward him like an arrow. "I try with them all." Her mouth opens wide and black. "Every single one of them!" Words fly out of it like bats from a cave, and Herb finds himself veering in his chair to fend them off. "I don't know how I could try any harder!"

"Sorry, Maggie. I know you do."

She withdraws and goes still. "No. I'm the one who's sorry, Herb." Her voice resumes its calm. "I didn't mean to shout. Really, I didn't. It's just that I have to shout to make you hear." She comes at him again. He makes an effort not to flinch. "Damn it!" she cries as he fails. "I'm not going to hurt you."

She reaches out with her napkin and gently wipes something from the corner of his mouth. Then she turns sideways in her chair and crosses her lovely legs.

"Like my new purchase?"

"Gorgeous," Herb replies, glancing at the generous length of leg exposed by the slit in her dress.

"Not the dress," she says.

"What then?"

"Oh, Herb, really." She sighs that sigh of hers that signifies deep exasperation.

"Buy something else?"

"I could bring a giraffe in here and you would never notice."

"A giraffe?"

"I could have an assignation right before your very eyes."

"A what?"

"Don't look like that," she says. "I haven't. Not yet. Now tell me, do you like it?"

"Like what, sweetheart?"

"Honestly, Herb! You really are too much! I have to drag you by an ear across a room and stand you right in front of something to make you see."

"What should I see, Maggie?"

"It's here in this room, I'll tell you that."

Herb looks at the top of the dining room door.

"Not there, Herb."

He looks at the brass fittings on the sideboard.

"Not there either."

"I don't see it, Maggie. Where?"

"Very well," she says, and sighs again. "I suppose it's time for another game. Guess."

He looks at the girls dancing around the unicorn in the tapestry on the wall.

"Cold."

He looks at the gold-rimmed platter on its shelf.

"Cold."

He looks at the chandelier above his head.

"Cold. Cold. Cold. How much longer must this go on?"

He turns in his chair and looks behind him.

"In front of you, Herb, not behind."

He looks at the roses in the middle of the table.

"Warm."

He looks at the candlesticks next to the roses.

"Hot."

"Hot?"

"You're looking right at it."

"At what, Maggie? I don't see anything."

"Oh, for God's sake!"

He can't help it. He flinches.

"And don't do that!" she cries. "I hate it when you do that!"

"Show me what you want me to see."

"This, Herb." She stretches out an arm, curls her long, polished fingertips around the base of one of the silver candlesticks, and draws it to her along the tablecloth. "This."

"That?" Herb ventures, thinking she can't mean that. It's a candlestick like any one of a dozen others she has about the house.

"Look at it, Herb. For once, will you look?"

He stares at the object in her hand. "Pretty," he says.
"No, Herb. It's not pretty. It's beautiful. It's magnificent.
It's a brilliant piece of work. Can't you see that? Can't you
see the beauty in it?"

"Sure, I can."

"It's Italian," she tells him. "Late nineteenth century.
Look at the silver, Herb, the shape. See how gracefully it's
designed? See how thin the silver has been beaten?"

"Yes, Maggie. I see it."

Herb likes it when she explains things to him patiently
and calmly as she is doing now. He can see things then,
when she takes the time to explain them, things he never
saw before. A little of the information she possesses about
Chinese vases or Italian candlesticks or any of the many
other esoteric subjects she knows so much about and he so
little seems to pass from her into him then, and to fill him
up and make him a more worthy man.

"See how the apex of each candlestick is shaped into a
butterfly?"

He looks at the place where Maggie is pointing. "Hey,
what do you know? Butterflies."

"See how the butterfly shadows dance before the
flames?"

Shadows of butterflies! Yes, of course. The minute she
says it, he sees them.

"It's lovely, isn't it, Herb?" Drawing the candlestick
closer to her, Maggie runs her fingers lovingly up and down
its shaft.

"Sure is."

"It's a thing of beauty, isn't it?" Slowly, she circles the
base with one long, perfectly manicured nail.

"It is."

"The lovely golden flames, the long shadows they cast."

"It's nice."

Butterfly shadows fly about him. Butterflies dance
before the flames. Butterflies play alongside the scantily
clad girls in the tapestry on the wall. Butterflies soar above
the Chinese dynasty vase and in and out of the crystal

goblets on the shelves. Butterflies swing from the pendants on the chandelier and pop like bubbles in the air. How can he not have seen them before?

"Are they new?"

"What?" Maggie cries, and glares at him, and in the violet glare of her eyes he sees that he has made a serious error. "Is what new?"

The trap is laid. He falls in. "The candlesticks."

"Have you ever seen them before?"

"I guess not."

"You guess not? You guess! Wouldn't you know?" Her fingers close on the silver base. "A beautiful thing like this!" She lifts the candlestick off the table and shakes it before him. "Wouldn't you know if you had seen it before?"

"Careful, sweetheart," Herb advises, as the butterflies make violent passes through the air.

"Careful? Why should I be careful, Herb? Tell me why. What difference does it make to you? What possible difference could it make?"

"Well, it could, it does. I mean . . . you might . . . it might—"

"It might what?" She lifts the candlestick above her head and waves it back and forth like a signal in the night. "Catch fire? And I might what? Burn the house down? And do you think I'd care? Do you, Herb?"

"Well, I—"

"I'll show you if I care."

"No, Maggie, don't!" But it is too late. She gives the candlestick a swing and hurls it like a flaming spear across the room. It lands on the floor beneath the window. Flames shoot up and catch the hem of the curtain.

"Josephine!" Herb shouts. "Come quick!"

"Be still," Maggie tells him, and takes his hand. "It's just a little fire. Nothing to worry about."

Butterflies swarm at the foot of the curtain. Butterflies scurry up the velvet brocade. Butterflies singe their wings in the sputtering flames.

Josephine comes in with a kitchen towel and swats at the curtains until the fire is out.

"Thank you, Josephine," Maggie says. "But you needn't have bothered. There was no emergency." Josephine turns on her heel and leaves the room without a word. The minute she is gone, Maggie takes up a chant. "'My little old man and I fell out,'" she sings and leans over and kisses Herb lightly on his lips. "'How shall we bring this matter about?'"

How can he not have seen?

"Everything all right, here?" It's Manny's voice, welcome and booming in his ear.

"Swell, Manny, thanks." Then the other room is back.

Maggie is weeping. Her tears course through him like rain.

"You'll never leave me, will you, Herb?"

"Leave you, Maggie? Leave my gorgeous girl?"

She pounds the table and glasses jump in fright.

"Don't call me gorgeous! How many times have I asked you that?"

She sweeps her knife and spoon to the floor.

"Is that all you see? All I am to you?"

"No, Maggie. No." Words desert him. His mind has joined another camp.

"You guys need anything, you shout." The voice is close overhead. A hand squeezes his shoulder.

"Sure thing, Manny. You'll hear us on Eighth."

"Maybe if I was different," Maggie proposes.

"Different how?"

"I don't know," she says, tears streaming from her eyes. "Smarter, maybe, with business sense. More like Ethel."

"Like Ethel? Don't make me laugh."

He doesn't know what to say. Her tears rend his heart. He longs to reach out, touch her skin, hold her hand. The moment is an agony.

"You guys think I'm blind?" He looked around the table. His table. Manny's room. Faces blurred before him.

"Blind drunk," Eddie suggested.

"Drunk as a skunk," Chuck concurred.

"Okay." Herb staggered to his feet. "'Night all."

"Where you think you're going?"

119

"Home."

"Not on your life."

Eddie tugged on the bottom of his jacket. Chuck had hold of his sleeve. Bill was steadying his chair beneath him.

"Sit down."

"Gotta go."

"Shank of the evening."

"Sit your ass back down."

Herb sat down. "That must be it," he said. "Blind drunk. Drunk as a skunk."

"'Course that's it, Herb."

"'Course it is."

"What else could it be?"

It couldn't be anything else. His friends must be right. He was drunk, like they said. They knew what was what. He looked about. Empty tables shrouded in white. Ghosts presiding over the room.

"You're the best," he told them. "You know that, you guys?" He smoothed the tablecloth with the flat of his hand. "The goddamned best."

Maisie was in her cloakroom, sleeping, probably, by now. Herb imagined her leaning back in her chair, her head resting against the wall, the bun in her weighty gray-brown hair serving as a pillow. It was time she relinquished the rule of her empire to the night and went home to the grown daughter she lived with in Queens. Manny was in the back somewhere, tallying up the day's receipts. They should all leave and let him close up, let Maisie go home. Certainly, he should leave. That was a given. He should for once in his life risk offending his friends, get up out of his chair, and do what was right.

Then something was pushing against Manny's front doors. Something small and quick and out of place. It disappeared for a moment, but Herb was sure he had seen it, then it was back again. Whatever it was, it definitely didn't belong here. He stared at the object, struggled to get it into focus. But his mind was a fog, he'd had too much to drink. It blurred before his eyes. It was moving fast, he saw that, and appeared nervous. He couldn't quite make out its shape. Fuzzy lines behind glass, distorted and wavy. Then it was on the other side of the glass, inside the door, zigzagging across the room. Lines now assuming a definite form, converging into a recognizable shape. A person. A small, furtive person. Well inside the room now and moving fast across the floor. A head, hooded in blue. Small, quick, bird-like turnings, right, left, right again. Sniffing the air like an animal getting its bearings. But not an animal or a bird. A man. A very old man or a child. A kid, thought Herb. And whoever he is, he definitely doesn't belong in here. This isn't his place. He doesn't know the layout or the routine. He's lost, confused. Sniffing the air like testing unfamiliar terrain. Hungry, maybe. Cold, too. Had to be in this weather. Wandered in off the street to get warm. He's moving fast now, suddenly seems to have a clear objective. Maisie's empire. He's headed straight for it. In search of directions. No, that's not it. Not directions. Herb goes stiff. Maisie's back there alone. Unprotected in a cloakroom that's all but empty at this hour. Wouldn't be more than five or six coats hanging on the rack—his and those of the guys at his table and Manny's and Maisie's own. And suddenly the coats and Maisie's chair and the emptiness of her empire drop in Herb's mind like coins in a slot and he's not drunk anymore and his mind isn't foggy or hazy or even a little mixed up. He's sharp as a tack and Maisie is alone, vulnerable, maybe even asleep, in an all-but-empty cloakroom with this small, lost, hungry and altogether out-of-place person coming her way.

Herb is on his feet, moving, shouting.

"Hey, you!" he calls and waves toward the running form. "Hold on a minute."

He's suffused with power. It falls on him from above like confetti. It fills him from within like helium.

"Hold up, I said!"

"Where ya going, Herb?" Chuck calls at his back.

"Who ya yelling at?" Bill wants to know.

"Sit down," Eddie commands. "Your drink's getting lonely."

But Herb is across the floor now, his friends' voices already distant in his ears. A running shape before him, the back of a sweatshirt, blue, thin, a hood pulled up over a head. Running forms slice the mirrors, his, the stranger's, then the voices grow louder, converge, and Herb knows the guys have put it together, have pictured Maisie, just as he has, alone and defenseless, and are on their feet, those splendid men, and almost at his heels. The knowledge spurs him on and, reaching the far side of the room, he comes up behind the intruder, close now to Maisie and captured like a spider in the glass all around him, thin arms, spindly legs, sharp black eyes. He sees that he is only a kid—a boy of fourteen, fifteen, at the most—and in the same instant sees the boy's hand go into his pocket and come out holding something bright that flashes silver-white before him and is multiplied in the glass, and he thinks foolishly of the endlessly multiplying cells Chuck had spoken of earlier, how much earlier it seems now, days, weeks, only these aren't any cells, this is something hard and menacing—a blade, Herb sees it clearly, a knife, the kid is brandishing— and all the flashing silver-white lines shimmer for an instant like minnows in the mirrors, then come together on the tip of that blade and go preternaturally still as the tip is pressed to Maisie's throat.

"What you got there, pal?" Herb calls out, keeping his tone inquisitive only, not harsh, not threatening, showing interest is all. "You looking for something? Something I can do for you?"

And the boy turned, frightened, confused, not having heard anyone come up from behind. He looked Herb in the eye, his own eyes, so wild before, freezing now, locking in place, his body momentarily paralyzed. Then he threw Maisie one last desperate glance and another, regretful maybe, at the few coats in her protection whose pockets, perhaps, he had meant to lighten, and ran back across the room, sheathing his weapon as he went, running through the big front doors and out again into the night.

Maisie had turned the color of ash. Her eyes were wide,

blank, unseeing. She didn't appear to be breathing. Herb leaned down, put a hand on her shoulder.

"You're all right, Maisie." He said it close to her ear as if it were a thing she should know and no one else. "You're all right," he told her again. "Breathe," he instructed, keeping his voice calm and even. "Just breathe. Take a breath."

She stretched out her arms, stiff, wooden.

"He's gone," Herb told her. "It's over, Maisie. Just breathe."

She waved her arms frenetically. They seemed not fully attached to her body. She spread her fingers wide. She stared, but still, she didn't breathe.

"It's all right, Maisie," Herb said again. "Breathe. Just breathe."

Wide-eyed, she beckoned Herb into her arms. And when he went, she drew him in, along with a breath of tremendous proportion. She held the breath longer than it seemed she should, made a strangled sound in the back of her throat, and finally let it out. Locking her arms around Herb's neck, she pulled him tight against her chest.

Then Bill and Eddie and Chuck were beside him, and Manny and Red and Stan were over in a flash. They took in the enormity of what had almost happened and with one voice erupted in wild cheers and cries of congratulations. Imprisoned in Maisie's fierce embrace, Herb felt a dozen hands pounding on his back.

"Good going, Herb!"

"Way to go!"

"What a guy!"

"Some eyes you got."

"Some legs."

"Eyes like an eagle."

"I never saw him comin'."

"Didn't know you could run so fast."

"You saved the day."

"The day, hell. You saved Maisie's life!"

Maisie, still in the throes of the initial trauma and refusing to relinquish her hold on Herb, now found herself nearly flattened by the blows delivered to his back and driving his weight down into her. Suddenly, she exchanged her death-grip about his neck for a violent shove against his chest.

"That boy . . . that boy . . . ," she began, pushing Herb away from her with a force equal to that with which she had only now pulled him close.

"It's all right Maisie," Herb told her. "It's all right. He's gone. It's over."

Water was brought, a passageway for air created. Maisie was helped out of her cloakroom and into a chair in front of it. Herb and the gang crowded around her. Stan held the glass of water awkwardly to her lips, and a chorus of concern went up, instructing her to drink, not gulp, to take small, careful sips.

"Easy, Maisie."

"Slow and easy. That's it."

"Sip it, Maisie. Slow, don't gulp."

"That boy . . .," Maisie tried again. "He . . . he . . . "

"Quiet. Don't talk." Stan pressed the glass against her lips. "Just take a sip."

"Back off, Stan," Manny told him. "You want her to drown?"

"Where'd he come from?" Maisie asked, gasping. "I never saw nothing. Nothing," she told them. "Then he's there." She fought for breath. "Everything's usual, then him."

"Easy, Maisie," Stan urged. "Have another little sip."

"Let her breathe, will ya, Stan?"

"My tips . . . my jar . . . " Maisie pushed the glass away from her and turned in her chair to point to the cigar box they all knew was on a shelf inside her cloakroom. "He wanted that."

"It's over now," Manny told her gently. "We're here with you. We're all right here."

"He wanted my tips."

"Well, he didn't get them, did he?" Manny took her hand in both of his. "Herb saw to that, didn't he?"

"Herb—" Maisie turned to him now with a look of such gratitude on her face Herb's immediate instinct was to run. "Herb," she said. And waved her arms loosely in his direction.

"Forget it, Maisie," Herb told her quickly, anxious to forestall any display of emotion in which he might be featured. "Don't try to talk. Here . . ." He motioned to Stan to offer the glass again. "Have another sip."

"My God, the knife!" Maisie cried. "The knife . . . " Her eyes shot wide as if she had only now remembered it. "He had it here." She grabbed her throat. "Right here. I felt the point."

As Maisie's eyes filled with tears, the men looked away. Stan stepped back, studied the water glass in his hand. Manny and Red, Chuck and Bill and Eddie lifted themselves from the hunched positions they'd assumed while huddling around Maisie's chair and found different areas of the room to observe. Herb stayed where he was, his hand on Maisie's shoulder, his eyes carefully inspecting the floor.

When Maisie could speak again, her voice trembled. "The look in his eyes . . . ," she began and covered her own with her hands as if the recollected sight were too much for her to bear. "A look like ice," she told them. "Dead it was. Not ice but stone. Ice melts. A kid so young already dead. He would have cut me sure." She reached out then and took Herb's cheeks in both of her hands. "A hero," she said, and tugged at his face. "A hero, that's what you are."

"Naw, Maisie. Not me." Herb's face burned beneath the pinch of her grip and the lavishness of her words.

"Yes, you," Maisie insisted. "Always a good man, now a hero."

Upon the repetition of the word, another wave of heat washed over Herb's face. "The guy was on my turf," he said. "That's all it was."

Maisie did alternating pulls on his cheeks, tilting his head from side to side like a pot by its handles. "You're a hero, you are," she told him. "You saved my life."

"You stop that now," Herb whispered in her ear. "The guys are listening."

"I be dead for sure."

"Hush, Maisie."

"You're a hero, that's what."

"No way. Not me."

"A hero, that's what."

Herb would have put his hand over her mouth to keep the word from escaping into the atmosphere of Manny's room, where he knew what would happen to it, but it was already too late, the room had already taken up the word. The tables and chairs seized it. The linens and cutlery grabbed hold and the mirrors and marble tossed it around while the gang recklessly bandied it back and forth.

"A hero! A hero! Herb's a hero!"

Without regard for truth or propriety, every man in the room was carelessly attaching his name to that word, combining the two in a loud, raucous chant, and repeating the chant over and over to the rhythmic clapping of their hands.

"Herb's a hero! A hero. Herb's a hero!"

"Cut that out, you guys," Herb shouted into the din.

"A hero! A hero," they carried on, ignoring him. "We got a hero in our midst. Our very own hero!"

"Hey, come on now," Herb begged. "Enough. Quit it, okay?"

"A hero! A hero!" they went on, deaf to his protests and pounding him mercilessly on the back. "Herb's a hero! A hero!"

They even started a crazy conga line, hands on the hips of the guy in front, snaking through the restaurant, repeating the chant and kicking out their legs every time they came to the word "hero," that sublime and awful word that had no business being anywhere near his name. Maisie sat in her chair, clapping her hands, spurring the guys on, and Herb stood helplessly beside her, praying they'd quit, yet, God forgive him, half-hoping they'd keep it up just a few seconds longer.

When the racket finally died down, Manny stood for drinks all around. Stan and Red made a sedan chair of their arms and carried Maisie, although she insisted she could walk perfectly well, over to Herb's table, where they set her down again and offered her food and drink.

"I don't dare," she said. "Not with how my stomach's actin'."

The entire episode and all it entailed, from the moment the boy was spotted at the door to the moment he ran back out through it and into the night again, was recounted from start to finish several times over, with each man presenting his own point of view and each point of view changing subtly or grandly, becoming larger and more encompassing with each recounting. Initially, Chuck said he saw nothing amiss until Herb had left the table, but later claimed to have caught a glimpse of something odd while he was still sitting there. Eddie said he was first on his feet after Herb, a point vehemently disputed by Chuck. Stan, who had been wiping glasses behind the bar, was closest to the door, but admitted his back was turned the whole time. "Otherwise I would have nailed him for sure." Red believed they ought to change their policy and lock up with ten or fewer inside, even if it wasn't closing time. "Only makes sense, boss," he argued, "with what we got in the till." "Never." Manny was adamant on the subject. "Not in my joint." "But, boss— " "You heard me, Stan. My doors don't get locked before four."

Maisie looked up from her chair. "I thought I was a goner for sure." She looked into each of their faces. "I thought he'd get my tips. I saw him looking at my box. Then he'd finish me off with his knife." She reached across the table for Herb's hand and finding it, squeezed hard. "A hero," she said. "That's what you are."

And then that notion was taken up again by the absurdly gratifying chant.

They called me a hero, Maggie. Me. Herb couldn't wait to see the look on her face when he told her.

By the time Maisie felt strong enough to leave for home, it was nearly three. Manny wanted to have her checked out at Roosevelt's where the kid of a friend of his worked the emergency room, but Maisie said she wasn't going to any hospital, so Manny called her house, woke up the daughter, alerted her to what had happened and made sure she'd be on the lookout for any possible delayed reactions that might surface when Maisie got home and require professional attention.

They all helped Maisie into her hat and coat then—a first, she said, in all the years that she'd been helping Manny's customers into theirs. They followed Manny onto the street where he got Maisie a cab, and Herb saw him press a wad of bills into her hand fat enough to take her to Poughkeepsie and back.

"A hero." Maisie whispered the word in Herb's ear one last time, then stepped into the cab.

She said it, Maggie. Me.

"Take a week off," Manny called to Maisie through the window. "Take two. I got you covered."

Finding themselves on the street and sobered by the unexpected turn of events, not to mention the biting wind, Eddie and Bill and Chuck took the opportunity to head on home once Maisie's cab had departed, but Herb, for reasons he could never afterward fully explain to himself, decided on one more for the road before doing the same.

"Sure, Herb," said Manny. "Place is yours. Stay all night if you like."

SEVEN

No, NOT ALL night, Herb thought, as Manny walked him back to his table, appealing as the idea was. Just a couple of minutes to clear his head.

"Anything you want, Herb," Manny said upon reaching the table. "Anything. It's yours." He pulled out a chair for Herb and helped him into it. "I'll be in the back doing the receipts. Shout if you you want me." Manny patted him on the back and walked off toward his office.

Unbidden, Red brought over another Dewar's-and-water and took his hat and coat away. Herb nodded his thanks, smoothed out the tablecloth although it didn't need any smoothing with the flat of his hand, and leaned back in his chair. A glass of Scotch in front of him. A square, glass ashtray so clean the indentation at each of the four corners pooled with prisms of light. His paper folded off to one side. An uncluttered expanse of clean white cloth before him. An appropriate view upon which to gaze and think.

A hero, they'd said. Why couldn't he be? Really be the man Maisie and the gang had said he was? He pulled a cigar from his inside left pocket, matches from the right front. A hero. Not just to go round and round with him in circles, but in actual fact be him. He lit the cigar and drew on it deeply. A man to make Maggie proud. In the configuration of the exhaled smoke, he saw the approximate shape such a man might take: broad shouldered, sturdy, taller than he, of course, and unafraid. Her knight in shining armor, she'd called him long ago. A newspaper like a sword beneath his arm. Why not? He didn't have to be tall. Capable, only, decisive and in command. A hero, they'd agreed, the lot of them. A man Maggie deserved. Brave and daring, with a saber or a ready word—a fist, if necessary—to present whenever the opportunity might arise to defend her honor or protect her from bodily harm.

Why not, Pops? Why couldn't that be me?

Metal man, she had also called him. A heart of gold, a tin ear.

We weren't made for it, were we, Pops? Neither you nor I. Hardworking, reasonable, that's us. Leave the heroics to somebody else. We go to work every day, pay the bills, come home loaded, maybe, but we always come home. Devoted family men. So devoted to our families we live the major part of our lives apart from them. That ever strike you as odd? Did Mother mind? She cooked and cleaned as if she accepted the division in her life, maybe even thought of it as the way life was meant to be. But Maggie minds. More than minds, she rails against it, and I see her point.

I see it, Pops, but can't bring it down. It's part of me, that division. Part of us. Built-in.

Herb clasped his glass in both his hands. The cigar protruded from between his fingers like another appendage. He stared into his Scotch. Swirls of pale, golden liquid. Islands of ice. It's who we are, isn't it? Doing business. Making money. Keeping order. That's what we're good at. Erecting boundaries and staying within. And why not? Step over the boundary, encounter chaos. *My bones are turning to chalk. I want to see your soul.* A world beyond our ken. *Touch me, Herb. Touch me here.* A longing for a different life eats like acid into his skin.

The king in his counting house, that's me, Pops. That's you. Walled up in the office. Our office, one and the same. We finance life, we don't live it. We package and pay for it and turn it over to others to live.

You'll never leave me, will you, Herb?

Leave her, how? She soars above my head, indecipherable, unattainable. But to make her proud. That would be something.

Here, tonight, at Manny's, he'd been a hero to his friends. He had routed an intruder, spared Maisie almost-certain harm. A not inconsiderable achievement. Herb sat back in his chair, puffed on his cigar, and sipped his drink. As soon as he finished his Scotch, he'd go home and tell

Maggie what the guys had said. They called me a hero, Maggie, he'd say, and her lovely eyes would twinkle. *Oh, Herb. What do you know about that?*

Then he saw the shoes.

Black and shining.

"Mr. Larrimore?"

White socks.

"Herbert Larrimore?"

Two sets. One planted on each side of his chair.

"You Mr. Larrimore?"

Black, shining shoes embedded in Manny's white marble floor as if they had some right.

"Sir?"

Maggie, he thought, and the Scotch wobbled in his glass.

"Sorry to interrupt."

Cops. Cops at his table.

Red had brought them over.

"May we talk to you a minute?"

No. They may not. No talk. No words. No sounds coming out of their mouths.

"We need to speak to you, sir."

No, sir. Not here. A hallucination, that's what Manny had said. That's what he'd told Red.

Red stood off a little way, looking scared. Scared of me, Red? Don't be. I'm not mad at you for having brought them over. You were doing your job, doing what Manny taught you. But you could tell them to go now, Red. Tell them there's nobody here wants to talk to them. Red looked white as a ghost. Whiter even than Maisie had looked.

Maisie. That's it. Herb took in a breath and let it out. He understood now. The memory of Maisie's stricken face had cleared his head. This had to do with her, with what had happened earlier. Thank you, Maisie. Thank you, God. It wasn't what he'd thought. Not anything to do with Maggie. Not what the black shoes and white socks had put into his mind. Thank God. Anything else he could handle.

"It's about that boy, isn't it?" he said, looking from one of them to the other.

"Boy?"

"He was just a kid. A hungry kid."

The cops regarded him without comprehension.

"Hungry and cold. Lost, too, probably, that's all." Herb laid his cigar in one of the ashtray's shiny indentations. "He didn't mean any harm."

"What kid?"

Herb looked back at the shoes, willing them to move, willing them to pick themselves up and turn around and walk back out the door. The shoes defied his will. They remained where they were, firmly planted on each side of his chair.

"That was nothing," he said with a wave of his hand as if to dismiss the boy and send the cops on their way. "She wasn't hurt. Scared, mostly. Besides, it's over now. You're too late."

"Who wasn't hurt?"

Black lines shivered in the white marble, but the shoes stayed put.

"Give him a break, for Christ's sake," Herb said. "He's just a kid. Go on now. Go back to your station."

"We're not here about any kid," one of the cops replied.

"I'm afraid there's been an accident," the other one said.

Herb wouldn't have this. It was like when the furniture changed in his apartment and the centuries disappeared, he wouldn't see it, wouldn't acknowledge anything of the kind. "Go on, now," he said again. "Let's forget the whole thing. Go on back."

"Would you mind coming with us, sir?"

"Manny," he called.

Stan had gone for Manny who was out of his office in two seconds flat.

"Right here."

"What is this, Manny?"

"It won't take long."

"What the hell's going on?"

"Beats me, Herb."

"Cops, Manny? Cops in your joint?"

132

"We need you to come with us."

"I'm not going anywhere."

"You want me with you, Herb? You want me along, I'm there."

"You tell them that. You tell them I'm not going anywhere."

"I'm afraid we have to ask you to come."

"Take your hands off my chair."

"You want me along, Herb, say the word."

"Tell them to go, Manny. That's the word."

"It's about your wife."

"Take your fucking hands off my chair!"

There was a shuffling of feet, a scraping of metal on marble.

"Give him a minute, can't you?"

"That's it, Manny. You tell them."

It was all right. Manny was here and Manny was smart. He'd know what to do. He'd have a plan. An escape route. A helicopter berthed on the roof of his restaurant for just such an occasion. The two of them would be out of here and in that chopper and headed for Mexico, the Keys, before those cops could say another word.

"If you don't mind, sir."

"I mind. I sure as hell mind. Tell them that, Manny. Tell them I mind."

"Take it easy, can't you?"

Easy, that's it. Manny was right. Everybody should listen to Manny and just take it easy. He wasn't going anywhere. He was where he belonged. The cops were the ones who didn't belong in here. This was his place, his and Manny's and Chuck's and Eddie's. The gang's place. Uniforms and guns had no business in here. Knives either. The kid was wrong to have brought a knife into Manny's place. He had made a bad mistake there, and it was that mistake that had thrown the night out of kilter. But it wasn't his fault, he was just a kid. His *wife*, did they say? No, that couldn't be. Cops at his table? *It's about your wife.*

"Ready now?"

His chair slid back. Marble slick as ice. Manny could open up a skating rink, charge admission. Section off a portion of the floor, rent out skates, let the customers go round and round. A second income couldn't hurt. Right, Pops? He'd mention it next chance he got.

"This won't take long."

They were moving his chair.

"Lay off, I said!" Herb grabbed the table with one hand, the chair's rung with the other. His elbow hit the ashtray, the cigar rolled onto the tablecloth. Long, dark veins spiraling through a thin, brown leaf. A burning leaf rolling across Manny's clean white tablecloth.

"It's okay, Herb. I got it."

Manny's hand closed on the cigar. His face was as white as Red's. Herb wanted to make a joke about that, about Red looking white. Manny would laugh and this would be over.

"All set now? Ready to go?"

Herb looked across the room at the bar. Stan was looking back. Another ghost. "Wait," he said.

"If you'll just come with us, sir."

"Wait just a goddamned minute!"

"Let him alone," Manny shouted. "Can't you see he's not ready?"

Right again, Manny. He wasn't ready. He had something to say. Something important to tell Manny. He made a gesture. Manny's big white face swooped low before him.

"She always liked you, Manny," he said it low. It was important to say it, important for Manny to know it. "The rest of the guys gave her the willies. Their eyes stung her flesh like nettles. Her words, Manny. What the hell are nettles?"

"You got me, Herb."

"But you, she always liked."

Manny squeezed his shoulder. "Thanks for passing that along."

One of the cops had his coat folded over his arm. The other held his hat. That wasn't right. Cops holding his coat and hat. For all the years he'd been coming to Manny's he had given his hat and coat to Maisie on his way in and had picked them up from her himself on his way out. That's the way it was supposed to be. Then some kid brings a knife into Manny's place and everything's thrown out of whack. Maisie had been sent home to Queens in a cab. Cops had come in and said something about his wife and now were holding his hat and coat.

"Manny?" he whispered. It was important to whisper. Manny turned his ear to Herb's mouth. "What the hell is this?"

"Nothing, Herb," Manny told him. "I'm sure it's nothing."

Manny was smart. He whispered, too. He had started this place from nothing, a greasy spoon, a hole in the ground when he took it over, and look where it was now. Broadway hot spot. Classiest joint in the neighborhood. His hangout. The place where he met his friends. Manny was his friend and Manny was smart. He understood why it was important to whisper.

"You're right, Manny. That's what it is. Nothing. That's exactly what. You stay here, take care of business, I'll be back."

"You sure, Herb?"

"Sure I'm sure. Finish the receipts. I'll be back."

"Here you go, sir."

A cop was helping him on with his coat. Another cop was handing him his hat.

They put him in the back of a blue-and-white like a regular hoodlum and took off. He didn't want to be taken out of a place where he belonged and led out into the wind and the cold and put into some squad car and driven off to some other place where he didn't want to be. He didn't want the city to see him like this. His streets. His town. He wanted to be outside on those streets, walking around like normal. Sixty-two years ago, he'd been born in this town. Just blocks from here. Hell's Kitchen, they'd called it then. Hometown kid makes good. His father would be proud. Wouldn't you, Pops? Mother, too, in all likelihood. He'd quadrupled the business, brought in over a million dollars in new revenue. Not bad, eh, Pops? Better than you expected? Make it in New York, you can make it anywhere. Tough streets. Slick tonight. Patches of yesterday's snow still at the curbs, yellow where the dogs had peed. They stopped for a light, people crossing peered in through the windshield for a look. Another bum taken off the streets. Another commendation for New York's Finest. But what could he have done, an old geezer like him?

He could open the door, jump out, race back to Manny's, polish off his drink, finish his cigar. The leaf was still burning. Dark veins, thin brown cylinder rolling across a clean white tablecloth. Manny had caught it, snatched it right up in his hand, the tip still glowing. He had left his cigar in Manny's hand. Left a perfectly good cigar in the hands of a man who didn't smoke. That didn't make sense. None of this made sense. Himself in a cop car. Escorted out of Manny's by cops on either side. What the hell was going on?

A hallucination, that's what. Not him, not his life. He was a simple guy who led an ordinary life. A quiet man. Maggie understood. She'd said she did. She'd said it was enough. *Happiest day of my life.* The cops had made a mistake, that's all. Got the wrong man. They didn't want him, they wanted somebody else. A simple case of mistaken identity. It happened all the time. Locking somebody up because he looked like somebody else. Especially if they were black. Even sending them to the chair. It happened. It had happened again. They'd made a mistake, that's what it was. They were after somebody else. Somebody that looked like him but wasn't him. Things in his life were as they'd always been. Work, home, the subway, Manny's. The life he'd been born for. Mirrors all around, marble underfoot. Everything as it was. His friends coming over, clapping him on the back, the joint jumping, chefs' hats swaying, chickens roasting, beef stew simmering, Maggie at home when he got back. Everything all right. Maggie off the floor and in bed. Maggie clothed, fed, feeling fine. Nothing bad had happened. Nothing terrible. Make it true. Oh, God, make it true. Say it, just say it. Say it's true, and I'll give you anything you want. A million bucks for your coffers. I'll raise it. I'll sell the business, the apartment, anything. I'll do anything you want. I'll go to church, to temple. Anything. Just make it true. Maggie took me to a church once. Easter Sunday. A dazzling sky, bright rays of sun braiding her hair. Took me right inside. *Look at the altar, Herb, isn't it beautiful? The stained glass, the lilies. Isn't it magnificent?* I'm Jewish, I reminded her. *So?* she said. *What is that, Jewish? What does that mean? Does it mean you can't come into a magnificent place like this and appreciate its beauty? We were married in a church, Herb. Remember? Happiest day of my life.*

Mine too.

Say nothing bad has happened. Say it, you fucker. Say it!

They drove east on 46th, turned up Sixth, and passed his old hotel on 54th. He could hop out at the corner, say thanks for the ride, fellows, go in through the revolving door like nothing had happened. They'd fixed it up now so you couldn't enter right off the Avenue and through the bar the way you used to. Now you had to use the entrance on the side street around the corner. That was all right. He didn't mind. He could do that, hop out of the squad car, duck around the corner, go in through the entrance on 54th and up to his old room on the second floor. The room was waiting for him, just like always. Nothing had happened, nothing bad, nothing had changed and nobody had said anything about any accident. *It's about your wife.* No, it's not. He wouldn't hear that, he wouldn't have it. His room was waiting. His first companion. A single room for a single guy. He'd loved it like a friend. He loved every last item in it—the old oak bureau whose middle drawer came out left end first and with a squeak, the narrow iron bed with the sagging mattress, the thin white curtain that blew with the window opened a crack across his face like a woman's stocking. But most of all, he loved the window itself, loved sitting at it, his feet propped up on the radiator, his news-paper in his hands, or standing by it, looking out. Watching the streets. Watching the city. And when it was time for dinner at Manny's, it was an easy walk whichever way he went—down Sixth a few blocks, past Radio City Music Hall and the RCA Building before cutting over to Broadway and across Duffy Square, or, the route he preferred for catching the action, straight across on 54th and down the eight blocks on Broadway from there—he knew the women working the streets and the men in the news-stands on the corners along the way. *Hi ya, Herb*, they'd call out. *How ya doing?* He'd pick up a paper and duck into a store for a fistful of cigars and continue on down Broadway, giant advertisements overhead, neon popping wherever he looked. He'd walk past the Capitol Theater, past Ripley's and Lindy's—the real one, where he'd first taken Maggie for cheesecake, not the cheap imitation they got now—past Loews and the Colony, Christ, he loved those streets, to the south side of 46th where he'd make a sharp right, walk west a quarter of a block, and there he was, the great double doors before him, his hand on Manny's initials etched deep in the glass.

But they didn't stop at the corner to let him out. They kept straight on up Sixth to 59th where they made a right, headed across town, the park on the left, the Plaza on the right, past the double-tiered fountain, the statue's naked shoulders, her hand raised to the sky . . . *Just like that, I wipe the slate clean . . .* past the places where the horses tethered to their hansom cabs would be parked in the summer—*Don't look if it scares you, Maggie. Don't look in their eyes*—then left on Madison and north. They drove all the way to 77th Street without exchanging a single word. They pulled up in front of his building and stopped. His building. Fred looking on. Pulled right up and stopped in front. As if they had a right. A squad car in front of his building. It wasn't right. Himself inside. Fred coming over to open the door. The poor guy wouldn't know what to think.

"It's okay, Fred." Herb said it fast, right through the window, seeing the panic in the man's eyes as he glanced in back and saw who it was. "It's okay."

Fred nodded, uncertain still. He, too, had gone white. He opened the door and stood aside, his white-gloved hand on the police-car door trying to make it seem like a regular taxi. Herb got out. The pavement swayed beneath him. Fred turned and hurried to the front door, just as he always did, leaving the door of a taxi one minute and arriving at the building's front door before the minute had elapsed so he could hold that door open, too. Fred in two places at once, as in a dream, having gracefully, effortlessly, lifted himself up off the curb and away from the cop car, straight up, it seemed to Herb, his feet lifting off the sidewalk, his body vertical, erect, floating as in a dream or a painting—he thought he had seen a painting like that in one of Maggie's art books—a guy's feet off the ground, his vertical body erect, floating, hovering, and, like Fred, turning from one place to land in another. And there's Fred, turning away from the car and toward the house, and floating over the sidewalk to the front door, and being simultaneously in one place and another, his white glove now on the car handle, now on the door handle, pulling open the building's heavy front door, letting them through. Letting Herb with Maggie on his arm into the lobby. Everything normal. Everything routine. The two of them, coming home late from dinner or a show, strolling into the lobby, arm in arm. Dinner, a show, a taxicab. *Can you believe that, driver? Can you? A filthy rubber band? A man of his caliber using a thing like that?* Fred at the taxi door, his white glove on the handle. Fred at the front door, pulling it open. Fred in two places at once. Maggie on his arm. The two of them crossing the lobby. Elevator gate pulled aside. *Old-world charm.* Jimmy taking them up. Her hand in his. His world in her hand. His key in the lock, the long white-tiled hall before them. *I've never been much of a dancer. Don't be silly, Herb. You're light as a feather on your feet.* Maggie in his arms, his hand on the small of her back. Going round and round down the long white hall. Like that. Not this. Not cops at his side. Cops in his lobby.

That's what he wanted. His life. His normal life. He wanted it back. He'd make it so. Will it so. He'd rise up on the strength of his own volition, the thread of his thought lifting him vertically off the ground, pulling him straight up the elevator shaft to the fifth floor. He glanced at the brass arrow over the door. Jimmy was taking somebody up. They'd have to wait for the car to come down. He didn't need the car, he'd rise on the force of his desire alone right up to the fifth floor where he'd go into his apartment and reenter his life. It was possible. It was. To change your life by thinking about it. By wanting it hard enough. Change it before it had happened. Change it now. Keep it from happening. Will it away. It was possible. It was.

They crossed to the elevator. His finger on the bell. A hand on his arm.

"No need to ring."

Jimmy wouldn't know what to make of the cops.

"We're not going up."

A touch on his elbow.

"This way, if you don't mind."

He minded. He shrugged them off. This was his building, his lobby, his elevator. Who the hell were they to tell him where to go?

They had him under the arms like a common criminal. They led him around behind the elevator and down a dark, narrow hallway he had never seen in all the years he'd lived here and into a passageway he had never even known existed.

"Watch your step."

They came to a door he didn't know was there.

"Through here."

Who the hell were they to be telling him to watch his step, to go here, go there, to be leading him down hallways and through passageways he didn't know anything about, to be pushing open some goddamned secret door?

"This way, sir."

They lifted him a little under the arms like some feeble old man who had to be helped over a step. Air like ice smacked him in the face and he was outside again and in the dark. Where the hell were they? What were they doing outside? Why was it so dark? What had happened to the street lights and where was all the traffic?

Brick walks, wooden fences, snow-cropped trees. This was wrong.

Yellow flashlights shining. All wrong.

"Over here, if you don't mind."

Brick walks? No horns or sirens? What the hell was this, the country?

"Just a little farther."

Back yards, tree roots, garden hoses.

"Careful there."

Tree roots? Hoses like in a goddamned garden? What were they trying to pull?

"Here we are."

"Ready, sir?"

A quick slicing sound. Tarp peels the air.

Tall buildings overhead. Black sky. Lights in distant windows like tiny TVs.

"I'm afraid we have to ask you to look."

Faces at the windows.

"One look is all."

Strangers gazing down.

"If you'll just take a look."

Not any location, not any city he had any acquaintance with.

"Is that your wife?"

Not the streets he had known all his life.

"Is it, sir?"

Not any place, not anyone he knew.

"Sir?"

No. Christ, no.

"If you'd just tell us, sir. Is that your wife?"

Not Maggie. Not her. Not his Maggie, his beautiful girl. Not in a place he didn't know. With strangers looking down.

Not with men in black shoes and white socks training yellow flashlights on her face. Not against brick walks. No. Oh, no. Not like that. No, Christ! White socks. Blood on the bricks. Not her. Not him. Nothing to do with him. A tarp pulled back. Oh, Christ, no! Slender and white. Palms up. *That's how you show an animal you mean him no harm.* Naked and flat. Nothing moving, nothing warm. Nothing soft beneath her head. She loved soft things. Silks and velvets. Feather boas, down pillows, cotton comforters. Not this. Not Maggie like this. Oh, Christ, not her! Not Maggie, his beautiful girl. He wants silks and velvets beneath her head, if it has to be anything. He wants boas and satins covering her. Waves gathering her in. Something yielding and soft cushioning her fall. Not this. Not concrete. Not bricks. Oh, Christ, no. Maggie, not like this.

"Sir? We have to know."

Not his whole world gone. Finished while he read a paper.

"Sir?"

Over while he smoked a cigar.

"Can you identify her for us, please?"

They called me a hero, Maggie. The guys, they—

"Is that—?"

Not Maggie lying there. Not Maggie naked on the bricks.

"Is it—?"

"No."

"It's not?"

Not Maggie with blood in her beautiful hair.

"That's not your wife?"

"I said no, didn't I?"

Who were they to be second-guessing him? They didn't know anything about it, not a thing. Not how she was his life, his world. All of it, not just a part. They didn't know anything about that. Not how she made him up, his existence, his name. Iron Henry, she called him. They didn't know that. They didn't know she made him stronger, smarter than he was. They didn't know she taught him about eighteenth-century Ch'ing Dynasty vases and furniture from France. They didn't know she said he could dance and he danced. They didn't know she changed his life, his religion, made him a lover, a husband, a father. They didn't know she showed him butterflies massing on the walls and ceiling of a room. They didn't know about that, these guys, these cops. And her Christmas tree, Christ! They didn't know a thing about that. Not a goddamned thing.

Close your eyes.

She plugs in the lights.

Open now.

On her command, his world lights up.

"Gee, Maggie, it's swell."

She did that. She did it for him. She stopped his breath with the beauty of a tree. They didn't know that. They didn't know anything about that. Not them, not these cops. They didn't know her eyes were the color of violets and her hair of sunset. They didn't know she turned men's heads or that her laugh rang like bells through all the rooms of their apartment. They didn't know anything about any of that. They stood with yellow flashlights pointing at the ground, the beams reflected in the polish of their shiny, black shoes.

"I'm afraid we have to ask you again."

Naked and slender and still.

"I gotta get back."

"Sir?"

"I'm going back."

"Back where?"

To where he belonged. To his hangout, his friends, his table near the open kitchen in the rear under the overhanging TV.

"Please, sir. One quick look."

"Manny's waiting." Manny was his friend. He couldn't keep his friends waiting. He had to be there for them when they came in. They might be coming in now, this minute, pushing open the heavy glass doors, sauntering over to his table, pulling out their chairs, lighting up their cigars, laying down their bets on a fight. They might be doing it this very minute, waiting for him, wondering where he was. He couldn't keep them waiting.

"Is that your wife?"

"How many times I got to say it?"

"We think it is."

"Who the hell are you to think?"

"Take it easy, okay?"

"Get your hands off me."

"If you'd just tell us— "

"I got nothing to say to you."

Not here. Not in some back yard like the country, not in a place he didn't belong, not with wooden fences and garden hoses and bricks on the ground. Not in a place without traffic or street lights where people who weren't his friends were looking down.

"I have to go."

This wasn't his city, his town. Ten minutes ago, he didn't even know this place existed. He knew the streets of his city like the back of his hand. They'd never turn on him like this. Never. Not ever. He knew that. He knew it! He walked a beat, he could tell these guys, like them. Like cops. Walked it from home to office and back, to Manny's and back. He could walk it any time, day or night, with his eyes shut. Madison to Park to Lexington, to the train, the Shuttle, up Broadway, past the guys in the newsstands, past the panhandlers at their posts, to 46th, to Manny's. A regular beat, like clockwork, like them. He was fair with the streets and they were fair with him in return. They'd never betray him like this. Never in a million years! Not his streets. Not ever. They wouldn't. He knew that. He knew it. Not ever. These cops didn't know that. They didn't know anything about it, not a goddamned thing.

"I'm going now." He tipped his hat. "Manny will have finished the receipts."

"Sir?"

"I can't keep Manny waiting."

"We need a positive i.d."

Herb leaned forward. "Cover her," he whispered. Manny would know why it was important to whisper.

"Pardon?"

"For Christ's sake, cover her!"

EIGHT

THE NIGHT DIDN'T exist. The following morning didn't exist. That afternoon was blank. No light. No darkness. Nothing. The next night and morning, nothing either. No sight or sound. Then from the window, out of nowhere, Pete. He went downstairs, talked to the man as in a memory. Then briefly, Ethel. Supplies and silence. Then again, nothing. A long, dark stretch like a tunnel and at the end of it, the pounding on his door. Her voice on the other side. The questions flying into his face.

"How could you, Dad? How could you? Just tell me that. *How?*"

The dark blue carpet rolling away behind her. The narrow stretch of corridor disappearing down the hall. The bulky jacket. The eyes tearing from the cold. The shiny, red nose.

"You want to come in?" A purple-and-white-striped scarf around her neck. A gym bag in her hand.

"To have *her* call? How could you do that? Her, of all people. *Ethel!* To make me hear it from her!"

"Or you want to stand out there and carry on?"

"What the fuck were you thinking?"

"Watch your language, okay?"

"To make me hear *that* from *her?* How could you, Dad? How?"

She glared at him, stepped forward, seemed to see the number on his door for the first time, stepped back.

"And what are you doing here? A hotel? You just left? Walked out? Went to a hotel?"

"Quiet," he said. "You'll wake the neighbors."

The wind had opened roadways in her hair. The jacket was made for someone twice her size. With the red nose and the old gym bag in her hand she looked like a waif, a runaway.

"Come in, I'll give you a tour."

"You think this is funny?"

He thought it would kill him, that's what he thought. He thought any minute now he would wake up dead.

"It never occurred to you, did it, Dad? What it would be like for me? No, of course it didn't. To pick up the phone and hear her . . . *her!* . . . telling me that. You never gave it a fucking thought!"

"That your new word?"

"You know what she said?"

"Come on inside."

"You want to know?"

"Come on in."

"'Don't tell.' That's what. Her exact words. 'Don't tell a soul. It might affect your father's business.'"

He turned away from her and walked inside.

"It's not a bad room," he said over his shoulder.

"Are you listening? *Your father's business!*"

"Same as I had when I lived here before. Same size and layout, only the one back then was on the floor below. Before you were born." He heard her footsteps cross the threshold. "I tried to get it back, but it was taken." He heard the door shut behind her.

"Bad for business . . . that's what worried her. That's why she didn't want me telling anyone. Why couldn't you do it, Dad? Just pick up a phone and call me yourself?"

How? How could he deliver news like that? Picturing her face, those big dark eyes, that sweet mouth. Break news like that across the miles? Hear her voice go dead when he said it? Just how, for God's sake?

A thud on the floor behind him. The gym bag, he figured.

"I brought you some stuff."

"Thanks, doll."

"Some shaving gear and a couple of clean shirts."

"That's swell."

"And a new toothbrush. I couldn't find your old one."

"Ethel brought it over earlier."

"Good old Ethel."

"She brought it with some other things."

"So, you don't need this stuff?"

"Sure I do." He turned and faced her. "I need it. It's just what I need." He held out his arms. She didn't move. He widened his gesture to include the room. "So, what do you think?"

She gave the place the once-over.

"It could stand a nicer bedspread and something on the walls."

"Now don't you start decorating."

"It's a hotel, Dad. What the fuck are you doing here?"

"Cut that out."

"Tell me what."

"I'm here, that's what. It's where I am." If he were a mole he would have dug a hole. "They got room service, maid service, barber shop, a bar. The bed's soft. There's a good lamp, a reading chair. What more do I need?"

"You need to be home."

"They'll even shine your shoes if you leave them in the hall overnight."

"How long you plan on staying?"

"Provided they don't get pinched first."

"How long?"

"Don't ask."

"I'm asking. When are you coming home?"

"I'm staying here."

She raised her arms, and let them drop. She gave her mother's sigh.

"All right. Fine. Have it your way."

She set her jaw.

"But a day or two, that's it. And you call downstairs if you need anything."

"Okay."

"Anytime, you understand?"

"Gotcha."

"Even the middle of the night if you're hungry."

"I don't eat in the middle of the night."

"But if you get hungry. If you wake up and want a snack, you call, okay? Don't wait for morning because you're afraid of disturbing somebody. They're there to be disturbed. That's why they're there. That's what you're paying for. Promise me you'll call."

"I'll call."

"Promise, Dad!"

"Okay, I promise. Now come over here." He waved her toward the window. "I want to show you something."

He opened the window wide. A blast of frigid air flew in, bringing snow off the ledge. "You won't believe this. I didn't at first. You can hardly see his face, but it's the same guy." From his old room on the second floor he had been close enough to the ground to read the headlines on the papers stacked by the curb. He could hear the ropes tear when Pete cut through them with his knife.

"Shut the window, okay? Snow's coming in."

Whoosh was the sound they made. *Whoosh* went the ropes when Pete cut through.

"That's him. That's Pete."

"It's blowing in off the sill."

The aroma of hot dogs and sauerkraut—two or three of which made his weekend lunches—of roasted chestnuts he didn't eat and pretzels he did, liking them best burnt around the edges and loaded with salt, wafted up from the pavement and in through his window which he never closed all the way, even in the winter, and flung wide in summer.

"The same guy, can you beat it?"

"It's freezing in here."

The stench of garbage in the summer—once for sixteen days running during a strike—and of hot tar being laid came up to him clear and unequivocal, but even that he didn't mind. Those were the smells of his city. Exhaust fumes, food carts. And the sounds of his streets. Paddy wagons and fire engines screaming up Sixth Avenue. Car doors slamming, ambulance sirens letting loose. High-heeled women racing down the street for cabs, guys duking it out on the corner after hoisting a few, Con Ed all the time working overtime.

"Dad, did you hear me?"

Seven years in a single room on the second floor of this hotel, but he couldn't honestly say he was ever lonely for there was always a guy to talk to at the front desk or on the door. Leaving for work in the mornings, coming back through the lobby at night, before and after Manny's, winter, spring, summer, fall, they never let him by without a wager on a game or a weather forecast.

"Come over here and take a look." He made a motion with his arm without turning around.

"See him, honey? See his hands? The old gray gloves with the fingers cut out so he can make change?"

"Close the window, Dad, it's cold."

Back in his room after dinner at Manny's and a nightcap in the bar downstairs, he'd lie in bed, letting the sounds of cars swishing down dry or rain-slicked streets lull him to sleep.

"And don't lean out like that."

That room was like a person to him. And if he ever brought a woman up, and that was long before Maggie—oh, Christ, to say her name, just to hear the sound of it in his head—the room would turn a blind eye to the event and take up with him again in the morning as if their bond were too strong to be broken by whatever might have transpired overnight.

"Sometimes, with a customer can't find the racing form or something on the rack, he sticks his head way out to show him. Like that! See him? There, that's him!"

"Who, Dad? Who are you talking about?"

"Pete! It's Pete. From when I lived here before. Years ago. See him, honey? Come have a look. It's him."

She was by his side. The long striped scarf wrapped backward around her throat, the ends crossed behind her neck and brought forward again to hang down the front of her body.

"That's him," he told her. "That's Pete."

"That guy?"

"One and the same. Same stand, too, only fixed up nicer now."

"Same guy from way back then?"

"That's what I thought—no way, can't be. But I took a second look and it was, so I grabbed my hat and went down. And sure enough, there he is, just opening up. Same old Pete. He remembers me right off. He's got a real cozy setup now. Aluminum siding like a regular house and a little flap he pulls down at night against the wind. And he's expanded into all the major magazines. It figures he'd have to, to make a go, but that's him, all right, that's Pete."

"Come on in now."

"Talking to him was like time played back. Anything intervening never happened."

Maybe it hadn't happened. Maybe Pete could fix it so it hadn't.

"Imagine that. Pete. After all these years. I walk up and he starts in like yesterday. Tried Florida for ten years, he says. Got a sister and brother-in-law down there. But he got bored, he tells me. Missed the streets."

"Come on, Dad. Come in and sit down."

"I understood right off. Sunshine, palm trees, what the hell? It's not the streets."

She put her hand on the window to lower it.

"Leave it."

She took her hand off.

"What good's a palm tree unless it's parked on Broadway?"

She tugged on his arm.

He wheeled around and threw her off. "Who the hell you shoving? Who you putting your hands on? What do you know about it? The streets or anything? Nothing, that's what. Not the streets, not Pete, not nothing!"

"Dad?"

She went white like the snow. Like Red. Like Stan. Another ghost. Phoebe? He'd done that? Scared his kid? Turned her white?

"I scare you, doll?" *His little girl.*

"No, Dad. I'm all right."

"Didn't mean to." He touched the fringe on her scarf, felt the big, puffy shoulder of her jacket. "You got her chin,

151

you know that?" He traced her jawbone with his finger. "The shape of her face."

"Come and sit down," she said. "Talk to me."

She pulled up a chair for him, pulled one close for herself. They sat facing each other, their knees almost touching.

"Pumpkin," he said.

"You haven't called me that since I was little."

He grazed the hem of her coat. "You want to take this off? Or you in a rush?"

"You know what else Ethel said?"

"Forget about Ethel. Give me your coat."

"She said in her religion it's still considered a sin."

"What sin? What religion? What the hell are you talking about?"

"You know what I'm talking about."

"Give me the goddamned coat."

"When are you coming home?"

"I am home."

"What about me?"

"You need a place? I'll get you a room."

"No jokes, Dad. Tell me what happened."

Tell her? How? Explain a thing like that? Martians were more plausible. A murder, maybe. He could tell her that. Her mother had been murdered. This was New York, after all. Old Wallace Kroenberg from across the hall was the prime suspect. She might go for it. Barged in in an alcoholic stupor, done her mother in. Like she'd seen a million times on TV.

He put his hands on his knees. "Long as I live, I'll never forgive myself."

"It wasn't your fault."

"A stupid accident like that."

"You think it was an accident?"

"It never should have happened. Window gates and she wouldn't have fallen."

"You think she fell?"

"I bought her everything else in the goddamned world, why not those?"

"She didn't want gates, Dad. She thought they were ugly. She wouldn't have them in the house."

"Ought to have made her have them."

"How? Hired the workmen yourself? She would have thrown them out. Nobody could make her do anything she didn't want to do, you know that. Besides, gates wouldn't have done any good."

"They would have stopped her."

"This time, maybe, but the next time—"

"There wouldn't have been any next time."

"If she was determined—"

"What do you mean, determined?"

"Determined, Dad. Determined to do it. An intentional act."

"How could it be intentional when it was an accident?"

"Dad, Ethel told me—"

"Shut up about Ethel!"

"For once in your life, can't you tell me the truth?"

"I already told you. She fell."

"Fine. That's the way you want it?" She threw out an arm. Her wristwatch got hooked in the fringe of her scarf. She had to tug on it hard to pull it loose. "Have it your way. It was an accident. She fell. And where were you?"

"What?"

"Where were you, Dad? When mother fell? Where the fuck were you? At Manny's? Is that where?"

"You watch your mouth."

"Where else have you ever been?"

She was sitting there with her coat on and that long, striped scarf thrown backwards around her neck. Purple and white. A college kid. A college scarf. He could take the ends of it and stuff them in her mouth. Or he could take her in his arms and tell her that he loved her, that he was sorry that he didn't know how to make this come out different or talk about it or even hold it in his mind without his head crumbling in on him like a cave. He could throw her out or he could pull her close and kiss her. First on the right cheek, then on the left, the way they'd been doing since she was old enough to stand. Right, left. First him, then her. She'd kiss his cheeks in the same order. Right, left. Him, her. When she went to school in the mornings, when he came home from the office in the evenings, when he left again for Manny's later that night, and again, around midnight when he came back from Manny's, if she was still up. The same routine. It never varied. They fell into it like clockwork. First him, then her, planting their kisses firm as trees, one after the other. It was understood between them that each kiss had to land solidly on the cheek, not graze the skin or be blown into the air. It was further understood that if either of them missed a beat or failed to make sufficient contact with a cheek, the whole routine had to be begun again from the beginning. They understood that. It was a thing between them. Their thing. Nothing had changed. Nothing at all.

"Give me your coat."

"Tell me what happened."

He held out his hand.

"Damn it, Dad. Can't you even do that?"

"Give it to me. I'll put it in the closet."

She stood up and followed him across the room and when they reached the closet he pulled open the door and shoved her inside. He shut the door and locked it. He leaned one hand against the door. He took the key and dropped it in his jacket pocket. The space between the closet door and the door to his hotel room was so narrow if both doors opened at once they'd knock against each another.

She started yelling before the key hit the bottom of his pocket. High, sharp shrieks fired off at the top of her lungs. *Dad! Dad! Let me out*! She banged on the door. Little fists pummeling hard. He stepped back and stared at the door. He thought he could see it bulge beneath the ruthless assault of her fists. He thought he saw wood splintering, her hands breaking through, their heels torn and bloody, shards of rough, dark wood protruding from her palms.

"Dad!" she yelled. "Let me out of here!"

He stared at the door, listening to her shouts.

"What are you doing? Open this door! Let me out!"

Her words were accompanied by hard, rhythmic poundings against the inside of the door. Deep, solid punches made with the sides of her fists.

"What the hell are you doing, Dad? What's the matter with you?"

She rattled the doorknob, kicked at the baseboard, went back to pounding on the door. For a while, she gave it single, evenly spaced strikes. Thunderclaps made, their sound would indicate, with one fist alone. Then she switched to a series of lighter, faster blows, as if using both fists in rapid succession.

"You let me out! You hear me, Dad?" She paused a moment then shouted again, releasing each word at a carefully spaced interval. "Do . . . you . . . hear . . . me?"

"I hear you fine," he shouted back.

"Then let me out and tell me the truth!"

She gave the door another round of vicious kicks and punches.

"Quit squawking and I'll tell you."

"Let me out and I'll listen."

"Listen from there."

He held both arms stiff before him and leaned into the closet door as in a runner's stretch.

"Accidents are what happen," he began. He would explain it as clearly as he knew how. "That's the nature of accidents." He would do everything in his power to make her understand. "They happen. They aren't intended, they happen, that's what. One after another, year after year, they happen, they go on happening. You can't control an accident."

"You open this door and let me out!"

"That's why they're called accidents, for Christ's sake! They happen by accident! They're not determined. Nobody determines anything. I send you to college to come home using a word like that? That's what I get for my money?"

"Money! That's all you ever think of. You gave her everything. You paid for everything. *Things!* Don't you get it, Dad? Things. That's not what she wanted."

"And what was? You know that, do you? You're so smart you know?"

"I know it wasn't your goddamned money."

"Then what? Tell me what. I would have given it to her if I knew. I never knew, Phoebe. I never could figure it out."

Now the banging began in stereo. It came simultaneously from out in the hall and from inside the closet. Hard, rapid blows against the door to his room, against the closet door. Delivered now in concert, now in syncopation. Blows building to a crescendo, breaking off, leaving space for the voices of strangers to come through. Strangers demanding entrance, demanding information. *What's going on? You all right in there?* And from within the closet, Phoebe, demanding to be let out.

For a long while, Herb stood between the door to his hotel room and the door to his closet, listening to the banging and shouting coming at him from both sides. Then he put his hands over his ears, turned around and leaned his back against the closet door. Slowly, he slid down the door until he was sitting on the floor. He stretched out his legs before him.

Phoebe's fists pounded at his back. Baby fists pounding like a linebacker's. Once those fists had been small enough to fit inside her mouth. One after the other she had stuffed them in, forcing them so far down her throat he'd been afraid she'd choke. "Feed her, Maggie," he'd pleaded. "Maybe she's hungry." *Maggie.* Oh, Christ. Don't think the name. Don't even shape it in your mind.

He dropped his head and pressed his hands over his ears. Still, the shouting and pounding came through. Phoebe at his back. Other fists, other voices, on the other side of the door in front of him. Judging from their sounds, those outside blows were launched by people of different weights and different heights. Some landed heavily, high on the door, others, lighter and more timidly, lower down. Strangers shouted at him from the hall. "What's going on in there?" "What's happening?"

"Who's asking?" he shouted back. "Who the hell wants to know?"

He sat on the floor, hands over his ears, back to the closet door, the vibrations from his daughter's blows running up and down his spine. People he didn't know pounded on the door to his room. Invisible fists threatened to break through. An unseen army was launching an attack. He was surrounded, outnumbered, outflanked, and outfisted. He thought about calling for Manny and the gang to come and even out the odds.

"What's the trouble in there?"

"Let me out of here, Dad! Let me out!"

"Who's that shouting?"

"Let me the fuck out!"

"You got a hostage in there?"

"You let me out!"

"He's got a hostage!"

"He's holding a hostage."

"Call the manager."

"Call 911."

A crowd of deeply concerned citizens had gathered in the corridor. Out-of-towners. Tourists, must be. New Yorkers would never get involved.

"Open this door, Dad. Open it now and I'll listen to you. I promise I will."

"Listen first, I'll open later."

"It's hard to hear in here."

"Shut up and you'll hear."

Herb stood up and placed the flat of one hand against the closet door, the flat of the other against the door to his room. With both arms outstretched, he dropped his head and stared at the floor. He'd put this to her in the clearest possible way. The way Chuck had put it to him in Manny's the other night.

"You know when you stand in front of your bathroom mirror?" He raised his head and called in to her through the closet door. "You're brushing your teeth and flecks fly out? You know what that's like? They fly into the mirror, right?"

"What are you talking about?"

"Flecks of toothpaste fly out. They hit the glass. You know they do. Well, that's an accident." Chuck would be proud. "Those flecks are accidents." Eddie and Manny and Bill would cheer him on. "They fly out of your mouth. They hit the glass. It happens to everyone. You can't stop it. It's unstoppable, you understand?"

"No, I don't understand. Now open the door."

"It's the human condition. Unavoidable, see? That's what an accident is, you hear me, Phoebe? That's an accident."

"Let me out of here!"

"It's not like you plan it. It's an accidental thing. I guess they don't teach you that in college. So you'll just have to take it from me. An accident is accidental. You don't determine it. What the hell kind of word is that? *Determined?* Like it's written down. Nobody writes it down, prints it out on paper. Maybe that you'll understand, that's the language you speak. Computers. Printouts. Nobody in their right mind would write it down on a piece of paper. Nobody would!"

Suddenly a space opened around him. The shouting and banging out in the corridor ceased. Phoebe went on yelling and pounding on her side of the closet, but out in the hall, all was quiet.

Herb opened the door a crack and peered out. A crowd had definitely gathered. When they saw his face, they backed away, looking guilty and ashamed, like people who sensed there was a value in minding their own business but had never fully taken the lesson to heart. Aside from those who had actually come out of their rooms to physically lay hands on his door, there were others, all up and down the corridor, watching from behind their doors, human heads poking from doorways like turtle heads from shells.

"He's coming now," somebody whispered. "Here he comes."

Then all the heads turned as one and faced the other end of the hall. A man rounded the corner from where the bank of elevators was located. A heavyset man. Manny! Herb's heart lifted. Manny had heard his call of distress, Manny was responding with the cavalry. But this man, the hotel manager, Herb presumed, was larger even than Manny. And now he saw that he walked with a limp. The man came down the dark blue corridor listing from side to side like a ship in high seas. He was so wide his body took up most of the space on either side of him, blocking from view the cavalry that was just behind. At the moment, there was only one in that number—Herb made out two feet advancing steadily on the manager's mammoth legs—but soon there would be others. Any minute now, when all his friends had assembled, there would be eight or ten times that number. But then the manager was down the hall and almost upon him, and Herb saw it wasn't the cavalry at all behind, but a lone employee, a man in uniform, a handyman, he supposed, bringing up the rear.

Red-faced, sweating profusely and breathing dangerously heavily for a man his size, the manager arrived at Herb's door. "What's the trouble here?"

"No trouble," Herb said. "Come on in."

Herb stepped back and opened the door wide to permit the large, sweaty manager and his small, brown-skinned handyman access to his room. Once they were inside, he closed the door firmly on the craning necks of the concerned citizens out in the hall.

"Let me out of here!" Phoebe shouted. "Let me out!" Her cries were more insistent now and seemed to contain a new element of hope, inspired, perhaps, by the sounds of voices other than her father's outside her prison door.

The manager gestured toward the closet. "Open it," he commanded.

Herb shrugged and turned his palms up. "No key."

The manager cocked his head at the handyman who immediately fished in his pocket and pulled out a link chain to which were attached twenty or thirty keys of varying size. The first key the man inserted unlocked the closet door.

Phoebe came out swinging. She backhanded both the handyman and the manager out of her way, then raised her fists to Herb. Reconsidering, she held them in check.

"You're crazy!" she screamed in his face. "Crazy as she was."

"Don't say that," Herb shouted. "Don't you call her that!"

Phoebe dropped her arms, opened the front door, and ran out into the hall.

"Don't you dare!" Herb called after her. "Don't you dare call her that!" He watched her feet skim the carpet and take the turn at the bend for the elevators. He stood where he was a moment, looking after her, then went back inside and shut the door.

The manager's name was Ross Penney. Carmine del Vecchio had been the manager when Herb had lived here. In answer to Herb's inquiry, Mr. Penney said he wasn't exactly sure what had become of Carmine. There had been six or seven intervening managers, he told him, and it was hard to know what had become of them all.

"Might've gone down to Florida to retire," Mr. Penney speculated. "Lot of people in the hotel industry do."

"Newsstand industry, too," Herb replied. But Pete hadn't stayed. Pete had missed the streets.

"How's that?"

"Nothing," Herb said quickly. "Sorry about the commotion." He looked into Mr. Penney's face and was glad he wasn't Carmine. He wouldn't have wanted Carmine to see him in a fix like this. "Bill me for the damage."

The handyman made a fast inspection of the closet door, front and back, hinges and lock. "No damage," he reported.

"Didn't think so," Herb said. "How could there be? Little fists like that? Baby fists. What's your name, pal?"

"Francisco." The handyman smiled. He had a gold eyetooth.

"Thanks for coming, Francisco." Herb shook the man's hand. "Thanks for your help. I'm sorry for the trouble. Sorry to have inconvenienced you." He dug into his trouser pocket and pulled out his wad of bills. He removed the dirty rubber band, licked his thumb, and peeled back the bills from the top. *It's not right.* Maggie's voice like angels in his ear. *A man of your caliber using a filthy thing like that.* He peeled past the singles, pulled out a couple of fives and pressed the fives into Francisco's hand.

"No, Mister, you don't have to." Francisco shook his head and pulled his hand away.

Herb grabbed his hand and forced the money into it. "My pleasure," he said. "For your trouble."

Francisco threw Mr. Penney a look.

Mr. Penney signaled approval with a nod. "Okay, Francisco. Now go check out that radiator in 1125."

Francisco took the money quickly. "Thank you, Mister. Thank you," he said, allowing Herb to shake his hand again. Then he opened the door and was gone.

Mr. Penney swung the door closed and turned to Herb. "Now you want to tell me about the problem here?"

"No problem," Herb replied.

"You put that woman in the closet?"

"Woman? No, nothing like that. She's a kid, just a kid. My daughter, in fact. You got kids?"

"Five."

"Then you know. They get a little excited now and then."

"You put her in that closet?"

"Put her in? No, she walked. Made a wrong turn. An accident, I'd say."

"Accident?"

"Exactly."

"I'm not partial to accidents happening in my hotel."

"Understood. Who would be? Not me, not partial at all."

"I wouldn't want to see it happen again."

"Me neither. Certainly not."

"Or anything like it."

"Nothing like it. No, not even remotely. Not even close."

"Accident, you say?"

"That's it. She gets by me, takes a walk, the door closes. Bang, it locks automatically. You oughta get it seen to."

Mr. Penney opened and shut the closet door a few times

in succession. "Seems okay now. Maybe you can do without a key."

"Without it? Sure. Whatever you say."

"All right." Mr. Penney's head waddled on his thick neck. "Long as that's understood."

"Perfectly," said Herb. "No key."

"You staying long?"

"Maybe. Last time I stayed seven years."

"Where? Here?"

"The room below on the second floor."

"*My* second floor?"

"Maggie moved me to the penthouse."

"Maggie?"

"I come in after work and Carmine hands me the key. Joe was sick that night, I remember, so Carmine's working the desk. I go up and the key doesn't fit. 'What's the matter with you, Carmine?' I have to go back downstairs and ask. 'All these years and you don't know which key is mine?'"

"You got a standing problem with keys at this hotel?"

"No, nothing like that. No problem."

The courtyard looms before him, Maggie lying on the bricks. The room took a dip, trying to throw the image off.

"You okay, Mister?"

"She moved me to the penthouse, is all. Imagine that, Mr. Penney. Me in a penthouse."

"Maybe you better sit down. You look a little green."

"She had them move everything up from my room. Not that I had much, you understand, but they moved it all. That penthouse was so high up it was like living in the sky. I felt the ground fall away beneath me in the elevator, floor by floor, as we went up. No, no chair, thanks. I'll stand. I looked out the window up there and couldn't hear the street sounds or smell the food in the pushcarts or read the headlines on the newspapers stacked in front of Pete's. You go ahead, sit if you want. It was like living in a different city. And then she moved me across town to a part of the city that had never been mine. Or hers either, for that matter. She was a country girl to start. Born on a farm but scared of horses.

Can you beat that? When I leaned out the windows in that East Side place my sleeves came away clean. Seven years here they'd been streaked with grime. No offense, Mr. Penney. I liked the grime. It was part of me, see? A tangible part. My own personal connection to the city. That's how I thought of it, no kidding. Like all the streets and buildings, bridges and tunnels had been ground down and sprinkled on my window sill just so I could carry them around under my fingernails and on my shirtsleeves wherever I went. Tangible, see? A part of me. The best part. Like she was."

"You want I should call somebody?"

"Who you got in mind?"

"That really your daughter? You want I should get her back?"

"How about we let her go for now? Maybe I done enough in that department for one day."

Mr. Penney walked to the door. Herb held out his hand. "Thanks for coming, Ross," he said. "Thanks for everything. Okay if I call you Ross? You call me Herb, okay? First names between friends, that's the way it ought to be. I stay long enough, we'll be friends." He shook Ross' hand. "Right, friend?" He shook it hard. "You're a good man, Ross, a good friend." He gave the hand another shake and kept on shaking it until Ross had to pull his hand free to get out of the room.

Herb stood in the doorway, watching Ross make his way, limping and listing down the hall. First the limp, the left leg pulling up short beneath him and shooting out, then the list, the enormous buttocks swaying from side to side, then the limp again. He watched until Ross had reached the far end of the corridor and rounded the bend for the elevators and disappeared. Then he closed the door. He walked back into the room and sat in the chair where he had been sitting before, a very long time before, it seemed now. He stared straight ahead of him. A thin light like a veil covered the room. He took off his glasses and pressed the heels of his hands into his eyes. He felt a terrible pressure inside his head like something trying to get out. When he took the heels of his hands away and opened his eyes again, it was nearly dark in the room. He couldn't make out anything clearly. The bed was rimmed by a kind of haze. The desk and the small, low table in front of him were covered in ripples of light and dark. On the table he could just make out the phone and a few magazines which, he imagined, were filled with stories of New York's nightlife and had been thoughtfully provided by the management, whom he now knew to be Ross, for the tourists who normally occupied this room. He sat in the chair in the dark watching the shadows deepen across the room until there was no difference between what had been light and what now was darkness. Then he leaned forward and dragged the phone to him across the table by its cord. He picked up the receiver and asked the switchboard operator to connect him to Pat, who was in another room in another hotel in another part of the city. He thought of telephone cords connecting hotel rooms to one another all across the city and across the nation and the world and he imagined that this was the only way anyone, anywhere, would survive.

NINE

THE KNOCKING AT his door reverberated through the room like a secret. He sat where he was, still and certain it would not be heard again. And then, miraculously, it was. It came like an answer to a wish he knew he had no right to make. He pushed himself up out of his chair, rising from it with difficulty, as though in the time he had sat there, and he had no idea how much time that had spanned—an hour, a day, ten years—he had sunk farther and farther into the chair until he was no longer sitting in it but had gone through it to rest beneath it, somewhere, on the floor. He struggled to his feet and walked across the room, which seemed like the terrain of an unfamiliar country beneath him. The dimensions of the room seemed to have changed, its length to be infinitely longer, its width remarkably narrower, the walls drawn more closely together since he had last walked between them. He put his hand on the knob and pulled open the door.

"Herb?"

Her face loomed before him like salvation. Her eyes were troubled. A vertical line bisected her brow. Those clear blue eyes swimming in sorrow. Sorrow for him, he saw at once, concern for him. He wanted to fall on his knees and thank her. He wanted to tell her how grateful he was that she had come so quickly—that she had come at all—it seemed he had only just put down the phone when he had heard the knock and there she was, standing in the hall outside his door, her face small and drawn, her eyes filled with concern. And in the same instant it seemed he had put it down in another lifetime and it had taken her an eternity to reach him. But she was here at last, and it was more than he had dared to hope.

"Herb, dear?"

She was wrapped in a full-length dark blue coat.

"Oh, Herb."

He was thankful for her face—the openness in it, the concern, even the line down the center of her brow and for the sadness in her eyes, too, and the feeling her face revealed to him—and he wanted her to know that. He was grateful for her hands and feet, for the snow on her shoes, for the long dark coat keeping her warm, for her body, safe, intact inside that coat, here and alive—that especially—alive, and he wanted to tell her that, but the words refused to come to him.

"I'm so sorry, Herb." She spoke again when he could not. "I can't tell you how sorry I am."

She placed her hand on his arm, and he thought they could stand there forever on the threshold of his hotel room, not speaking, not moving, the heat of her hand warming a place on the sleeve of his shirt and through the shirt, his body. He would be content if they never moved from that spot or spoke again.

"Manny called," she said after a moment. "He told me." Her voice was low. She was keeping the secret. She held his eyes a moment then moved her hand to his elbow and turned him around, steering him like a boat away from the door, which she shut behind her, and into the room. "I'm so sorry, Herb. I'm so terribly, terribly sorry."

She took her hand from his elbow and the world drifted away.

"Oh, Herb, my dear."

She came around in front of him and put her hands on his face and the world was back.

"I don't know what to say."

She moved closer and put her arms around his neck.

"This breaks my heart, is all."

He raised his arms and clutched at her coat. He felt her head against his shoulder. He clutched at the shoulders and sides of her coat. He took up fistfuls of the coat in his hands, grabbing bunches of the shiny, smooth material as if they were flowers, pulling on them as if to uproot them from the earth, then letting them go and grabbing others.

"I'm so sorry for you, Herb."

She took a step back, moving far enough out of his arms for a space to rush in between them and carve a hole in his belly. She lifted her face, and he saw that her eyes were bright with tears. Tears for him, who didn't deserve them. Sorrow swimming in her eyes for a man of so little worth.

"Pat," he said, words finally his again. "Not this. Anything but this."

"Hush, dear."

"Nothing's left."

"Hush."

"Everything's finished. Everything's gone."

"Let's sit down, all right? Let's just be quiet. We don't have to talk. We don't have to say anything. Let's just sit down and be quiet. Would that be all right?" She walked toward the closet. "I'll just get out of this coat."

He stood behind her and held the coat by its shoulders as she pulled down on the zipper. She bent forward slightly, taking the zipper all the way down to her ankles where it ended. There she gave one quick, sharp tug, freeing the zipper from its clasp. Straightening, she gave her shoulders a backward shrug and the coat slipped like a body from her arms into his. It was light, but lined with down and had a hood to keep her warm. Herb was glad Pat had a coat like this. She would need it to get through the harsh Chicago winters. He had a sudden image of her standing on a street corner at home, hunched against the wind and swirling snow, waiting for a bus, perhaps, her back turned to those fierce Chicago winds he had read about but never personally experienced, the hood pulled up over her head. He saw her entering her office building, crossing busy streets, walking in and out of stores, bags of groceries in her arms, brown paper bags and white plastic bags slipping against the shiny front of the dark blue coat that shielded her from the elements. He saw it like a series of snapshots, the snapshots turning fluid, transferring to film and becoming moving images. He saw her going back and forth to her job, back and forth to the nursing home to visit her father; he saw her getting on one bus and off another, going back and forth between one sensible, orderly occupation and another, always wearing the blue down coat with the zipper fastened from ankle to chin and the hood over her head.

He stood there, holding Pat's coat in his arms, seeing Pat there in the room before him and at the same time seeing her in Chicago doing things he imagined that paralegals did . . . taking down depositions, transcribing affidavits . . . carefully, meticulously, writing down statements, word by word . . . and he was glad that she had such an orderly life and so secure a job and was involved in such clearly articulated controversies between opposing parties, each of whom would have a distinct and defensible point of view and be represented by a licensed attorney and enjoy a constitutional guarantee to an equal voice before the law. A feeling of tremendous gratitude swept through him as he viewed what he envisioned as the neat parameters of Pat's life. He was thankful that her life was so well-contained and circumscribed by such clear-cut boundaries and that she owned a coat like this, lightweight but warm, full-length, and with a close-fitting hood, to see her back and forth between her various sensible occupations. He gathered the coat more deeply into his arms and pressed it against his chest. It deflated slightly as he pressed on it, like a raft losing air.

"I'll take it," Pat said, tugging gently on the coat. But he would not relinquish it. "It's all right," she told him. "I'll take it." He was so grateful to this coat for keeping Pat safe, for keeping her warm and alive. "You can give it to me," she said softly, looking straight into his eyes, and again, the secret lingered between them. "I'll just hang it up."

"They made me look," he told her suddenly. "The cops, Pat. They made me look."

"Oh, God, Herb. I'm so sorry."

"Her beautiful hair like sunset on the bricks."

"Don't think of it now, Herb. Don't think about anything."

"They pointed flashlights at her like guns."

She placed her hand against his cheek. Her touch was so light, he nearly screamed.

"It's all right," she said and took hold of the coat again. "You can give it to me now. I'll take it. I'll hang it up."

Gently, she pried the coat from his hands. She turned away from him and there was that wind again, carving out his belly. She prepared to hang her coat in the closet. The very closet in which he had earlier locked his daughter. He still had the key in his pocket. Pat's back was to him, her arms were raised as she adjusted the coat on its hanger. He could push her in, lock the door behind her, keep her safe forever. But he didn't need to do that. Pat's life was already safe. Her coat protected her. Her work protected her. She did slow, meticulous research. She took down notes in her careful, neat hand. Such small, careful lettering. He loved those letters. Loops like artwork. Long, straight rows of closely drawn letters. A row of her careful lettering appeared in front of him now, her handwriting dancing on the air before him. Letters like musical notes. Poems, arias. One note. One poem. He would remember it always. The only letter she had ever written to him. He might have been holding it in his hands this very moment. She knew how things stood between him and Maggie, she had written. How could I not? she asked in her small, neatly drawn letters. The question mark nearly broke his heart. She prayed for his happiness, she said. Every night of her life, she told him, she prayed. The paper on which she wrote was lavender. It had small flowers on long, thin stems along the border. The flowers wavered on the air before him as if in a wind. He wanted to reach out and steady the paper, to press it to his lips. She was writing, she said, to set him free. No strings, she wrote. And never any regrets. She wished him happiness. She wished him all the best. Always. All ways. She couldn't say it in person, she'd confessed. Some things were too hard to say. The loops on the 'h' and the 'd' in 'hard,' formed perfect symmetrical handles to the word. She didn't think she would be able to see him again for a long time, and she hoped, she wrote, out of respect for her feelings, that he would do her the kindness of not trying to contact her. Please, Herb, she wrote at the end, don't call. Don't write. She wanted nothing but the best for him, she added. She would always love him. Always. He saw the word before him just as she had written it: the first 'A' and the 'l' next to it so tall and neat. She had underlined the word twice. Twice. As if he could miss it.

Pat closed the closet door and turned to him, and he saw that same sadness in her eyes, that same vertical line bisecting her brow that had been there when she first walked in. Her eyes were dry now but her feelings were unchanged, and he felt unspeakably grateful to her for that—that in the time she had turned away from him and hung up her coat in the closet and turned back, she had not forgotten him, had not walked away and left him behind, had not reconsidered or amended her feelings for him in any way that he could see. Grateful for her constancy, he reached out and pulled her to him.

"There was blood on the bricks," he began, and then hardly knew what he was saying. "I saw a hose and I didn't know where I was. I looked up at tops of buildings I didn't recognize. Buildings, Pat, in this town, I didn't recognize. A city I didn't know. I felt I was flying away. People at the windows, strangers looking down."

"Oh, Herb, my dear. Oh, my dear."

He held onto her then and she didn't resist and it became his right. Did not the concern and sadness he saw in her eyes give him the right? Did not her lack of resistance confirm that right? He put his hands on her face. A sweet, pale, kind face that expressed feelings for him. Feelings that after all this time and all these years, had remained for him, constant, unchanged. He could take them for himself as they were meant to be taken.

She was soft in his arms and yielding. He traced her face with his fingers. He stroked her neck and arms. She was wearing a long-sleeved silk blouse that moved on her skin like water, and he was happy that her coat kept her so warm, even in this weather, that all she had to wear beneath it was a thin silk blouse. He felt the silk move on her body. He felt it move beneath his hands, on her arms and back. He put his hands on her shoulders and pressed them toward one another and toward himself, as if he would lift her up and pull her into himself in one smooth motion. He would guide her into him through his clothes, through his jacket and shirt and skin, and into his body, as if he could do that, as if nothing in the world could stop him, as if he were a man who could reach out and pull something sweet and good and constant into his life and keep it there safe and forever, as if it were his right.

"This breaks my heart, Herb," she said. "It breaks for you. It does."

She lifted her hand and smoothed back his hair, and he tilted his head to one side to let her do it. She moved her hand down from his hair to his cheek and he pressed the side of his face into her hand and let his head rest there. She held his head so firmly in that one hand she seemed to be telling him that he could let it go, let the full weight of his head and all that it contained fall into her hand, and promising that she would hold it, supporting its weight and the weight of his grief and loss in her one small hand for as long as he liked. He clapped his hand on top of hers and felt how small it was to be making such a prodigious promise, and he uttered a sound like a moan in the back of his throat and was startled to hear the sound.

"It's all right," she whispered. "I've got you."

He took her hand and turned it over and pressed his whole face down into it.

"What can I do, Herb? Tell me. Is there anything?"

He pressed his nose and mouth into her palm. He cupped her hand in his, bringing his fingers up beneath hers, forcing her fingers over his face, forcing them to cover his mouth and nose, pressing them against the rims of his eyes. He held her hand like a mask to his face. He breathed in the scent and moisture rising from her palm. He inhaled her through her hand.

"Anything?" she asked. "Anything at all?"

Other men live a life like this all their lives without ever wondering if they are worthy of it. They move into that life, appropriating its sweetness and goodness for themselves as if it were their right. He would be like other men and do the same. He would take this life as his own whether or not he was deserving of it. He and Pat would live here together, in this hotel. They would have everything they needed—food, drink, toiletries from the drugstore downstairs, clothes from the shops around the corner. Everything would be sent up to them. All their needs would be attended to. Pat would have her hair done, her shoes shined. He would have the newspapers delivered. They need never leave this room. They could lock the door and know their lives were entirely safe and contained. He would keep her warm and protected from harm. He was right to have locked Phoebe in the closet, he ought never to have let her out. He wouldn't make the same mistake with Pat.

"Are you hungry?" she asked. "When did you eat last?"

He lifted his head and framed her face in his hands. The heels of his hands rested on the line of her jaw, his fingers covered her ears. He pressed his hands toward one another, absorbing the feel of her through his fingers, his palms. His eyes were closed, he had left his glasses on the table. He didn't want to see anything now. He wanted only to feel, to soak up the sense of her through her bones and skin. Not to see, not to look. He had already seen enough. He had already been made to look. And the sight was more than a man—any man—should have to bear.

"Did you sleep at all last night?" she asked. "Did you eat anything today?"

Food, sleep. Good, normal things. A woman in his arms inquiring about his health, his needs. That's what other men had. Not yellow flashlights pointing like guns, not blood on the bricks.

"Do you want to go out?" she inquired. "Take a walk, get some air?"

A walk. Air. Good, sweet, simple things. A life like other men live.

"Herb?" The whisper again. The promise repeated. "You all right?"

"Yes." He nodded. He told her he was all right. But he wouldn't go out or let her out. He would lock the door and keep her safe. They would never leave this room. Everything in the world they needed lay within this room. He pressed her close and felt the hardness of her hipbones against him, the fleshiness of her thighs. She took a step back. He didn't want that. "No," he said. He didn't want her moving away from him. He didn't want her exercising any rights of her own. He stepped forward into her, moving her up against the closet door. He held her there, immobile, pressed like a flower between the door and himself.

"Herb?" she said. A note of alarm, new in her voice.

"No," he answered. He didn't want any notes of apprehension or alarm. He didn't want any words at all between them. He moved forward again, pressing her firmly into the door. He didn't want her escaping, going out from him into the wind and the snow and a world where violence fell from the sky.

The solidity of her body, the sweetness of her breath, that's what he wanted. The air in her lungs, the blood in her breasts. And the redness of her mouth. The nourishment that would come into his mouth from hers. The existence her existence would confer upon him. That's what he wanted. Breath and life and existence that would come and did come into him as if by right as he pressed his mouth to hers. That was all that he needed in this world.

After a moment, she pulled her mouth from his.

"All right, Herb," she said, and turned her head away.

He didn't want that.

"All right," she said again. "That was nice. But let's sit down now. Let's go in and sit down."

He didn't want her mouth pulled from his, her head turned away.

"It was nice, really, it was." She spoke to him softly. "It reminded me of the old days, but let's sit down now, all right? Let's go in and sit down over there."

No, it wasn't all right. He didn't want to sit down. He didn't want to move from this spot or go anywhere ever again.

She placed a hand on his chest. As if to form a barrier between them. With her other hand, she took his hand. She was holding him away from her with one hand while trying with the other to lead him across the room and to a chair. He didn't want that. He shook his hand free of hers. He didn't want to be held away from her, to let empty spaces sweep in like wind between them. And he didn't want to be led out of a space where they were safe and led into another that was exposed and open to danger. He didn't want a moment in his life from this moment on to pass without her body pressed to his, without her breath in his eyes, her lips on his, without being able to bury his face in her shiny, living hair or feel the pulse jump in her throat or run his hands over her warm, compliant breasts.

"No, Herb," she said, and attempted to turn sideways to him.

And he didn't want any opposition.

He turned her toward him roughly and ran his hands up the front of her body. It was his right. He ran his hands up her ribs and came to her breasts and cupped them in his hands. He pressed his lips to hers. He would hold her tight and keep her safe. He would keep her life from escaping, from going out into the cold and evaporating in the wind. And he would feel her yield to him as he deserved and as he knew she would yield, out of the goodness and generosity of her heart. He would feel the safety that other men feel as she let him into that soft, deep place within her where life did not vanish but begin.

"That's enough, Herb," she said softly. "It's nice, but it's enough. I want you to stop now." She was speaking quietly but distinctly, as if to a child. "Let's go in and sit down. Let's talk."

He shoved her back against the closet door and opened her blouse and put his hand inside the silk, inside her bra, and touched her bare breast. She gasped and pulled away, and he grabbed at the silk again and heard it tear, but her breast was soft in his hand, compliant and soft, as he had known it would be, and he did not want to let it go. He was a man like any other man doing this, a man who had a right, and he would assert his rights in the face of any struggle or resistance that might ensue. He heard her cries of protest and felt free to ignore them. He felt her try to move away and felt free to use his greater strength to hold her in place. She spoke his name again. *Herb*, she said, again and again. *No*, she said, *don't, stop*, and he ignored those pleas as well because they would deny him his rights, those same rights that other men took on a daily basis and as a matter of course.

He held her arms behind her back and pressed his body into hers. He moved her by slow, steady degrees away from the closet and into the room and toward the bed. And he felt the power of that, of moving an adult, struggling human being, across a room as if her weight, her life, were nothing in his hands. He moved her past the chairs, past the room's one standing lamp, past the low table with the magazines and the telephone on it, past the magazines as they slipped off the table and onto the floor, dislodged by her skirt or her leg knocking up against them as he walked her backward, their feet slipping on the magazines as on ice floes, his arms around her, holding her hands behind her back, and ignoring her sharp demands that he stop, that he let her go, that he think, only think! of what he was doing, demands that were growing tiresome now in their repetition and increasingly urgent, high-pitched sound. He moved her backward, pressing down on her, forcing her to bend back slightly from the waist as in a dance. He moved her backward like that, forcefully like that, across the room and up to the bed, right up to the edge of it where her knees gave way beneath her and she sank onto the mattress, and he placed her across it, stretching her out and handling her gently now, more like a dream than a dance now, arranging her carefully on her back, rolling her spine out from under her like a river, and lowering himself onto her. She could not get away from him

175

now. She could not evaporate into the dangers of the world. She was his. Her kindness and sweetness were his. The soft, hot, smooth flesh beneath him was his by right. She belonged to him and only to him. He pressed one knee between her legs and the other into the mattress beside her for support. He could climb into her like that, climb right up her body like a ladder and enter her yielding hot flesh.

"Stop this, Herb! Stop it now!"

She didn't mean that. *Touch me, Herb. Touch me here.* That's what she meant. She had taken his hand and thrust it between her legs. He hadn't understood at the time what she meant. It had seemed then a strange and ugly thing to do, but if that's what she wanted he would not deny her. And this now seemed right. This was something sweet and good and natural between them. Part of a normal life. And he, no less than other men, deserved a normal life. He didn't care how she struggled or pleaded, he wanted to be touched and loved in the normal way, the way other men were touched and loved. He wanted to touch a woman's breasts, to touch the lovely, tangled curlicues between her legs the way they were meant to be touched, the way other men touched them without ever once wondering if they were worthy.

"Stop it, Herb!" she cried. "What are you doing? Stop it this minute. Get off me. Get off!" she shouted "Let me up, Herb! Let me up, I said!"

He heard her voice as through a tunnel. It came rumbling toward him as if down a track. And then it stopped and backed up and came again and this time he heard it. Pat? This was Pat? Pat, calling out to him like that? Panic in her voice? Revulsion? Disgust? His Pat? His friend from years ago? Pleading with him like that? Screaming at him? Fear and revulsion in her voice? He looked down at himself as if into a mirror and saw what he was doing. He pulled back from her and saw that her face was wet with tears. Not tears of sorrow for him, but tears of fear and revulsion and anger. Pat? Repelled by him? His Pat? He had made her cry? Enraged her? He had done that? What was happening here? What the hell was going on?

"Oh, Christ." He took his hands off her. "Christ, Pat." He rolled off the bed and stood up. "Oh, Pat. Oh, Christ." He looked down at her disheveled hair and startled face. "Oh, Christ." He looked at the rumpled bedspread, at the torn place on her blouse, at her streaming eyes. "I did that? *I* did? To you? Oh, Christ." He looked at his hands and held them away from his body. "I did? How could I? Me? Did I hurt you, Pat? Did I? Oh, tell me I didn't. Tell me at least I didn't do that."

She covered her face with her hands.

"Oh, my God, I did. What's wrong with me? What's happening here? This isn't me, you know me, Pat. You know I'd never do this. Oh, Pat. Oh, Christ. I've made you cry."

She rolled onto her side and pulled her knees up to her chest. Her whole body shook as she sobbed.

"Oh, no. Oh, look at that. Look at what I've done. I couldn't have . . . you know me, Pat. You know I'd never— You know that. You know it!"

She held tight to her knees, folding herself into a ball that shook as she sobbed. Herb stared at the sight of her on the bed then looked away from the bed and out the window toward the streets and the city. The sky was dark. The snow had stopped falling. He could almost feel the air from outside on his face. Cold, smoky city air. Sounds lifted up to him off the street. Traffic rolling, horns honking, the city carrying on with the night. Pete would have folded down his aluminum siding and gone home by now. Times Square would be filling up, theater lights burning. Manny would be barreling down the center aisle, his arm around a customer. Red would be bringing somebody a drink. And in here? In this hotel? This room? An aberration, that's what. It had to be. Another hallucination. Something that could not really have happened. No way in hell had this actually happened. Never would he do a thing like this. Lock Phoebe in a closet? Lay hands on Pat? Never in a million years.

"You know me, Pat. We go way back. We have history between us. I'm not like this, you know I'm not. I'd never do anything to hurt you. You know I wouldn't. You know that."

She stopped sobbing and went still.

After a moment she said, "Who did it then?"

The question stymied him. "How's that?" he asked.

She lifted her head and looked him straight in the eye. "Who did it if not you?"

"Oh, no, Pat. No. You can't think that."

She let go of her knees and looked around the room. "I don't see anybody else here."

"But you know me, Pat. You know I'd never—"

"There's nobody else in the room, Herb."

"But this isn't me," he told her again. "I'd never do this." He moved his hand to reassure her.

She pulled away. "Don't touch me."

"Oh, Christ."

She scurried backward on the mattress.

"You're afraid of me, Pat?"

She raised herself against the headboard.

"Of me? Afraid of me?"

She crossed her arms over her chest.

"I don't understand." Herb looked toward the window again. It was shut. Outside were the streets. "What's going on?" he asked. "What the hell's happening here?" His throat was tight. Metal drummed in his ears. "I'm ashamed," he told her. He tasted acid in his throat. He sat down on the foot of the bed. "I got no excuse," he said. "None."

She pulled up her legs and pressed herself deeper against the headboard.

"With you or Maggie either."

"That's something different," she replied.

Her voice came to him as from across town.

"My fault all the same."

"Don't go taking that on."

"I could've gone home. Maybe been there before—I tried to leave. I did. I told the guys I had to go. I got up lots of times, saying I had to go, had to get home, I remember that. I tried. They pulled me back. Each time they pulled me back down and made me stay. Not that I'm blaming them. Best damned bunch of guys in the world. It was me, Pat. Me. I should've left anyhow. I should've gone home. I never was any use to her."

"You gave her the world, Herb."

"She gave me more. Before her, I was what . . . ?" He lifted his shoulders and let them drop. "Business, policies, facts, figures? That's it. You know, you saw. Still am, I don't pretend any different, but she took an interest. She tried to fill in the gaps. Even took me to an opera once. Me, at an opera . . . can you imagine?"

Pat smiled.

"Oh, there it is. That smile. I thought I'd never see it again. Christ, I'm so sorry. Can you ever forgive me, Pat? Can you?"

"Tell me about the opera."

"I didn't understand a single thing that was going on on that stage. But inside, here . . . " Herb tapped his chest. "It shook me. Really shook me. I didn't let on, I don't know why. Stupid. Scared. I should have. That was a big mistake. One of millions. I should have told her how it shook me."

Pat uncrossed her arms.

"She had nothing when she met you," she told him. "You gave her everything you had in life."

"Things."

"What?"

"Things. That's what Phoebe said. I gave her things. And never the right ones. She didn't have to tell me that. I would have, Pat, if only I'd known what they were. You know I would have. But I never knew, never could figure it out."

"She wasn't an easy woman to understand."

"Beyond me, that's for sure. All those fragile things in the house. All that decorating. I didn't get it. 'Beauty,' she said. 'Beauty wherever you look. I can't do anything about your streets or your subways,' she told me once, 'but I can surround you with beauty at home.' It was lost on me, and that's the truth."

179

"Beating yourself up won't do anybody any good."

"And you, just now. I don't know what happened, Pat. It's like it wasn't me. That's no excuse, I know. It's like some other guy took over. Can you forgive me, do you think? Is there any way you could?"

She smiled again, not wide enough to show the lovely gap between her two front teeth, but a smile all the same. "I never could stay mad at you, Herb," she said.

"Oh, that's great. That's just swell." He went to hug her and stopped himself, guessing she wouldn't be able to tolerate his touch just yet. "Thank you, Pat. Thank you. You're a peach, you are," he told her. "But for me to do a thing like that. And to you, of all people—" He threw his arms out wide. "What am I now, a brute, a crazy man? Is that how I think a man acts? To treat a woman like that? Misuse her? Manhandle her? That was never me. Not my style. I respect women. You know I do. I like them. And this—To force a woman? Hurt her? Force my will on her? Is that me now? At my age? Sixty-two years old and that's what I've become?"

"Don't, Herb. Don't do this to yourself." Pat got off the bed and came around to where he was standing and took his arm. "Let's sit over there, okay?"

"Her rages threw me, Pat. Really threw me. I'd freeze right up, then run."

"Let's sit in those chairs over there, all right?"

"They were like fits, those rages. You ever see one of those? The way she'd fly off the handle?"

"I did."

"There was no way in or out of them."

"Come on, Herb." She led him to a chair and helped him into it. She turned on the lamp and pulled up a chair for herself.

"Like storms you just had to let run their course," Herb said. "I was no good at all to her then. Not much at other times either. Froze up like ice. Never knew what to do."

"How could you, Herb? How could anyone?" Pat leaned forward in her chair. "Maybe I shouldn't be telling you this, and I hope I'm not out of line, but I think you ought to have another angle to consider. Once . . . ," she began and her voice went soft and distant. "And this goes a long way back . . ."

She was telling him a story, he thought. *Once upon a time* . . . And the image of Rapunzel unbraiding her hair and throwing it out the window appeared before him.

"Maggie and I were up for the same show . . . not just us, dozens of girls . . . " Pat's voice came clear again. "A cattle call, it's called. Anyway, they were looking for dancers and we're all arranged on the stage according to height. Maggie's a few lines behind me . . . they put the tall girls in back . . . and the choreographer's in front, running us through the routine, and then he steps back and has us do it on our own. Just a simple tap number, nothing complicated, and we're all into it . . . the lines moving evenly, taps clicking pretty much in synch across the stage . . . when suddenly I hear this big commotion behind me and the rhythm's broken and the beat shot all to hell. A lot of the girls just stopped cold and stood aside. Others tried to keep it together, going on as long as they could like nothing had happened, and that's what I tried to do, too, but then Maggie came crashing forward from the back, breaking through the lines, and that ended that. She charges downstage, doing this wild dance . . . really wild . . . whooping and hollering like some kind of Wild West number, shooting out her arms and legs . . . all she needed was feathers. And it's nothing remotely like we're supposed to be doing. No beat to it at all, Herb, no rhythm. It wasn't a dance anymore, just something crazy."

He tried not to see it. To keep his eyes on Rapunzel before him, to focus on her unfastening her golden braids, to watch the long, wavy hair swinging in the wind.

"Like something had snapped inside her," Pat went on. "Snapped right off. And she goes up to the choreographer and carries on like that right in his face. He was shocked, you could tell. We all were. Nobody knew what to do. Then she quit. Like that." Pat snapped her fingers. "Stopped on a dime. Dead silence on stage. That's it. It's all over. Nobody moves, nobody speaks. Over, just like that. The end. She and I went for coffee afterward and in the booth she says, 'What's the big deal? I felt like doing it,' she tells me. 'So I did it.'"

Pat's features went pale. They seemed to quiver and recede before him. Her voice drifted off, then returned.

"It scared the hell out of me, Herb. Honest to God, it did. I should have told you then. You two weren't married yet. It wasn't a normal thing to do. Truth is, I was scared. Not for her, for you. You were already head-over-heels. I worried what you were getting into. I should have warned you, I know I should have. I was wrong to keep quiet."

"Forget it," Herb told her. "It was nothing. A mood, probably, that's all. She was acting up. Like you said, she always was high-strung. That's all it was, Pat. Nothing."

"It was something, Herb. It was definitely something. I knew it then. And there were other things, too. Laughing jags. Uncontrollable, like when a kid gets the giggles and can't stop. But over things that weren't funny. And not even giggles, but great, loud, whooping shrieks . . . more like shrieks of pain than laughter, and her eyes going all weird. And crying jags, too. For days at a time. It wasn't normal. Even then I knew it. And that means it went a long way back. All the way, maybe, to when she was a kid. Long before you knew her anyway. Or me. It was already established in her childhood, that's what I'm trying to say. So whatever it was, it wasn't your fault."

"Moods, Pat, I swear. That's all. There was never anything wrong with Maggie but moods."

"Okay." Pat drew herself up in her chair. "If you say so."

"Sure, that's all it was. Moods. But even those I couldn't help with." A sudden wave of nausea hit him. His stomach cramped, his head went light.

"Just let me say this, Herb." Pat's voice sounded loud, then so faint he could hardly hear it. "Normal moods don't need help. And those weren't normal. I saw a talk show about it once. Things like that. Spending sprees, like Maggie went on, and gambling. The people on the show were big shoppers, too, and heavy gamblers. Went through the kids' education fund, the entire family savings. They talked about the depression hitting, the despair taking over. About not eating or sleeping . . . or sleeping 'round the clock—she did that, too, I remember—not leaving their rooms for weeks. It's not just moods, Herb. It's got to do with the poles. Swinging from one to the other."

Her voice was so distant now he had to reach for the words. A cold sweat broke out under his arms. "Look, Pat," he said. "Suddenly I'm feeling— "

"Bipolar, that's it."

He felt hot, then cold. Objects in the room went dark, then bright. "All of a sudden I feel kind of sick. Could you give me a minute?"

"Why, sure, Herb. You don't look so good. I'm just saying, don't go thinking it was your fault."

Herb made it into the bathroom in time to raise the lid. His stomach cramped and heaved and even with nothing in it since dinner the night before last, emptied its contents into the bowl. Water and foam splashed onto his shoes. He waited for the second eruption, which came seconds after the first, then pulled the flush and lowered the lid and sat down on it. His hands and knees were trembling. His head seemed to be coming apart. He leaned forward and placed his head between his knees, stayed down a moment, then reached over to the sink and groped for a washcloth. He ran some cold water on the cloth and pressed it to his forehead. He put his feet up on the lip of the tub and sat there a while longer with his feet up, the washcloth covering his eyes.

When he felt steady enough to stand again he raised the lid of the toilet and made use of the facility. Afterward, he rolled up some toilet paper and cleaned off his shoes, then washed his hands and face at the sink, and brushed his teeth with the new toothbrush Phoebe had brought over for him, years ago, it seemed now, leaving his old one untouched in the holder.

He stood for a long while leaning on the sink, letting the feel of the cool porcelain climb up through the heels of his hands. He lifted his face and stared into the mirror. Specks, all right. Bluish-white dots splattering the glass. When he'd had that discussion with the gang at Manny's—in another lifetime, it seemed now—his life was already over, only he hadn't known it at the time. He'd been thinking about the look on her face when he told her what they'd said. *A hero, Maggie, me.*

A sound like a gulp issued from the back of his throat, and before he knew what was happening, his elbows had buckled and rough, hard sobs were coming out of his mouth. He had to lay his forearms flat on the sides of the sink to steady himself. Never to see her again? Never to touch her silken hair or hear her golden voice? Oh, Christ, Maggie. Never in any way to share a life with her? What was life then? She was everything to him. Glistening, exotic, fine as the light at sunset, and equally unattainable. There were parts of her he never could have. He'd accepted that long ago and determined to make up for it the only way he knew how. Things. He'd offer her things. He'd give her the world. It was how he loved. Only it wasn't enough. He saw that now. Not nearly enough. He put his hand over his mouth to muffle the sounds he could no longer restrain.

"You all right, Herb?" Pat was tapping at the door. "You need anything in there?"

"I'm all right," he called back. "Give me a minute, okay?"

He looked into the mirror. Was she despondent? the cops had asked. Were there other men? What the hell were they talking about? Routine questions, they assured him. Do you know of any reason? they asked again and again. What men? What reason? They were asking the wrong questions. Phoebe could have told them what they should have asked. Where was he? Where the hell was he?

He turned away from the mirror, then forced himself to turn back. A businessman. A working stiff. Dark eyes. White shirt. Clean when Ethel had brought it over, soiled now. He had put on a clean, white shirt that morning, a jacket and tie. Out of habit, he supposed, as though dressing for the office. And for the first time on a weekday in his entire business life he had not gone to the office. He would never go to it again. This was the end of that life for him. The end of life as he had known it. He hadn't read the paper that morning either. He'd asked the clerk at the desk the night before to send the *Times* up to his room in the morning, so he could read it first thing, another lifelong habit, and there it lay, on his doorstep, until Ethel arrived, having made that misguided call to Phoebe he'd told her to make, and brought it in. She'd handed it to him with a look of open astonishment on her face: a paper at his door, unclaimed?

He hadn't slept in the bed either, had just laid down across it without pulling back the spread or taking off his shoes when the cops had finished with him, around four in the morning, it must have been. He had found his way across town, and to this hotel. It seemed an instinct in him to head west.

Oh, Maggie. They had never slept apart. In twenty-two years of married life, no matter the anger or resentment she felt for him at the end of the day, she had never once forced him from the bed or banished him to the couch. Some part of her, her back, her hip, her foot, was always touching him at night. Touch through the night, they both needed that. Despite the vast differences between them and what, he supposed, his friends at Manny's would consider the utter unsuitedness of their union, they had filled that need for one another—the comfort of bodies mutely settling into place side by side in the dark.

Later, much later, Phoebe had arrived, her face cold and red, snow on her shoes, a gym bag in her hand. There was a commotion of some sort, he recalled, and Ross and Francisco had appeared, and after that he'd sat watching the snow fall with the light and listening to the sounds outside his window grow faint as the snow hushed the city and calmed the streets. At some point he realized the snow had stopped falling and was piled thick as a phone book on his window sill and knew it would have covered the streets below, leaving a thin, crunchy layer on top that would remain unbroken for the briefest of times until the first footfall came along to make an imprint. And then it was dark and Pat was knocking on his door. And now his eyes were blinded by tears. Open and blind. *Why do you never see?* A day. One day. Less than twenty-four hours. Oh Christ, Maggie! A life.

TEN

JIMMY TOOK HERB up the five flights in the elevator without uttering a single word. Herb stared at the back of the man's head, at that place on his thick neck between his hairline and uniform collar where the wool chafed and left long red marks like fingernail scratches on his skin. This man, who had been conducting his passage from lobby to fifth floor and from fifth floor down again to the lobby for twenty-two years, and with whom Herb had discussed every significant political and sporting event of those years . . . with the exception of any that might have taken place within the last six days and of which Herb had little memory and less knowledge . . . did not now deign to speak to him.

For Christ's sake, Jimmy, Herb ached to shout, don't be like that. Deaf to the stifled, anguished plea, Jimmy maintained his silence. His resolute muteness was reinforced by the unnatural stiffness of his shoulders and by the rigid, forward positioning of his head above those shoulders. Even the red marks on the back of his neck underscored his steadfast determination not to let a word escape from his lips and travel to Herb's ears. He stood with one white glove on the elevator's brass controls like a robot, not a man, not a friend. Say something, can't you? Herb longed to scream at his back. I know you're mad, but we're friends, after all, we've always been friends. It was Jimmy's conversation over the years, his thoughtful comments on the prospects for rain or sun, his assessment of the Yankees' chances for the pennant, the country's chances for an improvement in its political leadership, his evaluation of the great boxers of their time, going all the way back to Sonny Liston and progressing through the careers of Joe Frazier, George Foreman, and the incomparable Ali . . . including a mention, because it was impossible not to mention while the scandal lasted, the infamous bite Mike Tyson had taken out of

Evander Holyfield's ear . . . that had awakened Herb to the defining questions of his time and readied him for the day ahead.

Okay, I know. You're right. I left her alone. I shouldn't have. It was wrong of me, I know. Unforgivable at a time like this. But, Christ, Jimmy, what could I do?

In this very elevator, taking her from floor to floor as she passed from year to year, Jimmy had overseen the full span of his daughter's life. It was only natural, Herb understood, that he would feel protective of her now and furious to the point of speechlessness with him for having stayed at the hotel for the better part of a week. But couldn't he see his side of things? And he had tried. I did, Jimmy. I called her several times and I took her to lunch. But I couldn't come back here. I couldn't enter this building, walk through that lobby. Can't you see how I couldn't?

It was Jimmy who, from the time Phoebe had started going to school alone until the day she progressed to public transportation, had hurried her out to the station wagon the school sent around that pulled up to the curb in the mornings. It was Jimmy who had made quick trips back upstairs with her and taken his turn waiting while she ran inside for a forgotten homework assignment, a sweater or lunch box. It was Jimmy who had appraised, pronouncing fit or not, every piece of outdoor equipment purchased as a birthday or Easter or Christmas present or any other kind of present for Phoebe that left their apartment and entered his elevator to take up its rightful life in the parks and playgrounds of New York—every sled and bat and mitt, all those ice skates, field-hockey sticks, tennis rackets, the various knee pads and helmets, Frisbees, and skateboards, the roller blades that Herb was dead set against and Jimmy said she'd get the hang of in no time, the whole line of increasingly streamlined, multigeared, and expensive bicycles that had begun with the shiny green Italian two-wheeler Maggie had recklessly bought for her when she was only three years old and Herb had thought she had no business getting near for another decade at least. "Not to worry, Mr. Larrimore,"

Jimmy had assured him the first day Phoebe had been allowed outside with the Italian bike. "She can handle it. You'll see."

And Jimmy had been right. By the end of that day, the training wheels were off and Phoebe was riding on the remaining two as if she'd been born for the Tour de France. From the very beginning, it was Jimmy who had correctly assessed Phoebe's needs and potential and taken special care for her comfort. In her first year of life, seeing her whiz by in a baby carriage with Maggie or some nursemaid at the helm, Jimmy would note if she was riding too high or too low on the pillow, if the blanket was tucked too loosely or too tightly across her chest, if the sun was likely to shine in her eyes, and would reach in and adjust the pillow, blanket, or carriage hood accordingly. It was Jimmy who had folded Phoebe's hand in his white glove while she waited to be driven off to her first sleep-away camp; Jimmy who had kept track of the boys and girls he called her posse that she traveled with throughout high school; Jimmy who ticked them off by name for Herb when he came home from the office so he'd know who was who when he got upstairs. It was Jimmy who had seen Phoebe off to dentists and doctors and on her first real date, and right up to the day last fall when he saw her off to college, it was Jimmy who had found something to say to Herb about how smart and pretty she was, how big she was getting, how the years were flying, and how many hearts she would break in her time, and now, just because he hadn't been home in six days—is that it, Jimmy? Is that why?—the man had absolutely nothing to say to him.

Have a heart, Jimmy. How could I come home? You tell me that. It's like a wound you can't touch or even look at right away. I came back as soon as I could. But Jimmy's wide stance and stiff back proclaimed a disinclination toward forgiveness. Oh, come on, man, give it up. You weren't there. You didn't see. Not that I'd wish that on anyone. And the funeral—Herb was grateful that was still mostly a blur in his mind. Thank God Ethel had handled it.

Just as you'd guess, Jimmy, not a hair out of place. Might've been officiating at a board meeting. White roses everywhere. The one occasion Maggie would have found them appropriate. Phoebe under my arm the whole time, inside the church, outside in the snow, seeming to shrink and grow taller by degrees, now a little weeping kid, now an amazingly brave young woman, God, I was proud of her, and all the time like someone I didn't quite know but felt intensely protective of. None of it seemed real.

How could it be, Jimmy? How could that be her? 'Mrs. L,' as you called her, beneath that smooth, shiny lid, under that hard, cold ground. Open up that box, dig up that earth, and there she'd be. No, Jimmy, it wasn't possible. Not her. Not that. I was polite, you know I would be. Always the gentleman, as she said, but inside I was raving. Metallic man, she said that, too. I thanked them all for coming, said how I appreciated their presence and kind words. About the only ones I knew were Manny and the guys, but I thanked them all, and then I had to get out. In the middle of the reception, I couldn't take any more. Ethel had arranged this big spread in the boardroom—food, drink, the works—and suddenly I couldn't breathe. I looked around, saw everybody eating and drinking, carrying on like nothing had happened, like the world would go on as it does, and I had to be out of there and somewhere else. So I went to the hotel. My old place, you know it. And I stayed for six days. Okay, it was wrong. Don't hate me for it. It always felt like home. And I couldn't be here, you know I couldn't. In the days since I went to the office a few times, though I never thought I would again, and took Phoebe to lunch once at the Oyster Bar. I made a stab at an apology there. For what, I'm too ashamed to tell even you. What kind of man does that—locks his kid in a closet? But she was gracious enough to appear to accept it, although I couldn't have come close to the right words. If there are any for something so outside the range of acceptable human behavior.

Jimmy pulled the car to a halt, rather more abruptly than usual, and opened the gate at the fifth floor. He turned and threw Herb a look. Maybe his silence on the ride up was meant to be merciful, but the look he threw then sure as hell wasn't.

Herb stepped out of the elevator and angled his head tentatively toward his apartment. "She all right?"

"You asking me?" Jimmy pulled the gate shut.

The elevator descended, leaving Herb alone on the landing, his front door facing him. He stared at it, taking in the number above the peephole, the peephole itself, the knob beneath. Then he turned and looked at Wallace Kroenberg's door across the hall. Maybe he could get his eighty-year-old, rheumy-eyed neighbor to rouse himself from whatever alcoholic stupor he was likely to be in and come over and help him break the ice, for there was bound to be a lot of ice that needed breaking. Maybe a man of Wallace's years and experience could explain to a girl Phoebe's age that her father's life was over now, that he wouldn't have been any good to her even if he'd been around the last six days, that the man who had come home to her was a shell of the man who had left and that she'd have to take it on faith that he was aware of his profound deficiencies and regretted them with all his heart.

Herb turned from Wallace's door and looked at the black and white tiles beneath his feet. He was standing in the hallway outside his apartment door as Phoebe had stood in a hallway outside his hotel room. Tangled hair, a red nose, a beat-up old gym bag in her hand. She'd looked like a runaway. They were both runaways then, truants from another life. But she had come home, and now, so had he. He put his key in the lock and turned it swiftly to the right. He pushed open the door, and found her waiting for him in the hall. She was wearing jeans and a sweatshirt and gathered herself up stiffly at his entrance—a flesh-and-blood statue with galleries of empty rooms falling away behind her.

"Hi ya, doll," he said.

"Hi ya, Dad," she replied.

She submitted to his part in the ritual kissing of the

cheeks, but when it came time to do her answering part, she turned her face away and walked ahead of him down the long white hall and into the dining room where she disappeared.

He went to the closet to hang up his coat and place his hat on the shelf above, and a piece of himself broke off and sank like a stone as he opened the door. Everything of Maggie's was gone. Every one of her hats, handbags, scarves, jackets, down and woolen coats was gone—even the dark ranch mink that Herb had loved seeing her in and that Phoebe had only last year persuaded her on the ground of animal rights never to wear again. Every item that had belonged to Maggie and habitually hung in that closet or lay on its shelf had been removed. All the things she wore or carried or wrapped about her neck or placed on her head, that bore her perfume and her own personal identifying sweet scent and from which Herb, upon coming home at night and placing his hat and coat in that closet, had taken an almost-physical comfort, were gone. Maggie's things, gone. Maggie's things, hanging or lying next to his in that closet all those years, gone. He'd come home from the office, open that door, see and smell her garments hanging there, and all the different people she was when she wore them rushed toward him at once. The vivacious and coquettish Maggie. The Maggie who swiveled her hips and told him not to touch as she modeled a new outfit before him. The Maggie who sat on his lap and nibbled at his ear. The perfectionist Maggie who redid the house again and again and stared at a room at four in the morning, tapping a finger against her upper lip and saying, "It's not quite right." The Maggie who sailed dishes and lighted candles across a room. The Maggie who didn't leave the house for days. The Maggie whose moods he could never decipher, whose terrors and despairs he could not penetrate. They gathered in that closet and rushed when he opened it like a wind into his arms. Then his hand would reach out and caress the silks and wools and furs, as if by stroking those pelts in a darkened closet with no one to see he could both pet his gentle, loving Maggie and soothe the wild creature she now and then became when she wore them. But all her clothes were gone. Only her scent remained. Empty wooden hangers rattled on the rack like chattering teeth. He took down a hanger and hung up his coat. Life-sized spaces swung like ghosts on either side of his coat. He breathed in the sweet residual smell of Maggie's things—part wool and fur and leather, part powder and perfume, part Maggie's own personal odor—and wondered if Ethel had done this, attended to the disposal of Maggie's belongings as she had to her body, and with the same cruel efficiency, or if it had been Phoebe's doing.

Herb closed the closet door and walked into the dining room. Phoebe was on her hands and knees beneath the Christmas tree. Her hair was pulled back into a ponytail. Exchange the jeans for pedal pushers, the ponytail for a bandanna, and it might have been Maggie twenty years ago on the floor beneath that tree. She was looping red silk ribbons about the slender glass necks of long-legged reindeer standing two by two on a bed of cotton before a miniature of Santa's sleigh. But that's her mother's job, he thought. *Don't look Herb. It's not quite finished yet.*

Phoebe glanced up at him from the floor. "Mother didn't finish," she said, as if it had simply slipped her mind.

Phoebe, on her hands and knees, maybe six months old and having just learned to crawl. She scurries about the apartment like a crab in frilly white bloomers, himself racing behind. "Catch her, Herb!" Maggie commands. "Don't let her in there!" He doesn't know why she needs to be caught or which rooms have been designated off-limits, but the urgency in Maggie's voice allows no time for questions. He runs down the hall after the fleeing child, careening around corners, bumping into walls, astounded by the baby's speed, and enjoying the feel of himself in pursuit. She turns and sees him coming, throws him a look of outright defiance—*Catch me if you can!*—lets out a squeal that slices the back of his eyeballs with its sharpness and takes off again, faster than before. She can lead him a merry chase even then. But he never knows what to do when he catches up with her. He doesn't dare pick her up for fear of dropping her and can't grab an arm or leg and risk dislocating a tiny limb. So he runs until he gets ahead of her, then turns and stands still, just stands there, awkward and lost, legs together, stiff as stanchions to block her path. Even this she takes as a challenge. Squealing, she goes right and left, searching for a way around, and he moves as she moves, right, left, taking quick, small steps, barely inches at a time, his legs like trees in front of her face, until her mother comes and scoops her up off the floor.

Her mother. His Maggie. Crushed against a city street. Streets he had walked all his life, dead sober and blind drunk. Day or night, he felt safe on them. He and the streets had an understanding. Long ago, they'd struck a bargain. Their sounds and smells were part of him, a tangible part. He knew when to stop and converse with a guy seeking change on a corner, when it was safe to intervene in a public altercation, when it was more prudent to move on. He trusted the streets and they were fair with him in return. But this hadn't been fair. It was never part of their bargain. To turn on him like that? On her? What could have made them do it? Becoming suddenly stealthy and treacherous, rushing at her without warning, without giving her notice or time to think—maybe even reconsider? Not his streets. They wouldn't have done it. They would never have betrayed him like that. But the cops had made him look. The evidence was there before him.

He snatched the ribbon out of Phoebe's hand. "Get up," he ordered. He couldn't have her there, down on the ground before him like that. "Get off the floor."

"I'm doing this," she told him.

"Do it later."

He reached for her hand, she pulled it away. He knew he'd made some big mistake with her somewhere along the line, but he couldn't figure out exactly what it was or what to do about it now and he wished she could just let it go.

He dropped the ribbon and walked into the living room.

"How about a little light on the subject?" He switched on a lamp.

She came up behind him and switched it off. "I like it dark."

"Don't start."

She threw him a look. Her mother's look. It froze his heart. In an instant the look would be a word, a shout, a scream, an instant later, flying objects, broken china, shattered glass.

But this was Phoebe, his daughter.

"Sit down," he said.

She went to the sofa and arranged herself in a corner.

Out of habit, Herb would have preferred to sit in his green leather chair by the window, but paternal obligation, as he saw it now, led him to a seat on the sofa beside her.

He couldn't think of a thing to say.

She stared straight ahead.

"What'd you do today?" he finally asked.

The fine hairs at her temple seemed to take little pouches of skin with them as they were pulled back along with the longer hairs into the rubber band around her ponytail.

"And you?" she returned the question. "What'd you do today? Or the last *six* days?"

The ponytail reared up and swung to one side as she turned to face him. "No, don't tell me." She held up a hand as if to block his words. "Let me guess. It was too much for you. You couldn't take it . . . me, this house. You had to be where you felt safe."

"Honey, I'm sorry."

"A fucking hotel!"

The ponytail swung back the other way.

"And afterward, you went to the office, took care of business, followed your routine."

"Listen, Phoebe— "

"Did you or didn't you?"

"I went to work, yes."

"Sold policies, paid out claims, played the market, right?"

He didn't answer.

The hair snapped back.

"*Right?*"

He shrugged.

"Did you know," she continued, "that playing the market is an essentially aggressive act?"

"Honey, please—"

"It's how certain men express anger. The quiet, gentle man turns killer on Wall Street. Is that you, Dad? Did you make a killing in the market today?"

"If you'd just listen—"

The ponytail took another vicious swing.

"That's what they say, isn't it? Make a killing? Did you, Dad? Did you make a killing? Did you drive her to it?"

"Oh, for Christ's sake."

"Then tell me the truth. What happened? Why was she so unhappy?"

"She wasn't unhappy."

"Shit, she was right. You're blind as a bat."

"Hold it, doll."

"Was it because you were never home?"

"I was home."

"Always at the office."

"Somebody had to pay the bills."

"And not just the office."

"Manny's, you mean? You don't understand business, sweetheart, never did. Neither did your mother. A lot of it gets done in restaurants. She could have come along any time she liked. I always told her that. She could have had dinner and watched a fight."

"She hated fights."

"Only because she didn't understand them. I tried to teach her a little about them . . . weight divisions, title-holders, previous wins and losses, that sort of thing . . . but she wasn't interested. 'You go,' she'd say. 'You watch with your so-called friends.'"

"Who were your friends that night?"

"What night?"

"You know what night. The cops came and got you. Ethel told me. Who were you with?"

"The gang, I guess. The usual fellows."

"Nobody else?"

"Not that I remember."

"Just the fellows?"

"That's what I said."

"Not a woman in your gang?"

"Now you listen here. There was nobody else. Not ever. Nobody but your mother."

It was true the way he meant it. Sure, he'd gone to Manny's. More than he should have maybe, and he'd stayed late some nights, drinking beer, watching a fight or a game if there was one on worth watching, and talking to the guys. But it was only because he felt at home there. He liked the food and the company and the atmosphere. He liked not having to watch what he said or count his drinks or worry about somebody holding something against him in the morning. But nobody but Maggie ever had his heart. Not his heart. Nobody. Not ever.

"Why then? The truth, Dad. Or isn't that on your commodities index?"

"I told you the truth."

She clutched the pillow at her side. He grabbed her wrist.

"What? You think I was going to throw it?"

He let her go.

"A simple gesture makes you flinch. And you, a man. Imagine what it was like for a child."

"You had nothing to worry about."

"Is that so?"

"She'd never hurt you."

"That's what you think."

"Don't get smart."

"I never knew if I'd be hugged or hit."

"She dressed you in ribbons and lace."

"You walked out the door and the ribbons turned to belts, the lace to sticks. *Sticks,* Dad. She collected them in the park and brought them home as weapons."

"I don't believe you."

"Of course you don't. You only believe what you read in the *Wall Street Journal*."

He wasn't up to this. He had done his best. What more could he do? Drop it, just drop it, he wanted to say, whatever it is you've got against me. Why couldn't she do that? Why couldn't they go back to the days when they didn't have to speak to be understood, when she would give him her hand without any fuss, just slip it into his, light as smoke when he wasn't looking, when she could sit with her books and he with his papers and hours could pass and nobody had to say a word to hold a conversation?

"You should've taken me with you."

"To Manny's? I took you lots of times." Shirley Temples, shrimp cocktails while he nursed a Scotch. He wanted those days back.

"You were happy there," she said.

She never spoke a truer word.

"All your friends around, famous people coming over, saying hello. Waiters bringing you just what you wanted without having to ask. I liked being there, seeing you happy."

"I needed a place."

"So did I."

"You were a kid. Your place was at home."

"And yours wasn't? Weren't we a family? Or were those men at Manny's your family and not us?"

"It was always you. You know that. You and your mother. Whatever you needed, that always came first."

"Things again."

"That's enough of that."

"You gave us things!"

"You'd rather starve?"

"Objects! Possessions!"

"Damned right I did. I gave you everything you ever wanted. Something wrong with that?" He had fed and clothed and housed them. He had their teeth straightened, their eyes examined. He got them vaccinations and flu shots. He sent them to allergy doctors, yoga masters, chiropractors and nutritionists. He took care of them, that's what he thought he was supposed to do. He made possible the antiques dealers and furniture restorers, the seamstresses and hairdressers, the private schools and after-school activities, the music lessons, summer camps, movies, theater and operas, the clothes and vacations and anything else they ever wanted or needed or thought they needed—any appliance, stereo, delicacy, service, or piece of art they took a fancy to, even the piano nobody in the house knew how to play. *Things.* Yes. He gave them things. He gave them the freedom to do as they pleased, the confidence that comes from knowing there's a roof over your head, a meal on your table, and that all the essentials of life are yours for the asking. Yes, he did that. He gave them things, and along with the things, hope for the future and a reasonable expectation that their hopes would be fulfilled. And where was the crime in that? That's how he operated. He didn't know how to do it differently or where else to look for the meaning of love.

"Don't be so hard on me, doll."

"And don't call me doll!"

He stared at her, baffled by the command. What the hell was wrong with her? He had always called her doll. She loved it when he called her doll. They both loved it. It was a thing between them, their thing.

"Phoebe, I—"

"You were never there."

He was the head of the family, he kept them healthy and safe. That was his job. He kept them secure and protected from harm, not falling out of windows, not crashing down onto the concrete below. He did his job. Only he hadn't. As it turned out, he hadn't.

"We lived in the same house," she was saying to him now. "But you were like a boarder. You came in to sleep and shower and went out again to eat. It might as well have been a hotel."

"I've always been partial to hotels."

"No jokes, Dad. I remember when I was little how mother would go around the apartment, straightening up all the rooms, plumping cushions, angling chairs just so, putting flowers in vases like she was having a party. Then at five-thirty exactly, the front door would open, and you'd walk in. Just you. The whole party. You'd walk through the living room and sit over there in your green leather chair by the window. You'd open your magazines and newspapers and never even notice the flowers or the cushions or how nice everything looked. You'd skim the magazines but read the papers through from cover to cover . . . sports pages, financial pages, even the obituaries . . . and when you'd finished one paper, you'd throw it on the floor and pick up another and throw that one on the floor too when you'd finished reading it."

"Don't be angry with me, doll."

"And when you'd read them all, you'd get up and go in to wash and shave and put on a clean white shirt for Manny's. Sometimes I'd watch you through the bathroom door if you'd left it open a crack. You did everything in order—washing, shaving, brushing your teeth, dipping your comb in water, parting your hair. The routine was as important to you as the news of the world or the stock market closings. And it was important to me, too. I counted on your routine. Your hours, your locations, the places you'd be, the routes you'd take to get there and back. Even the kissing routines. They were like bars around me. I felt safe inside. And when you were ready to leave, you'd put on your hat and coat and give me a great big grin. You never looked happier than when you were on your way out the door."

"It wasn't like that."

"Oh, Dad, Daddy, why? Didn't I matter? Did those men matter more?"

"Of course they didn't. It was you and your mother. Nobody else."

"She'd come after me when you left, both arms swinging."

"Don't tell me that."

"Striking out wildly, slapping at my head, face, back—hitting whatever part of me she could reach. And when she'd finished she'd burst into tears and beg me to forgive her. She said she didn't mean it. That it wasn't her doing it."

"Stop it, Phoebe."

"Somebody else made her do it, she'd say. Voices told her to. People told her to. She saw things, Dad, she heard things. She spoke to people who weren't there."

"She did not."

"She did! Goddamn it, I'm telling you the truth!"

"Who asked you?" He threw up his hands and turned his back to her. He looked out the window. The sky, growing dark, beckoned to him. The rhythms of the city, slowing down now as they did every night at about this hour, called to him. He and his shadow self could politely excuse themselves, get up from where they sat, execute a little turn about the room, and head for the door. He loved the streets at this hour. With the city bridging the gap between the end of its business day and the beginning of its night life, an interlude opened around him, quiet and private, and taller than he, like his own personal shelter. He could walk down a block, insulated by the sudden stillness, and take his time easing into the syncopated Broadway rhythms waiting for him up ahead, just on the other side of the interlude. He wanted to be out on the streets now, horns and sirens drowning out talk of a woman turning lace to sticks, striking a child and speaking to people she couldn't see. A woman swinging from pole to pole. Bipolar, Pat had called it. He didn't want to know about that. Long ago he had made it his business not to know anything about a woman like that, and if every now and then, despite his best efforts not to know, such a woman stood before him—eyes flashing, agitated, towering above him, it seemed at those moments, arms like the wings of a giant moth battling the air—he kept her voice masked, her motives vague, her features indistinct, careful to avoid any chance of recognition. If he had said something, done something to provoke such an outburst, he couldn't for the life of him figure out what it was. She was a storm then, an avalanche, a raging flood, erupting without reason or warning, sweeping through the house, knocking fragile objects off their shelves, sending him, reeling, out the door. What could he do at those times but what he always considered a favor to them both—pick up his hat and take his leave?

"Sometimes late at night . . . "

"Quit it, Phoebe."

"After she had quieted down I'd get out of bed and go into your bathroom. It was the one room in the apartment she never went into. I'd lower the lid on your toilet quietly, so she wouldn't hear. Remember how she used to yell when you let it slam? I'd sit down and put my feet up on the edge of the tub and breathe in deep to catch the smells of your toothpaste and aftershave."

"Knock it off, I said."

"Squib toothpaste. Lilac Vegetal. Those were magic smells to me. Your water glass on the sink where you'd left it, your toothbrush in its holder. I'd finger the towels you'd used before going to Manny's, hanging there, still damp and wrinkled on the rack. I'd tell myself no matter how drunk you were or how late it was, you used that glass and that toothbrush every night of your life before going to bed and it couldn't be much longer before you'd come home and use them again."

He wished he'd been a different man. Stronger, braver, a better father, maybe even some hero type. Kids deserve heroes. But he was who he was and that wasn't any hero, despite what the gang at Manny's had said. He didn't think he had ever done a single thing, other than pay the bills, that another man might be pleased to point to as a measure of his family valor. Maggie knew it, if Phoebe didn't. Sometimes he'd catch a look in her violet eyes, a kind of aching, longing, mournful look that seemed to be asking why couldn't he be that knight in shining armor she sometimes took him for, for real? He'd put on his hat and coat then, tuck his paper under his arm, never sorrier than at such moments that it was made of newsprint and not the fine, flashing high-grade steel she'd prefer, and head quietly out the door.

"I used to think it was my fault," Phoebe went on, the sound of her voice now like needles in his ears. "That if I was nicer to her or more patient, or thought more about her nerves, like she was always asking me to, she'd be different. But she just got worse."

"That's enough."

"She got crazier every year."

"Don't call her that."

"Crazy, Dad. Crazy."

"Don't you dare."

"Maybe if you'd been around . . . If you'd seen what was happening . . . If you'd done something—"

"What could I have done?"

"Something! Anything! Taken her to a doctor—"

"She had plenty of doctors!"

"Not the right kind. If once . . . just once . . . you'd acted like a man—"

"What the hell do you know about men?"

"More than you think." Phoebe threw up her arms and waved her hands through the air. "They don't walk out the door and pretend not to see. They don't take people away! They don't let them die!"

Herb saw the flailing of his child's arms. He saw her mouth opening and closing. But he didn't feel the air move as she struck at it with her hands or hear the words as they came out of her mouth. She might have been an opera singer he was watching on television with the sound turned off. Or he might have gone stone-cold deaf. For he didn't hear any other sounds either—not in the room where they were or coming up from the streets outside. Not the Madison Avenue bus releasing its air brakes as it stopped on the corner, not the gradually increasing rush of traffic through the streets indicating that evening's interlude of quiet was coming to an end, not the sounds of people yelling for cabs or horns blaring or police sirens wailing or ambulances claiming their right-of-way. Silence encased him like a tomb. Under the circumstances, he figured there was only one thing to do: Rise from the couch, bow low to his unhappy daughter, raise his arms to his lifelong phantom partner, and glide off into the night. Never to return this time. That seemed sensible and right. Not this before him. Not these words, not these lunatic accusations. For Phoebe's voice now, as after a three-second delay, resumed its normal sound. Words as hard as pieces of concrete thrown up by jack hammers riveted his attention. *He* took Maggie away? *He* let her die?

"So that's it," he said, his own voice almost unrecognizable in his ears. "That's what you've got against me. I knew it was something . . . but this!"

"Just tell me the truth. That's all I want." Her voice was low now and sadder than he'd ever heard it. "The truth's always been scarce in this house," she went on. "Mother with her antiques, creating worlds that never existed . . . you with your newspapers in front of your face . . . me with my books . . . everybody hiding. Look where it got her."

"Don't you talk about her."

"Why not? She wasn't just yours! You didn't own her."

"Lay off!"

He threw up a hand to silence her. "You think I did that?" He shook his head to clear it. "That's what you think? *I* let her die? Christ, it makes me sick to say the words." He let his hand drop back into his lap. "Don't you know I would have given anything for it to be me instead? Don't you think it kills me, a stupid accident like that?"

"Now we're back to accidents."

"And you be still! You've had your say. A few goddamned gates and she'd be here today." Herb felt his voice soar up out of reach and fly away. He stared out the window, waiting for it to return to him.

"You have the whole world ahead of you," he said after a while. "And I'm happy for you, doll, don't get me wrong. But your mother was my world. They might as well have come in with bulldozers and taken it away. I'll never get over it."

"Nobody ever gets over it."

He took off his eyeglasses and pinched at the bridge of his nose where the small bones ached. "If there was any way to make this easier for you, baby, you know I would. One goddamned fall—"

"She didn't fall."

"Oh, Christ, Phoebe."

"She jumped out that window, Dad. She jumped. That's the truth. Truth isn't beauty and beauty isn't safety, the way mother thought. She jumped and left us behind like we weren't worth living for."

He could have smacked her then, right across the jaw, or taken her by the shoulders and shaken her until her eyes popped out of their sockets. Instead, he drew in a breath, released it and, almost inaudibly, replied, "Don't you think I know that?"

It took her a moment to understand. "Know it? How?"

He put his glasses back on his head and hooked the stems behind his ears. "I saw her in the courtyard, remember?" His Maggie. His beautiful bride. "I read the note."

"What note? I didn't know she left a note."

"I sent the super up with the key. The police found it on the table next to the bed." Their bed. Their room. A room he would never go into again as long as he lived.

"You never told me she left a note."

"It was addressed to Henry. They didn't know who to give it to."

"Henry?"

"Iron Henry, remember? She used to call me that."

"From the fairy tale? The princess who hurled a frog against the wall?"

Herb shrugged. "You got me there, but it's fitting, isn't it—a woman who liked to throw things?"

"Iron Henry, sure . . . ." Phoebe's head bobbed in little assenting motions as the story came back to her. "The loyal servant . . . he fastened iron bands around his heart when his master was turned into a frog . . . then the master got his human form back and the servant was so happy the iron bands burst from joy."

Herb couldn't help but smile. "The cops never in a million years would've figured that one out."

"But you knew?" Phoebe cried. "You knew all along? All the time you were going on about accidents and gates?"

He didn't know what to say to that. It was a failure in him, he acknowledged, something cowardly and weak, a disconnection inside that let him create a diversion or skirt an issue on the ground of sparing somebody's feelings or preserving the peace or making something simple that wasn't while giving his phantom partner time to cut in and lead him away.

Phoebe waited a moment, then graciously let it go. But she wasn't quite finished yet.

"What did she say in the note?"

"She asked me to take care of you," Herb replied, his voice holding steady as he answered as if that request were reasonable enough. "She asked me—" he began again, and his voice gave out as if Maggie's second wish took the life right out of him. "To forgive her."

"Oh, God. Dad, I'm sorry, I'm sorry. I'm so sorry. It wasn't your fault, I know it wasn't. I know that. I know how you loved her, I do." She scooted toward him along the couch and threw her arms about his neck. "I don't blame you. Really I don't. Forget what I said. I didn't mean it." She was hugging him tight. "Forgive me. Please, forgive me. I didn't mean it. Honest, I didn't. It was a stupid thing to say. I just wanted the truth. From you, not Ethel. I should have heard it from you."

Something lined up inside Herb at that and locked into place. He pulled back from her, feeling it lock, and met her eyes. "You're right," he said. "You should have heard it from me."

He drew her to him then and held her for a long time. They sat, wrapped in each other's arms, not speaking or moving, while the sky darkened and the sounds of traffic rose from the street outside.

206

After a while Phoebe moved back from him, a flash in her eye, the ponytail swinging. "I could quit school," she said. "Stay home, take care of you . . . raise the baby."

"*What* baby?"

"No baby."

"What baby?"

"No baby, Dad. I just wanted to see if you were listening."

"What goddamned baby?"

"There isn't any baby, Dad. Honest. Not that there couldn't be."

"What the hell do you mean by that?"

"There could be, that's all."

"How? How could there be?"

"How do you think?"

He stared at her. She laughed.

"No, honest, Dad. Just kidding. Inappropriate humor runs in the family."

"It's not true?"

She swung the ponytail.

"But it got your attention, didn't it?"

"Say it!" Herb demanded. "Say it's not true."

She hesitated, smiling broadly.

"Say it, Phoebe. Goddamn it!"

"Okay, it's not true."

"Not even possible?" he demanded.

She grinned and cruelly withheld her answer.

"Damn it, Phoebe!"

"Okay," she relented. "It's not even possible."

"You swear?"

"I swear."

"Thank God." She was still his little girl. Untouched, intact. He sighed in relief. But could she be lying? Could she have seen how the mere possibility destroyed him and said that it wasn't true when it was? Could she have spent less than four months at college and come back having learned how to put a duplicitous spin on things for his sake?

"I could take the semester off," she was suggesting now. "Not go back after Christmas, get a job."

"You have a job," he told her. "Finish school."

"Who'll look after you?"

He looked into her face and felt unspeakably proud of her. This fine young woman his daughter had become. His daughter. To this day that got him. His? *Of course she's yours, Herb. Go on, take her. She won't break.* A kid in whose blood his own genes ran. And Maggie's, too.

"I don't need any looking after," he told her.

He'd like her to know what a pleasure it had been. A real pleasure, he wanted her to know, having had her in his life. And unexpected, too, he'd like to tell her, for until she came along he'd never thought fatherhood was actually in the cards for him.

"Give me a minute, will you?" he said and squeezed her hand. "There's something I gotta do. Go get changed. I'll take you to dinner."

He waited until she had left the room, then he got up from the sofa and walked into the piano room. He looked at the oriental carpet beneath his feet. He saw the richness of the colors, the intricate weave of flowers. He looked at the gleaming rim of parquet floor between the carpet and the wall. He forced himself to look. He saw her sitting there, her back against the wall, her bare buttocks on the floor. He didn't pretend to understand. Maybe he never would. But he was a father and had a daughter still young enough to need him. He went up to the Chickering baby grand piano, raised the lid and struck a note. Sour, he supposed. With his tin ear he couldn't tell for sure, but he knew that piano hadn't been tuned in years and his was the only note struck on it since Phoebe quit taking lessons at the age of twelve.

He walked through the living room, turning on lamps as he passed and noting as he never had before how the square of marble, stretch of wood, patch of fabric, or edge of glass closest to the lamp jumped with life as the light came on. The colors in the paintings on the walls suddenly appeared so vivid to him he wondered if Maggie had recently had them cleaned, if one did such a thing with paintings. A small green pyramid made of marble, a paperweight, maybe, standing on the table at the near end of the couch popped into focus before him. He was struck by the almost-translucent paleness of the green and by the weight of the pyramid in his hand as he picked it up to examine. He put it down and his eye was caught by a wooden figurine of a dancing girl on the far end table. Walking toward it, he saw that the girl was suffused by a glow that seemed to come from within the wood itself. Next to the figurine lay a glass dish with bright strips of color floating through the glass. He stopped and picked that up, too. Colors like moving lights swirled through the dish, the slimmest strips of reds and blues and golds. It held him as in a spell.

He carried the dish over to the mantel and set it down next to a clock he couldn't remember ever having seen before. The clock was tall and white, apparently carved entirely from alabaster, and covered by a large glass dome. A two-foot, pure-white clock beneath a dome of glass? Sitting in the center of his mantel? And he had never seen it before? He stepped up close and studied its face. He checked it against his watch, and understood that it didn't tell time. But why should it? Time was a detail with which Maggie had never been particularly concerned. This clock's function, Herb realized, was not to count the hours, although it may well once have done so. Today, it sat on his mantel beneath its dome of glass, its sole function to please the eye. A function it performed perfectly. He paused before it, struck by its beauty. Of no use whatever, but undeniably beautiful.

He walked through the open sliding doors and into the dining room, passing shelves of china cups and saucers so thin they seemed more blue than white and cut-glass crystal from whose facets diamond-shaped rainbows scattered. The Christmas tree stood in its corner before him, complete in his mind's eye. What Maggie had begun Phoebe would finish. He saw the reindeer, their tall glass legs poised in their prancing, standing on the mirror placed on the floor and framed by cotton to simulate a frozen lake in a bed of fresh snow. He saw the red silk ribbons tied to the reindeer's slender necks, forming the reins to Santa's sleigh. He saw the multicolored ornaments all in place on the branches, the lights and tinsel hung, the angel aloft, the room lights turned off, the tree lights on. *Gee, Maggie. It's swell. Are you sure, Herb? Are you sure? You're not just saying that?* Every year it took his breath away.

He walked down the long white-tiled hall toward their bedroom in the back. Shadowy outlines of himself bounced off the walls as he walked by and locked into place within him. He could feel them locking, one after the other as he walked, shadows becoming substance within. He passed the cutoff to the kitchen, the den and the library. He passed Phoebe's room on his left, the large bathroom she and Maggie had shared on his right. With each step he took, he felt the shadows lock and interlock within him, turning to tissue and bone, turning to sinew and cartilage and ligament.

At the end of the hall, he came to the bedroom door and stood still before it. He stared at the door, knowing he couldn't go in, knowing he had to. He put his hand on the knob and turned it gently. The door swung open before him. Odors of Chanel No. 5 and Charles of the Ritz hung above him like a wreath. He crossed the threshold and his legs turned to feathers. He lifted an arm, held it out shoulder high, let his fingers graze the wall for balance, and switched on the chandelier. Peach satin headboard, peach satin footboard, the satin scored by the light as by a pin. Maggie's silver-handled hairbrush lay on the dresser top. Next to the brush, her comb and jewelry box, her lipsticks and powders, her large collection of perfume bottles, arranged in graduating size. The silver edging the comb and brush gleamed in the light of the chandelier. The marble on the dresser, the glass of the perfume bottles and on the mirror above glittered before his eyes. He picked up the brush and held it until the silver grew warm in his hands, then gently laid it down.

He walked across the room toward the windows. The bed had been neatly made, the spread pulled tight and smoothed over the pillows, the carpet vacuumed. Had Phoebe done all this, or had the housekeeper whose wide, heavy jowls he could see clearly before him but whose name he could not at the moment recall? At the windows, he hesitated. The curtains were drawn. Polished cotton, glazed by a kind of sheen and imprinted with tiny blue and purple flowers, they matched the bedspread and stretched from wall to wall. The structure above them, made of the same material as the curtains and arching in a series of graceful loops toward the ceiling, was called a valence. He had a sudden recollection of Maggie telling him the name. *Look at it, Herb. Isn't it pretty? I designed it myself.* She had designed a valence, a thing he would never in his life have given the least thought to, would never even have known existed if she hadn't pointed it out, and she had designed it, thought it up and designed it herself—a graceful arch stretching from one end of the room to the other. He followed it with his eye and saw that it was beautiful. Waves of amazement and pride overtook him. Quickly, he stepped forward and pulled the cord and with the sound of tearing silk, the curtains parted. A rush of violence opened to him like an embrace. He stepped forward to meet it.

Five nights before, standing with the cops in the court-yard below, he had looked up at the buildings overhead and had found this window and had thought, as he'd thought only minutes ago, that he would never again enter this room. Certainly he would never cross to this window, never stand where she had stood, looking down, following the trajectory of her gaze and seeing with his own eyes the tops of trees and roofs of brownstones as she had seen them, and from the very angle at which her eyes had looked their last. He opened the window wide and leaned out. Old snow lay on the ground and on the rooftops. Snow edged the wooden fences and lined the cracks between the garden bricks. He felt the stone of the building's façade beneath his hands. He felt the pull, the sudden vertigo. It was like falling in dreams, he imagined, and he had done that hundreds of times—the quick drop, the opening like a trap door in the stomach, the soaring panic and jerking awake with a start and in a cold sweat at dawn—only for Maggie it had not been a dream and day never dawned.

He leaned out farther still and looked at the ground five flights below. A gray haze circled the courtyard lamps. A cat jumped a fence. He moved his eyes and found the place on the bricks where she had been and forced himself to look and to keep on looking until he could hold the sight. His eyes filled and the place was gone. He blinked and brushed the tears away and the place was back. It had been cleared of her body. The blood had washed away in the snow. He stared at the spot until she was there again, naked and crushed against the bricks. He stared hard and kept on staring until she was there no more, and then he brought that place up from the ground. Flight after flight, tenderly, he reeled it in. And when it was on a level with himself he fixed it in the very center of his mind's eye as with a lock and key. He would hold it there until he could incorporate it, as he knew he must if he was to go on, into some vision of life that was generous enough to accommodate truths he couldn't yet grasp and complexities that might always elude him. *My bones are turning to chalk . . . I hear them crumbling. Touch me, Herb. Touch me here. I want to see your soul.* He was an ordinary man with an ordinary man's capacity for understanding.

In her note she had asked for his forgiveness. Now he asked for hers.

He stood there a moment longer, gazing out into the night, his hands on the windowsill. She had asked him to take care of Phoebe. He made that promise easily, then made her another. The ground blurred before his eyes and the cold stung the rims of his ears. He drew his head in and shut the window. He went into his bathroom and followed the routine he had followed every day of his life since the day he began working for his father. He brushed his teeth and washed his face and shaved. He ran cold water over his comb and parted his hair. He put on a clean white shirt and knotted his tie and did up the buttons on his vest. He adjusted the hang of his jacket, turned off the light, and left the room.

He walked down the hall, past Phoebe's room on his right, the master bath on his left, past the library and the den, past the dining room and the cutoff to the kitchen. He walked into the living room and found Phoebe waiting for him there. Every light in the room was blazing. She had plumped all the cushions on the sofa and chairs.

"Place looks great," he told her. "You look great."

He looked at her, bathed in the dual light of the table lamps and of the street lights coming up now from below, and she came into such sudden, sharp and almost-painful focus before him, it was as if he were looking at her through a pair of powerful binoculars he had only that instant learned how to adjust. She seemed almost to sparkle, the way the mica-studded pavement at the foot of the fountain in front of the Plaza sparkles in the sun on a cloudless day.

"You're something, you are," he said.

That inexhaustible and mysterious mix of city light by which he had made his way all his life that rises daily from its streets and population, taking color from its chrome and glass and concrete surfaces, vitality from its noise and perpetual motion, that never, even on the blackest night, allows the city to go entirely dark was opening his eyes now and revealing her in brilliant, even excruciatingly sharp detail. He saw that she was taller than he had thought, five-six, he estimated, whereas before he'd given her no more than five-four or four-and-a-half. She had taken down the ponytail and brushed out her hair so that it hung loose about her shoulders, and he saw that her hair and eyes were actually darker than he'd believed, closer to bittersweet chocolate than chestnut, and that her eyebrows were full and dipped down slightly at the ends rather than continuing straight out toward her temples. In the way she stood before him, her arms easy at her sides, in the straightness of her legs and hips and in the way her head angled to one side and her gaze caught his and released it and caught it again, he saw that she was full of grace and it was as if he had never seen her before.

"What, Dad?" she asked. "What are you looking at?"

"You," he replied. "I'm looking at you."

And that smile, Christ! *His?* He'd had a hand in that?

He walked up to her and took her in his arms and felt overwhelmed by her unutterable sweetness and the gift she was to him. He held her close a moment, then out at arm's length. Her hair and eyes were shining and in their light he saw that he had been given another chance, or a chance he'd had all along but only now saw how to take.

She has changed into a blue blouse and a dark skirt that falls to her ankles and bears the outlines of flowers of some kind, tulips, he'd say, yes, definitely, tulips. The skirt sways as she moves and the lamplight picks up the pale, gentle shapes of the bulbs in the skirt. She takes a step back and raises her arms to adjust what he thinks may be a barrette in her hair. It falls to the floor and the light glances off it and he sees that he is right, it is a barrette. She bends to retrieve it and, turning her back to him an instant, fastens it around the band of hair at the left side of her head from which it has fallen, and he is overcome by the gracefulness with which she bends and straightens and by the astonishing resiliency of spirit he takes this to portend. For a moment he wishes to do nothing but look at her, to let her figure fill his eyes and to feel his chest swell with gratitude as he takes her in. Then he says her name. "Phoebe," he says, and she turns toward him in a series, it seems, of separate but simultaneous actions, now her hips turning, now her waist, her shoulders, her arms, each moving slowly, separately, yet somehow all at once and in easy, overlapping movements. Her head turns and her long, dark hair flies out and forward, swirling from shoulder to shoulder, covering her face as it flies, covering her eyes. The lamplight ripples through her hair, burnishing and lightening it until it is the color of sunset, and he thinks for an instant, Maggie! and then she has turned fully toward him and her hair settles down about her shoulders, and he sees that it is not Maggie, not at all, although certainly she is there, too, forever in his child's face, that lovely, open face that now faces his, and he sees the light and promise in her eyes and makes her the same promise of love he had just made her mother. Then he smiles and cocks his head and juts out an elbow and takes his daughter on his arm and walks with her through a room he has never seen in such detail toward the front door and dinner maybe at Manny's.

No, he reconsiders.

"How about Sardi's?" he says. "Or 21? Or Gallagher's for the biggest, juiciest steak you've ever seen?"

"I don't eat meat, Dad," she tells him.

"Since when?"

"Eighth grade."

Eighth grade? That was what, five, six years ago? He had a lot of catching up to do.

"You name it, doll. I'm buying."